The Omega Trap

An Annabel Staple Mystery

Maggie Peck

First published in Great Britain in 2024 by Willow Bodge Press

A CIP catalogue record for this title is available from the British Library

Paperback ISBN: 978-1-7396111-2-5
eBook ISBN: 978-1-7396111-3-2

Cover design by Franky Peck Graphics

Willow Bodge Press
Willowbrook
Suffolk IP13 9RH

THE ANNABEL STAPLE SERIES

For Geoff

PROLOGUE

Sir Richard Dunne found Rosemary Hutton irritating, always had, probably always would. But she was useful. At least, she had been in the past and he hoped she would be now. Damn her, she always sat with her back to the sun – looked like she was wearing a halo. Anyone less angelic would be hard to imagine.

'Yes, you've let things slip,' she continued their conversation. 'The "proverbial sieve" comes to mind. We have all the bright ideas and then we let them slip through our fingers.' She raised one shaking arthritic hand. The June sunshine shone through the gaps in her fingers sending shadows trembling across the table between them. 'Over to Russia ... or China ... or bloody Timbuktu.'

Sir Richard gritted his teeth. As a member of the security service he felt the criticism keenly. It was what they were supposed to do – catch spies. The PM had said something similar the other day, only slightly more colourfully. And that was nothing to the flack they were taking from the Americans.

It wasn't for the lack of trying. He happened to think they were actually pretty good at it. But the whole nature of spying was that you were never absolutely sure it

was going on until you got the proof. And to do that …
you occasionally had to be prepared to try something
unorthodox.

Which was why he was now sitting in the quiet, comfortable sitting room of Rosemary Hutton. He knew her
Special Operations Executive, MI6 background and she
had been legendary in the service, but he was shocked by
how frail she'd become – osteoarthritis he'd been told.
He was wondering if he'd wasted his time driving all the
way out to Ayot St Lawrence to see her but she still had a
reputation for getting results. It was worth a try.

'I presume you have suspects in mind,' said Rosemary.

Sir Richard shifted uncomfortably.

'I can't be expected to help unless I know who they
are,' Rosemary pressed.

Sir Richard knew this. His reluctance had been for
show. 'We've got our eye on Gerald Harcourt,' he said.

Rosemary raised her eyebrows. 'Foreign Office man,
fifties, rowed for Oxford. A bit pompous.'

'Yes.' Sir Richard had been ready to provide this information if needed but was not surprised that Rosemary
already knew of the man.

'Interesting. Access to a lot of information, plenty
of contacts, regular visits abroad. Yes, I can see why he
might be under suspicion,' said Rosemary. 'Any particular reason why he's included?'

'There have been rumours. He's losing popularity as
a house guest.'

'As a house guest? Why?'

'We've made discrete enquiries, the suggestion is that 'things' have gone missing, but nobody is prepared to be more specific. They just find reasons not to invite him again.'

'And you think it may be because he's been stealing documents?'

'It's a possibility. He and his wife used to be regulars on the weekend house party list of wealthy industrialists. Not so much of late.'

'Hmm.' Rosemary was silent for a few moments. 'Anyone else?'

'Alexi Galkin.'

'White Russian,' said Rosemary. 'Grandparents fled Russia under the Bolsheviks, moved to Austria. Parents fled Austria under Hitler, settled in Britain. I shouldn't have thought he had any love for mother Russia. I presume that's where you think the secrets end up?'

Again, Sir Richard was forestalled. Rosemary's almost encyclopaedic memory for people and facts could become irritating. 'We think so. Yes, unlikely on the face of it, but questions have been raised concerning him.'

'Questions?'

'Certain contacts he's been cultivating recently. Sudden trips he's made. Correspondence we've intercepted and don't understand.'

Rosemary frowned. 'I'd like to see those transcripts.'

Sir Richard shifted uncomfortably again. 'I'll see if that can be arranged.'

'He's worked with my lot in the past,' said Rosemary.

Sir Richard knew that she meant MI6. 'Yes, but he may have been turned.'

'It's not unheard of,' agreed Rosemary. 'Nobody else?'

'Not today,' Sir Richard attempted a joke.

Rosemary regarded him stony-faced. It looked for a moment as though she would say something. Then she sat for some time staring at the picture on the wall over the fireplace. It looked like a Cézanne but it couldn't be, surely? Sir Richard took a sip of his coffee and waited. The heavy earthenware cup felt thick and unpleasant on his lips. Why didn't she have decent porcelain cups? Then he looked at her hands. She probably couldn't handle anything more delicate.

'What we need …'

Sir Richard perked up. This was what he wanted to hear.

'… is a tethered goat.'

He visualised a terrified animal tethered to a platform in a jungle, the hunter in a nearby tree waiting to shoot the tiger as it pounced on its prey. 'What would we use as the bait?'

'Oh,' Rosemary waved her hand, 'some recent innovation. I'm sure you can come up with something suitable.'

'Not something we'd want to lose!'

Rosemary raised her eyes to the ceiling. 'Do try for some imagination. Of course not something we'd want to lose. It's got to be tempting though.'

Sir Richard considered this. 'How would it work?'

'It'll take time to set up. We'll have to lay bread-crumbs, hint at the "goat" in the right quarters, subtly of course. Make sure your two suspects get to hear of it. Set the trap. Lead them to it. Make it easy for them. See if they … *bite*.' Rosemary grinned like a crocodile.

'All right. But where … and how?'

Some time later, Sir Richard left Rosemary's house and walked to the waiting, chauffeur-driven car.

Rosemary's plan might just work but he didn't entirely trust her to pull it off. Perhaps it would be wise to take some precautionary measures, just in case. Rosemary wouldn't need to know about them.

He almost felt sorry for Rosemary. She must find it dull stuck out here after being at the centre of things for so long. His visit was probably the most exciting thing that had happened to her in a long time. Then he re-called the cold glint in her eye and the crocodile smile and he shivered.

He allowed himself a brief pause to take in the view of the ruined church and the general tranquility of Ayot St Lawrence in the early summer sunshine. How pleasant it would be to retire here … but not yet, and perhaps one of the neighbours might be a deterrent.

CHAPTER ONE

Two or so months later, the telephone rang in the hall at Haddens. Annabel heard it from the kitchen and hurried through to the hall shouting out, 'I'll get it.' Mrs Summers, her housekeeper, appeared on the upstairs gallery, raised a hand in acknowledgement and disappeared back to her housework.

Annabel still had to remind herself that this beautiful Tudor house in Hertfordshire actually belonged to her. Brought up in a Victorian end-of-terrace house in Shepherd's Bush, she had inherited Haddons just three months ago from her father Alec Stanhope who she thought had died in the Second World War. The inheritance had plunged her, at the age of twenty-one into a life of wealth, mystery and, at the time, danger.

'Annabel?' Rosemary Hutton's crisp but beautiful voice was instantly recognisable and Annabel's heart sank. Rosemary was an old friend of her father from their Special Operations Executive days in the second World War and, as Annabel had come to discover, one of the chief sources of clients to the Stanhope & Baxter firm. It was sure to be a job and Annabel's confidence in that department was at rock bottom. Ferdy's work at Stanhope & Baxter seemed to consist mainly of serving writs and debt recovery in London. He called it the company's 'bread and butter' in that it paid the bills, but it wasn't the sort of work that she either wished, nor was encouraged by Ferdy, to get involved in. Annabel was starting to think that her career as a private eye was over before it had begun.

'Ferdy's not here,' she said.

There was a slight pause. 'Is there any reason why I can't speak to you?'

'No, of course not. It's just that I thought –'

'Actually, it's you I wanted to speak to. I've got a job for you.'

'For me?'

'For both of you. But I want you to persuade Ferdy to take it on.'

Annabel didn't know what to say to this.

'He might be reluctant,' Rosemary continued. 'but it'll do him good. Won't say more now. Two o'clock tomorrow? That's good.'

Annabel replaced the phone on the hook and stood staring into the mirror above it for some time. Light blue eyes under straight brows stared back at her under thick straw-blond hair. She knew that she resembled her father closely because everyone who knew them both said so, but looking like him and filling his shoes were two entirely different things.

Rosemary enjoyed being cryptic but this stretched the bounds. However, if Rosemary was willing to employ her, perhaps her career wasn't over yet. What job could it possibly be that Ferdy would be reluctant to accept? He was a 'try my hand at anything' sort of person.

She returned to the kitchen where she had been endeavouring for some time, and so far without success, to open a padlock using only a thing that looked like a hairpin. Ferdy had made it look easy. Annabel regarded it with determination. She inserted the hairpin-like thing and jiggled it around. To her astonishment, the padlock clicked open.

'Yes!'

Full of confidence she closed it and tried again. Nothing doing.

The weather the following day was sunny with a light breeze that just lifted the dark green late summer foliage. Brought up in London, Annabel was still getting used to life in the country and she found the changing rural scenery fascinating. The crops in the fields were now a biscuit brown. Ferdy and Annabel were driving to Rosemary's house in Ferdy's ivory-white MGA. The hood was down and Annabel caught wafts of burnt toffee from the dried out fields that they passed.

'So, she didn't say what the job was about?' Ferdy broke the silence.

Annabel shifted uncomfortably in her seat. She hadn't told Ferdy what Rosemary had said. Surely, it was up to him to decide if he wanted to do a job or not? Rosemary was inclined to make everything so complicated and was probably imagining problems where none existed.

'No. Might be interesting?'

'Hmm.' Ferdy kept his eyes on the road.

'Not something we'd want to turn down,' continued Annabel. His silence was making her jumpy.

'Why ever would we want to turn it down?' He glanced at her in surprise.

'I just said, we *wouldn't* want to.'

Ferdy drew in to the side of the lane and switched off the engine. 'What aren't you telling me?'

Annabel hesitated. 'She said you might be reluctant to take it on but that it would do you good.'

Ferdy lifted his eyebrows in surprise. 'Can't think what that might be.'

'No. I couldn't either.'

Since her father's funeral he seemed to have retreated into himself. She was afraid he regretted asking her to join him in Stanhope & Baxter. He had insisted on sharing the company's profits fifty-fifty and she had done very little so far to earn that money. And he had no other source of income whereas she had the money she had inherited from her father – although it was still tied up in probate. John Trevor, her father's solicitor, was covering day to day outgoings for her in the meantime. Ferdy's father Sir Terrence Baxter, originally of Baxter Electricals but now so much more, was one of the richest men in the country and had been paying Ferdy an allowance, but after Sir Terrence had run off with, and then married, Ferdy's girlfriend Sarah, he had refused to accept it.

They drove into Ayot St Lawrence and drew up in front of Rosemary's house. Ferdy stopped the engine and a peaceful silence settled around them. Rosemary's orderly and geometric box-hedge and paving-stone front garden belied the corkscrew mind of the owner. As Annabel knew from previous visits, the back garden would be a profusion of country garden plants and wild flowers – Rosemary's self-proclaimed yin and yang.

She preceded Ferdy up the path and rang the bell by the green front door. They waited. Both knew it could take a while, but, in fact, the door was opened after only a moment by Phoebe, Rosemary's partner, who greeted them in a distracted fashion.

'Raspberry jam on the turn … you know where to find her.' She disappeared back into the kitchen. The sickly sweet smell of raspberries trailed behind her and hung in the air.

Rosemary was sitting in her usual chair with her back to the window so that her face was in shadow. She waved them to the sofa opposite where the sun fell full on their faces. Annabel was relieved to see that there was a tray with coffee pot and a plate of biscuits on the coffee table between them. She was hungry and had been afraid that Phoebe might have been too preoccupied to worry about refreshments.

'Thank you for coming,' Rosemary said. 'Coffee? Perhaps you would like to pour?'

Rosemary's arthritic hands looked more claw-like than normal. Annabel reached for the pot but Ferdy got there first. As he busied himself pouring the drinks Annabel looked around the room and saw the painting that her father, Alec, had left Rosemary in his will, *Poplars along the Loire* by Cézanne. Rosemary had hung it over the fireplace. It looked good there.

'Fear can be quite an aphrodisiac,' said Rosemary who must have noticed where she was looking. 'Alec and I had sex in just such a place as that. During the war, you know.'

Ferdy spilled coffee on the table.

'Oh, really?' Annabel knew she had coloured up; yet another piece of information about her father. So, Rosemary hadn't always preferred women.

'Happy memories.' Rosemary gave a satisfied little smile. 'Well, to business,' she continued. 'I am sure you must be aware of the problem caused by espionage in this country?'

Annabel had heard of Burgess and MacLean who had defected to Russia in 1951. She'd only been seven years old at the time but had grown up with the uneasy knowledge that members of the intelligence service had spied against their country. A sense of unease that was only intensified by the recent and very public defection of Kim Philby. Then there was the scandalous Profumo Affair just two years ago. And wasn't someone called Blake sent to prison for spying? But Rosemary probably knew a lot more about such things. As had her father, Alec Stanhope.

'We are, up to a point,' said Ferdy but didn't elaborate.

Annabel appreciated the 'we' whilst hoping that the extent of her own knowledge wouldn't be tested.

Ferdy got out his cigarettes. 'May I?'' he asked.

In response Rosemary indicated towards a nearby ashtray. She looked on sadly as Ferdy lit his cigarette with Alec's lighter.

'Is that was this is about?' he asked, expelling smoke.

'Before we go any further,' Rosemary turned to Annabel, 'have you signed the Official Secret's Act?'

Annabel laughed, 'Of course not!'

'That'll have to be remedied,' said Rosemary.

Annabel stared from Rosemary to Ferdy. 'You have?' she said to him.

'I have,' he confirmed. 'Just needs a drop of your blood, nothing to worry about.' His face was at its most unreadable.

Rosemary looked up at the ceiling and Annabel realised she was being teased but still … the Official Secrets Act! Just over three months ago she'd been a secretary in an accountant's office – and bored out of her mind, she reminded herself.

'Do you want me to leave?' she asked, bitterly disappointed.

'I think we'll trust you. But see that she signs it,' Rosemary added to Ferdy. She leant forward, hands on knees. 'I want you to be my eyes and ears on the ground in a sting operation to catch a suspected spy.'

'Sounds interesting,' said Ferdy.

To Annabel, it sounded difficult and possibly

terrifying but she noted the slight puzzlement in Ferdy's voice and shared it. They hadn't heard anything so far to suggest that he wouldn't want to take on the job.

'I presume this isn't your job alone? Is it MI5?' Ferdy continued.

Annabel was impressed. Perhaps he did know quite a bit about spying. But surely Rosemary was retired now? And wouldn't she have been MI6?

'Correct,' said Rosemary. 'They consulted me.' Her tone suggested *and about time too*. 'They have two suspects in mind. I suggested a sting operation – and that's where the two of you come in.'

'Who are the suspects?' asked Ferdy.

'One is a man from the foreign office, Gerald Harcourt …'

'Never heard of him,' said Ferdy.

'And the other is a Russian,' Rosemary paused, 'Alexi Galkin.'

Ferdy started forward in his seat. 'Alexi! He hates communist Russia! They must be mistaken.'

Rosemary's eyes glittered. 'Exactly what I said. But apparently he's been behaving suspiciously – receiving strange telegrams, taking sudden trips.'

Ferdy shook his head. 'But Alexi – he and I go way back.'

'I am aware of that,' said Rosemary.

'Do we know what was in the telegrams?' Annabel asked.

Rosemary looked at her. 'We do.' She handed over a sheet of paper. It contained five lines.

Canale Casablanca
Friedrich Tunis
Nain Caracas
Holbein Amsterdam
Vermeer Barranquilla

'And these were all separate telegrams?' asked Ferdy.

'They were.'

'Over what period of time?' asked Annabel.

'The first was four years ago. The rest, spread out between then and now. No particular pattern.'

'Could be some sort of code,' said Annabel. 'The first word in each case looks like a name. At least two are artists. And it looks like the second is a place. Did he go to the place in question after receiving the telegram?'

'He did.' said Rosemary. 'And all the names are of artists.'

'Could just be a list of paintings in different galleries around the world,' said Ferdy.

'Could be,' agreed Rosemary.

'Or maybe private collections?' said Ferdy. 'Alexi loves his art. He'd think nothing of travelling to see some particular picture.'

Rosemary looked at him with a certain degree of sympathy. 'It's never easy thinking ill of a friend. But,' her voice became brisk and businesslike again, 'that is why we have set up the sting operation. It's as much about clearing the innocent as catching the villain.'

'What about Gerald Harcourt?' asked Annabel. 'What suspicions are there concerning him?'

Rosemary told them what Sir Richard had said.

'So, he's become unpopular,' said Ferdy. 'I know what those weekend house parties are like. My father had them all the time. It's where all the business gets done. The Harcourts wouldn't have been the only visitors. Why pick on him?'

Rosemary shrugged her shoulders. 'Apparently things have gone missing more often than not when he and his wife have been guests. Rumours spread and mud sticks. Anyway, it's enough to raise questions.'

'Things?' asked Annabel.

'Things unspecified,' Rosemary admitted. 'I know it's tenuous and they may be being overcautious. It may be a case of light fingers. It may, on the other hand, be something more serious.'

'OK,' said Ferdy, 'How would it work?'

'It'll be another weekend house party. Both suspects will be invited, along with several other guests who will be invited as cover, and yourselves, of course. Documents of a sufficiently tempting nature will be, er, dangled.'

'So, as far as they are concerned, they believe themselves to be normal guests at someone's house but, at some time during the weekend they will attempt to locate and copy documents that they have been given every reason to suspect might be found there,' said Ferdy.

'Correct.'

'But how will they know about the documents?' asked Annabel.

I can assure you that they will know. Considerable effort has been made over the past few weeks, in the most subtle of ways, to ensure that they know.'

'What are the documents?' asked Ferdy.

'Blueprints, some sort of recent innovation in electronics, I believe. Suitably tempting.'

'But what if we fail and the documents do get copied?' Annabel asked.

Rosemary looked at her. 'What we want is a name. That's all.'

'So, when you say you want us to be your eyes and ears on the ground, that is literally it. We just bring back a name and let them get away with it?' Ferdy's voice betrayed his dislike of the proposal. Annabel wondered if this was the reason why Rosemary had thought Ferdy might not like to take on the job.

'And react to any unforeseen circumstances,' said Rosemary, a touch airily.

Unforeseen circumstances?

'What unforeseen circumstances do you anticipate?' said Ferdy.

Rosemary shrugged, 'You know the nature of these jobs. The pay will be good.'

Ferdy sat for a few moments in silence, a frown on this face.

'I presume that the host is in on this?' he asked.

Rosemary shifted in her seat. 'Naturally. But apart from the host and his wife and yourselves, nobody else will be in the know.'

'And who, exactly, are they? The hosts.'

Rosemary shifted again. 'The hosts are your father Sir Terrence and his wife Lady Sarah.'

Annabel gasped. She looked sideways at Ferdy. He sat still as a rock and his lips had tightened into a thin white line.

'No,' said Ferdy.

'Let me just explain.' Rosemary's voice was cold as steel.

'No point,' Ferdy interrupted. 'We're not taking the case.' He got up and walked out.

Annabel got up too. Rosemary looked annoyed but not as annoyed as Annabel might have expected. They heard the front door open and close.

'You're going to have to work on him,' said Rosemary turning back to Annabel. 'He'll come round.'

Annabel gaped at her. 'No he won't! You heard him. And, quite frankly, I'm amazed you even considered us for this job given the history between him and his father.'

'That is *precisely* why I did choose you. This nonsense between Ferdy and his father and Sarah has gone on long enough. They need to resolve it, if not for their own sakes, for yours.'

'My sake?' Annabel stared.

'He'll never be able to move on until he has resolved things with Sarah and his father,' Rosemary spoke with finality. 'Plus,' she continued, 'having you and Ferdy there at his father's house is the perfect plan in every other respect. Now, this is what you're going to do.'

Annabel left the house in a thoughtful mood. The car was still outside – which was a relief – but Ferdy was no-where in sight. She had been quite a while, and it was hot out there on the road. Perhaps he'd gone for a walk? Annabel decided to wait in the churchyard; it looked cool and shady. As she got closer she was surprised to see that the church was a ruin. The tower remained but the roof of the nave was gone and the flint walls partly demol-ished. It looked as though they had been like that for a long time. She opened the low metal gate that separated the churchyard from the lane and stepped through.

As soon as she was beneath the old hawthorn trees she felt her spirits lift – in direct contrast, it seemed, to the lowering of the ambient temperature. She was sure that Rosemary was right about Ferdy having to resolve things with his father and his stepmother Sarah before he could move on. And it would be silly to pretend that she herself had no vested interest in that. The age-old setting, the tall trees behind the church, told her that anything was possible given time.

Ferdy appeared from within the church, passing out through the arched doorway that had once contained a door. He walked, head down, hands in pockets, his slim, youthful, frame giving off a sense of contained strength and vitality. As he emerged into the sunlight his brown hair took on hints of auburn and gold that shone out against the dark interior. Annabel watched in appreciation. He looked up, saw her and walked in her direction. Annabel waited until he was alongside then turned back towards the lane. He fell into step beside her.

'I didn't know,' she said.

He looked searchingly at her. 'No, you didn't. What did she say? You were in there a while.'

'I think she still thinks we might take the case.'

Ferdy snorted. 'Of course she does. This is just the start.' He held open the gate for her.

'She means well,' Annabel offered.

'Does she? She has her own agenda.'

'"For queen and country"?'

He laughed abruptly. 'That, of course.'

'It might be an opportunity to mend things with your father.'

'Did she say that?'

Annabel was silent.

'Extend the olive branch?' continued Ferdy. 'Why should it be me that makes the first move?'

Annabel decided not to respond to that one either.

'That sounded pathetic,' he sighed. '*Why does it have to be me?*'

Annabel tried to think what her old friend and neighbour Enid would say: 'It's never good to let bad feelings take over.'

He was silent.

'Do you miss him? Your father?'

He shrugged.

They were back at the car by then and Annabel winced as the leather of the car seat burnt the backs of her legs – the downside of an open-top car. That notwithstanding, she loved this car with its red leather dashboard and seats, its wire wheels and gleaming chrome details.

'Have you done this sort of case before, with Alec?' Annabel asked, as Ferdy started up the motor and they drove out of Ayot St Lawrence.

'Since you're going to be signing the Official Secrets Act I'll come clean and say yes, I have. Kind of hard not to when I was working with Alec.'

'But you're working with me now,' said Annabel. 'I don't know anything about spying.' She took a deep breath. 'I don't feel ready for this. In fact, I'm amazed that Rosemary has involved me at all.'

'I think you'd be surprised what you can do. You found your father's money.'

'But this – trying to catch a spy – is different altogether.'

'Actually, not so much. You're still keeping your eyes open, noticing things, following clues. But anyway, we haven't said we'll take the case and my vote is still to say no, especially as Alexi is involved.'

Annabel considered this.

'Knowing one of the suspects wouldn't make it any easier,' she conceded. 'You seem pretty sure that Alexi Galkin couldn't be a spy.'

Ferdy laughed, 'Come to think of it, I wouldn't put anything much past Alexi. I just think it impossible he would ever spy for communist Russia. He hates them with a passion. His family lost everything when the Bolsheviks came to power.

Annabel tried to imagine what it must be like to have to flee your country; to lose your home, perhaps all your possessions; to never be able to go home. It might make you desperate enough to try to buy your way with stolen secrets. But surely the Bolsheviks came to power at the start of the century?

'Just how old is Alexi?' she asked.

'Six years older than me,' he paused. 'Yes, I can see what you're thinking. He was born in Austria. I'm not sure if he has ever been to Russia but he is fiercely proud of being Russian – the old Russia, that is.'

So Alexi was thirty three. Annabel thought about his background. It sounded sad.

'What about you?' asked Ferdy. 'Doubts aside, would you like to take the case?'

'I think I would,' she said.

'You would? Why?'

'"For queen and country", of course. Also, I'd like to meet your father.'

'Oh?'

'Dorothy says you take after him. I want to see what you'll look like in thirty years' time.'

Dorothy was Ferdy's younger sister. She and her brother had both been badly affected by their parents' divorce but whereas Ferdy had broken off all dealings with his father, Dorothy had tried to maintain a relationship with him and his new wife.

'Maybe Rosemary's right,' said Ferdy.

'Don't tell *her* that!'

Ferdy grinned reluctantly. 'Christ no!' He drew an audible breath. 'I meant, maybe it is time. All right, I'll think about it – but only "for queen and country".'

'Handsome and distinguished,' said Ferdy after they'd driven a few miles.

'What?' Annabel was confused.

'How I'll look in thirty years' time.'

'You're going to have plastic surgery between now and then?'

'Ha!'

Annabel settled back and looked up at the trees passing above their heads. She smiled.

A week later Rosemary phoned Haddens again. Annabel answered the phone.

'Well?' Rosemary asked. 'Have you managed to persuade him?'

'I'm not sure that either of us are that keen,' said Annabel.

'I'm going to have to have an answer. There's too much at stake.'

'Do you have a date in mind?' Annabel asked.

'It's all set up for the last weekend in August.'

It was all set up. Annabel felt steamrollered. 'And if we say no?'

'A lot of people will have wasted their time and a spy will continue to do their work unhindered.'

Annabel said she would speak to Ferdy.

CHAPTER TWO

The following day, Annabel was in the kitchen at Haddens with her housekeeper.

'Mrs Summers,' she asked, 'do you know Rosemary Hutton?'

''Course I do.'

'What do you think of her?'

'Fine once we'd come to an arrangement.'

Annabel was fascinated. 'What arrangement?'

'She doesn't involve me in any of her shenanigans and I send her two pots of my rhubarb and ginger chutney once a year. Cheap at the price, in my opinion.'

'I've never tasted your rhubarb and ginger chutney,' said Annabel hopeful of an offer.

'No, you haven't. Now, if that's everything, I'll be off. I've the vicar coming for lunch.'

No doubt, *he's* going to be offered some rhubarb and ginger chutney.

Annabel went into the library. The valuations of her father's assets and estate were gradually coming in and John Trevor, her solicitor, had asked her to have a think about what might be sold to help pay for estate duty.

'Well, those can go,' she said looking at the pieces of jade in one of the display cabinets. Not only were they ugly, in her opinion, they were also a troubling reminder of her father's problems. He had started to collect jade after he discovered that his art works were being replaced with reproductions. The reproductions could also go but she didn't suppose they would be worth anything.

The door bell rang putting a hold on these thoughts. She was expecting Ferdy but when she opened the door both Ferdy and his sister Dorothy were on the doorstep. Two cars stood on the drive,

Annabel embraced Dorothy in delight. She would like to have embraced Ferdy too but they hadn't quite reached that stage. They exchanged chaste kisses on the cheek. He smelt male and citrusy and he was freshly shaven.

Dorothy was wearing a dress with white, blue and red colour blocks set within a black grid. It reminded Annabel a bit of a Mondrian painting she'd seen once. It looked expensive. Annabel had made a bit of an effort herself due to Ferdy's impending visit. She believed she looked good in her blue mini skirt and white *broderie anglaise* top – both bought in the sale – but was humble enough to realise that Dorothy had eclipsed her.

'You look nice,' said Ferdy.

Perhaps not entirely eclipsed.

'Yes, you do!' Dorothy beamed. 'Doesn't that colour suit her?' she appealed to Ferdy.

What? The white?

'It does,' said Ferdy. 'Matches her eyes.'

Must mean the blue. Or maybe both.

'OK, that's enough,' she said. 'Anyone would think I never make an effort.'

Dorothy laughed over-loudly. She sounded nervous but what had she got to be nervous about? Annabel offered coffee and they went through to the kitchen. On the way she hung back and 'looked' a question at Ferdy. He shrugged his shoulders. He had no explanation.

Annabel put the kettle on the Aga hot plate and Ferdy sat down at the table. Dorothy sat down too but then got up and paced.

'Seems an age since I was here last!' she said.

'It was last week.'

'Oh! Was it?'

Annabel would have had her normal brand of instant coffee if she had been on her own but she made a pot of real coffee for her visitors. She'd just about worked out, through trial and error, how much coffee to put in to make a drinkable cup but still felt slightly anxious. At this rate the tension in the room would become unbearable. She placed pot and cups on the table and sat down. Dorothy sat down too. Her leg jiggled an audible rat-a-tat-tat with her shoe on the stone floor.

'I have news,' said Dorothy.

'Oh really?' said Annabel.

'Tell all,' said Ferdy.

'I'm engaged.' Dorothy smiled shyly at them.

Annabel leapt up. 'Oh Dorothy, that's marvellous! That is … I presume to Matt?' Matthew Lloyd had been holding a torch for Dorothy for years but Dorothy had become disillusioned with the thought of marriage following her parent's divorce.

'Of course to Matt!'

'Well done, Dodo.' Ferdy gave his sister a big hug. 'Got there at last.'

'Yes,' said Dorothy. 'I'm so happy. We both are.'

She did indeed appear to glow.

'Have you fixed a date?' Ferdy asked.

'Not yet but we're thinking of next April. I was wondering,' Dorothy turned to Annabel, 'if you'd be my bridesmaid?'

Annabel flushed in surprise. 'I'd be delighted. That is, if you're sure?'

Dorothy beamed. 'That's wonderful! And don't worry about the dress. It will be nice, I promise. I shan't expect you to wear anything hideous. Probably blue but I haven't quite decided yet.'

'Where will it be held?' asked Ferdy.

'I'm not sure about that either. It's really early days. I'd like it to be at the church where we grew up, you know, at Mum's, but I'm not sure if she can cope. You know what she's like. She'll want to be involved but she'll get all worked up.'

'I'll be happy to give you away,' said Ferdy, 'that is, if you want me to.'

Dorothy coloured, 'I'd really like that Ferdy,' she said, 'but Matt thinks I should ask Dad. In fact, he wants to ask Dad for his permission. He's old-fashioned that way. He wants a formal engagement at Dad's …' Dorothy's voice trailed away. Silence hung heavy over the table.

Annabel glanced at Ferdy. He had raised his face to the ceiling. His eyes were closed.

'And you want me there too,' he said.

'Of course I do!' Now that it was out, Dorothy clearly felt she could relapse back into self-justification. 'And Annabel too, of course. Don't you want to come?' Dorothy had adopted her 'little girl lost' look. It was very effective.

'Cut that out, Dodo.' Apparently, Ferdy had his own armour.

Dorothy grinned but then pouted. 'I thought you'd be pleased that we've got engaged!'

'I am, Dodo. I am. So when is this … event … going to happen?'

'Dad has suggested the last weekend in August.'

Annabel gasped. Ferdy lowered his cup slowly to the table. The last weekend in August was the weekend of the proposed sting operation.

'What is it?' asked Dorothy. 'Have you something else planned?

'No, we have nothing else planned,' said Ferdy slowly.

'Well, I know it means going to Dad's and I do know that's going to be hard but …' Dorothy took a deep breath, 'don't you think it's time?'

'I'll think about it.'

Dorothy left shortly afterwards having achieved her objective, if not yet having received a definitive answer.

Annabel and Ferdy watched as she drove away, her black and white checked headscarf fluttering in the breeze.

Annabel, who had barely been able to contain herself since Dorothy had mentioned the last weekend in August burst out, 'I cannot believe that your father has allowed the two events to happen on the same weekend!'

'Oh,' Ferdy laughed hollowly, 'I can believe it all too well. He'll think it's economic use of time.'

'But what if the "unforeseen circumstances" turn out to be dangerous. Has he thought of that?'

'I don't suppose there will be any danger. We're just there to *watch*, remember.'

'Well, but it's not impossible. And presumably your father knows that. Has he no concern for Dorothy's well-being? And how could he be so unkind to her! She'll be expecting to be the centre of attention when in reality she'll just be shoe-horned into something that your father probably thinks is *far* more important!' Annabel realised that her voice had risen.

'Welcome to our world,' said Ferdy.

Annabel looked at him in horror. She was starting to understand what life had been like for Ferdy and Dorothy growing up.

'I'm just wondering what Rosemary had to do with it all,' he continued. 'The screws are being turned.'

'Rosemary? But how could she have anything to do with Matt and Dorothy getting engaged?'

'You'd be surprised. Oh, not in the fact itself, but in

the mechanics of it, yes. I've said no to her. Can I also say no to my dear sister?'

'We're being manipulated.'

Ferdy laughed. It wasn't a pleasant sound.

'Do you think Dorothy knows that she and Matt won't be the main attraction?' Annabel asked.

'Probably not.'

Annabel couldn't imagine Matt agreeing to anything that might put Dorothy in danger, however unlikely. 'She's ruthless, Rosemary, I mean. She seems to be quite happy to put your entire family in danger if it means she gets what she wants.'

'Yes. Yes, she is. In any event, I think we've just been given our excuse for being there.'

'Excuse? Do we need one? After all, it is your father's house.'

'And Alexi, for one, knows that I haven't seen him since he left my mother.'

Two days later, Ferdy and Annabel were waiting by Marlborough Gate on the north side of St James' Park. A black car, un-showy but quietly expensive drew up on The Mall and a man got out of the back seat.

Ferdy whistled under his breath. 'She's really pulled out the big guns this time.'

'What?' said Annabel. 'Who?' She didn't recognise the man and he didn't look that impressive. She reassessed that view as he walked towards them. He had an air of authority and assuredness.

'Sir,' said Ferdy.

Annabel wondered if she should curtsey. The moment passed.

'Baxter,' the man nodded a greeting. 'And Annabel Staple, I believe? I knew your father.'

Annabel was too used to people saying this to be surprised. What did surprise her was that this man called her by her name, Staple. Most people who met her for the first time assumed her surname would be Stanhope.

The man looked around with apparent pleasure at the sunshine and general greenery. 'Shall we walk?' The question was rhetorical. He set off down the curved path towards the lake and they fell into step beside him.

It was indeed a beautiful day; the trees were wearing their late summer foliage which cast deep shadows across the dried out lawns. Annabel glanced back. The car had gone. She hadn't noticed the man arranging a collection time. She had slotted into place to the right of Ferdy, leaving him to walk beside the man, whose name she still didn't know. She wasn't sure what she would find to say to him, so was happy to remain a bystander. Not that Ferdy was required to say much either. The man kept up a gentle flow of platitudes as they ambled south towards the lake.

They crossed the bridge over Blue Lake and continued down to Birdcage Walk. Annabel wondered if the man would ever get to the point. But perhaps his mere presence was the point. They arrived at the southern edge of the park and Annabel was fascinated to see the man's car draw up. Smooth as a well-oiled clock and bang on time.

'I'll be seeing your father later today,' the man said to Ferdy. 'I'll tell him we'll go ahead? It's really very important, you know.'

'Yes, sir,' said Ferdy, accepting the inevitable.

'A pleasure to have met you,' the man said to Annabel. 'A great shame about your father.'

He stepped into the car which drew smoothly away. Annabel and Ferdy stood in silence watching it depart. Annabel took a deep breath. Such rarified company had left her feeling starved of air. Ferdy, she observed, was looking resigned but not particularly happy.

Annabel found her voice. 'Who *was* that man?'

'Actually I don't know his name. Alec knew him – referred to him as 'Jehovah'. I've only met him the once.'

Annabel looked at him, 'So, we're taking the job?'

Ferdy sighed. 'It would seem so.'

It was what Annabel wanted but she was concerned for Ferdy. 'Are you all right with that?'

He shrugged. 'I don't appear to have been given a choice.'

Hooked but not committed. Suddenly, Annabel was angry on his behalf. 'Well, I think it's entirely up to you. If you don't want to do it, we don't do it!'

He grinned lopsidedly. 'Oh … it's probably time.'

Annabel stood self-conscious and defensive in her best

blue dress. She had bought it in the January sales and only worn it once.

Dorothy looked at it critically. 'No.'

'What do you mean, "No"?'

They were in Annabel's bedroom at Haddens and the sun was sending shafts of light onto the polished wood floor. It felt pleasantly warm under Annabel's bare feet.

'Believe me, it won't do. Not at Dad's. Everyone will dress for dinner and they won't be wearing last year's high street cast-offs.'

'But nobody will know. It's as good as new!' Annabel protested.

'That model was in the shops last year and if I know that, everyone else there will know it too. At least, all the women will.'

'What a fuss!' Annabel complained. The prospect of 'dressing for dinner' was daunting. For the first time she wondered how she would manage in the house of a very rich man. 'I suppose you think I ought to buy something *haute couture*?'

It appeared that Dorothy had failed to register the sarcasm in her voice. 'Thank goodness!' she beamed. 'I was afraid you were going to get all silly and start saying you couldn't afford it – which of course you can, now.'

Well, I walked into that one. Humbly, she begged Dorothy's advice. She would need it.

Which was why, two days later, Annabel trailed reluctantly behind Dorothy as she swept into a small boutique in New Bond Street – a street Annabel had never visited before, not even to window shop. At first glance the shop, to Annabel's eyes, seemed virtually empty. Just two meagre rows of clothes along each wall and a central pedestal-type thing with one handbag and a pair of shoes on it. At least they were matching, Annabel acknowledged. But where was the choice?

Dorothy was busy being greeted by the woman in the shop, effusively, it seemed, and by name. Annabel sneaked a peak at one of the dresses on the stand and visibly recoiled at the price on the tag. She'd never dare wear something that cost that much! She'd be bound to spill something on it before she'd worn five minutes. Surreptitiously Annabel wiped her hand over her skirt, afraid to even touch the merchandise in case her hands were sticky.

'Dear Dorothy tells me you have a weekend party coming up.' The woman appeared beside her taking in, with a practiced eye, the sum of Annabel's clothes which she must have known cost relatively little, maybe even as little as one of those headbands artfully hung from a cherub on the wall. Annabel gave her credit for not blanching but recognised that this was purely because of Dorothy's introduction.

Dear Dorothy was hovering nearby pretending to look at a pair of checked cigarette trousers but Annabel was not deceived.

'Yes, I have,' she said. Now that she was here she might as well make an effort. Out of the corner of her eye she could see Dorothy relax. 'I'll need a dress for the evening.'

'I'm sure we can help,' the woman purred.

Yes, I'm sure you can. Already, Annabel missed the anonymity of her usual high street shops.

'With that figure and hair …' the woman stepped back, finger to lips, 'something simple, I think.' She suddenly darted over to the far wall and came back holding, reverently and in both arms, a slip of a dress in a soft yellow.

Actually, that's quite nice. Annabel reached out to it.

'But with those eyes … blue. Definitely blue.' The woman hung the yellow dress on the end of the rail and darted away again, this time to a room in the rear – that explained the lack of choice – and reappeared with a different dress in ice-blue.

'Try them both on,' Dorothy urged.

The changing room was a revelation: large and spacious with a huge mirror, a chair and a small table with a box of tissues upon it. From a peg on the wall hung a scrap of fine muslin. Annabel wondered what it was for.

It was a far cry from the scrummage of the communal changing rooms Annabel was used to: ten or twenty girls struggling into and out of clothes, the floor a mass of discarded clothing, hand bags between feet, shrieks of laughter, body odour, a motley assortment of underwear on show.

This changing room was hers alone.

'I'm next door,' Dorothy called. 'Trying on those trousers.'

Annabel began slowly to undress. The dresses were her size. The woman hadn't even asked. She put on the yellow one first. The zip opened and closed with a whisper. It was fully lined and slid over her skin like a caress. She looked at herself in the mirror. And looked.

'Which one have you tried first? Is it nice on?' Dorothy called.

'Yes … it's nice. The yellow.'

'There's a big mirror out here,' said the woman.

This one isn't big enough?

'May I see?' Dorothy's voice came from directly outside.

Annabel emerged reluctantly and was greeted with a stunned silence.

'You look *amazing*!' Dorothy was almost hugging herself with delight.

'Very nice,' said the woman with quiet satisfaction. 'I have shoes that match that perfectly.'

Of course you do. But she was quietly delighted by her own appearance. She would buy this ridiculously priced article of clothing, she decided, if only to see Ferdy's face when he saw her wearing it.

'Try the other one on,' Dorothy urged.

'Why? I like this one.'

She saw a lack of comprehension on both women's faces and, bowing to the inevitable, returned to the changing room.

Oh dear. She knew it was a mistake to try it on.

She stepped outside.

'You're just going to have to buy both of them,' Dorothy pronounced.

'That just came in today. I haven't had a chance to put it out yet.'

Dorothy's indrawn breath was audible and reverential.

CHAPTER THREE

I t was Friday morning and Annabel and Ferdy had been driving alongside a high stone wall for some distance, and had just passed a signpost for Saffron Walden. There were fields to their right full of ripening wheat and barley and the occasional tree overhead bestowed a welcome coolness to the otherwise warm air. Their two suitcases were strapped to a rack on the boot. Just as well it wasn't raining; sports cars were impractical if you had luggage to carry. They had been silent for some time now, both occupied with their own thoughts.

'Must be almost there now,' said Ferdy.

'You really haven't been before?' Annabel was surprised. 'Not once?'

Ferdy cast her a look. 'New wife, new home.' They rounded the corner and came upon a wide entrance with a solid looking gate. No house name as far as Annabel could see. 'Same security,' Ferdy added dryly.

He drew up in front of the gate and they looked at a mounted camera and an intercom panel. Ferdy pressed a button, the panel crackled into life and a disembodied male voice said, 'Could you just confirm your identity please, sir.'

'Ferdinand Baxter and Annabel Staple,' said Ferdy.

'Straight up the drive please, sir, and follow the signs to the house.' The gate opened automatically and Ferdy drove through. Glancing back, Annabel saw the gates closing smoothly behind them. She felt a momentary disquiet. The trap suddenly felt all too real.

'Do you think they know that you're the boss' son?' Annabel asked as they proceeded as directed.

'Well, they do now.'

There was no sight of the house from the road but Annabel was used to that now. Her father's house was the same. It seemed the richer you were, the more you valued your privacy. Annabel had loved the fact that she could go from her parent's back door to that of her neighbour Enid's in twelve paces but she had to admit that she also loved the space and privacy of Haddens.

The house when it eventually came into sight was unexpected. So unexpected that Ferdy stopped the car. 'Art Deco, who would have thought …' he said.

Ultra modern with white walls, clean lines, large and small windows some of which were round, like portholes, curved glass-brick walls, metal poles supporting porches. It was deceptively small in that it was only two storeys high and didn't have a pitched roof but it stretched away on both sides of the entrance in a shallow curve, into the surrounding birch and pine trees.

'Omega House,' said Annabel. She too had been expecting something older, but the name suited it. 'It looks like a ship.'

'Does a bit,' he agreed.

'It's not like your old house?' Annabel asked.

'No. The house we grew up in, where my mother lives now, is Georgian.'

Annabel, clenching her hands in her lap, sensed Ferdy glancing over and unclenched them. She was supposed to be supporting him.

'They won't bite, you know,' he said.

'Of course not.' She wondered if he was reassuring her … or himself. 'But anyway, the danger is going to be from one of the guests.'

'That's the plan. Dangle the cheese and the mouse will come.'

'And the enticing morsel? Rosemary mentioned blueprints. We don't know exactly what, do we?'

'No, but I imagine it's a whopping hunk of gorgonzola not some piece of –'

'Not a paltry triangle of cream cheese?' Annabel cut in.

Ferdy grinned. 'I was going to say Cheddar, but you've got the idea.'

'I like Cheddar,' said Annabel. She also liked cream cheese. Let's face it, she liked *any* cheese.

Ferdy started the car. '*En avant* and all that; into the lion's den.'

'There'll be mice and lions?'

They emerged into a spacious forecourt area with an island bed of large stones and heather. Annabel hoped that the simplicity of architecture and planting would be reflected in the food. She wasn't holding her breath on that score.

There was a man waiting on the steps leading to the front door.

She felt Ferdy tense. 'My father,' he said.

Annabel was pleasantly surprised. It looked as though Sir Terrence was making a real effort to be welcoming. He couldn't have been waiting there on the off chance of their arrival; the man who spoke on the intercom must have alerted him, no doubt by prior arrangement. Annabel began to feel hopeful about one part, at least, of the weekend's activities. Sarah wasn't there, but perhaps that was also by design?

They drew up and got out. Sir Terrence stepped forward and they walked to meet him. It looked for a moment as though Sir Terrence would attempt to embrace his son but Ferdy made no corresponding movement and the moment passed.

'Ferdy, I'm glad you were able to come.'

Annabel imagined Ferdy's mind running through all the arm twisting and machinations behind his presence there, but he contented himself with, 'Hello Dad. You're looking well.'

He was indeed looking well. Dapper in beige trousers and a pale yellow V-neck cashmere jersey over a white shirt, he was, as Dorothy and Ferdy had said, an older version of Ferdy. The face had filled out, the eyes had seen more, there was an authority and presence which Ferdy lacked but the spark that lay within Ferdy and which made him who he was, lay within the older man too. It was masked, at present, by an expression which puzzled

Annabel until she identified it as unease. Unlikely, in a man who had the ear of government, you would have imagined.

'And this must be Annabel Staple.' Sir Terrence turned to her. His voice was even but his eyes were cool. Annabel had wondered how necessary her presence was at this weekend. Now she wondered if she was there under sufferance. 'I knew your father.' He didn't sound as though the acquaintanceship gave him any pleasurable memories and Annabel wondered if he had resented Alec's hold over Ferdy. Annabel waited for the usual comment about her striking resemblance to Alec but Sir Terrence was silent. 'Sarah is looking forward to meeting you,' he continued smoothly. 'She is just seeing to Jonny ... but do come in.' He led them up the steps and into the house.

At first glance, Annabel felt as though she had stepped into a mausoleum. The entrance hall was wide and deep. The house must be considerably larger and deeper than the exterior had given one to expect. Everything was white, the walls and ceiling and the floor, which looked as though it was made of marble. A white staircase curved away to the left of the front door towards the upper floor. There was a marked lack of clutter. One huge modern picture, in tones of orange and brown, added colour to the otherwise austere space.

They became aware of footsteps upstairs. A young woman with Jackie Onassis style hair and what looked, to Annabel's admittedly uneducated eye, like designer clothes came down the stairs. She walked slowly and appeared to be concentrating on her feet on the stairs so that it wasn't until she reached the bottom of the flight that she looked up. Under beautifully arched eyebrows her eyes wore an expression in which reserve and determination were equally apparent. Annabel had never seen such perfect skin. She was blond. It wasn't even Annabel's type of messy straw blond; it was perfect blond, smooth and shiny. Annabel imagined that it stayed exactly where it was supposed to stay. She took all this in with misgiving and then glanced at Ferdy. He was also looking and his face wore its usual unreadable expression. Then Annabel looked at Sir Terrence and was surprised to see that he too was looking at Ferdy and from Ferdy to Sarah and back again.

'There you are, my dear.' Sir Terrence stepped forward. 'They have arrived, you see!'

Sarah reached the hall floor and walked towards them. The swelling at her waist showed her condition. 'Yes indeed. Hello Ferdy,' she said in a soft voice. Annabel thought she saw an element of assessment in Sarah's eyes, quickly replaced by cautious friendliness. Sarah held out her hand which, after a momentary hesitation, Ferdy shook. 'And you must be Annabel. I am so pleased to meet you.' Her voice had a slight regional accent which Annabel couldn't place.

They stood awkwardly.

'There's coffee in the drawing room,' said Sir Terrence.

Sarah led the way into the second of the doors at the rear of the hall which opened onto a huge room with a predominantly white and grey colour theme. A large grey sofa and four cream armchairs were grouped around a rectangular glass topped coffee table in front of an open fire place with white marble surround whilst four large windows looked out over a vista of grass and trees. The central two were French windows whilst the outer two had deep window seats covered in a grey fabric that matched the sofa. The only colour in the room was provided by another huge modern picture over the fireplace, this time in shades of bright blue and orange, a richly polished oak floor and a turquoise rug under the coffee table. Again the room was very bare of possessions. There were no books and few other paintings on the walls.

'Minimalist,' said Ferdy.

'The advantage of starting afresh,' said Sir Terrence. 'There is very little here that we have not chosen ourselves.'

Sarah tensed.

'Indeed,' said Ferdy coldly.

Annabel accepted a cup of coffee, white no sugar, and a seat on the sofa. There were no biscuits. It would appear that the minimalism extended to the food. However, at that moment the door opened and a young woman came in bearing a tray on which sat plates and biscuits and a cake. With raised spirits Annabel accepted a slice of the lightest looking lemon sponge she'd ever seen. It floated onto her plate and came with a cake fork and a neat little paper napkin. Annabel regarded the cake fork dubiously. It seemed she would have to use it. She did so, then chased the resultant piece around the plate.

Ferdy was looking at a sideboard to the left of the fireplace with a glass top. It looked like a display case to Annabel. 'Some things have travelled with you, I see.'

'Yes. There were some things that your mother didn't want … and that I would have been sorry to lose.'

'Would you like to see?' Sarah asked Annabel.

Annabel abandoned her cake, got up and looked into the display case. It contained lots of little boxes many of which had pictures painted or enamelled on their lids. They were pretty, she supposed, and if you were going to collect something it made more sense perhaps than football cards which is what Frank, her stepfather, had collected.

'What are they?'

'Snuff boxes. People used them before cigarettes came along.' She lifted the lid and took one out. 'This one's my favourite.' The scene depicted was of a shepherd and shepherdess standing together under a tree – a bucolic image of love.

'So, let's talk about why we're here,' Ferdy said, abruptly.

Sir Terrence shifted uncomfortably. 'Perhaps you'd like to settle in first? Then we can talk.'

'I can show you,' Sarah said.

She sounded over-eager. If everyone was going to be this much on edge the weekend was going to be tough.

They finished their coffee and followed her back into the hall. Their suitcases were no longer there.

'I've had them taken up to your rooms,' Sarah explained. She led the way up the stairs. They were also uncarpeted and to Annabel's eyes they looked dangerous. Sarah climbed them warily. 'It's the only thing I don't like about this house,' she said. 'Be careful, they can be slippery. There really should be a handrail. We would've arranged for one to be fitted as part of the work but it never occurred to us at the time.'

'How long have you lived here?' asked Annabel. making conversation to mask Ferdy's silence. He was looking about him, his expression a veneer of politeness overlaying a patent dislike of all that he saw.

'We bought it … just after we got together' – a glance at Ferdy – 'but then we had a lot of work done. We've only just moved in properly this year. We love the Art Deco style.'

'The name's unusual – Omega House.'

'Yes, it is a bit.' She paused as if to say more but then remained silent.

Annabel gasped as they reached the top of the stairs. It opened out into what appeared to be a huge space divided into smaller areas by mid-height partitions running at right angles to the outside wall. The partitioned areas were occupied by comfortable chairs and sofas in bright blues and orange colours whilst the end walls and partition walls held a great many paintings but what took the breath away was the view from six large windows which stretched away to the horizon across extensive lawns, a large lake and beyond that, fields and woods.

Sarah smiled at her. 'Yes, we love it. We put in the partitions to give more hanging space for Terry's paintings.'

'Must be hard to heat,' said Ferdy.

Sarah turned to him, 'Oh no! It's all beautifully insulated.' She led them towards the left into a long wide corridor with doors stretching away to the left and right. 'You're now in the bit that we built on. We've put you in the first two rooms here. I hope that will be all right? We thought you'd like to be as close to everything as possible.' She opened the first of the doors. 'This room is for you Annabel, and Ferdy, you're next door.' She stepped back. 'Come downstairs when you've settled in.'

Annabel entered her room. It was large and contained a double divan bed, a dressing table and two chairs. The colour scheme was soft earthen colours; pinks, creams and beiges. It was warm and welcoming.

'It looks like a hotel room,' said Ferdy. He had followed her in. He didn't sound impressed.

'Does it?' Annabel had never been to a hotel. If this was what they were like, she wanted to stay in one. She noted with delight a box of tissues on the dressing table. She explored the two doors in the room. One led to a walk-in wardrobe. She opened the other.

'Ferdy!' She stopped in wonder. 'My own bathroom!'

Ferdy peered over her shoulder and sniffed.

'Let's look in your room!'

They did so and found a mirror image but for the colour scheme which was in tones of grey and blue.

'Girls and boys,' said Ferdy. 'A bit stereotyped isn't it?'

His reaction filtered through Annabel's delight. 'You don't like it?'

'It's … impersonal.'

Perhaps it was a bit impersonal. But she still liked it.

'At least we'll sleep.' Ferdy indicated the heavy curtains that hung floor to ceiling in front of the deep window embrasure.

Annabel returned to her bedroom where she unpacked her things discovering further wonders; scented drawer liners which reminded her of Mrs Summers, writing paper with Omega House on it in a clean modern font, padded coat hangers and shoe trees. She washed her face and hands in the bathroom where she found three different sized ochre-coloured towels, scented soaps and, wonder of wonders. a cream towelling dressing gown.

A tap on her door a while later and Ferdy entered at her call.

'Ready?'

'Ferdy! I have a dressing gown! Do you?'

'I do. In fact, all manner of stuff.'

'Well, I think it's amazing!'

'Glad somebody's pleased,' he grinned. 'But my guess is she had an interior designer job-lot.'

'Well, if so, she can add in the personal touches later.'

'That's very true.' They set off down the corridor. 'Forward … into the valley of death …'

'… and other stirring, call-to-arms speeches.' She sensed, rather than saw, his grin widen as she preceded him down the stairs. It was a staircase for making a grand and confident entrance. She wished it had a handrail.

CHAPTER FOUR

'How did you get mixed up in all this?' Ferdy asked his father.

They were in what Annabel presumed was the dining room having lunch. Annabel was surprised that the room wasn't larger. She wondered how meals would be managed when everyone else was there. The table sat four comfortably – at a pinch it would seat six.

Sir Terrence patted his mouth with his napkin. 'I was approached.'

'By Rosemary Hutton?'

Sir Terrence inclined his head. 'She thought I'd have a vested interest in catching someone who was selling our ideas to the Russians.'

'Which you do.'

'Which I do.' It looked as though he was going to say more but changed his mind. 'The rest,' he shrugged, 'was obvious. I'm an industrialist, I give house parties. I have the perfect set up.'

'And you knew that we would be involved?'

'That was a … detail … I was happy to accept,'

Annabel wondered quite how happy he had been. How difficult had it been to persuade him? She recalled the way that Sir Terrence had looked from Ferdy to Sarah and back again. Was he frightened about losing Sarah back to Ferdy? How successful was their marriage?

'After all this time,' said Ferdy. 'Patriotic fervour wins the day.'

'I had other reasons. And you accepted too. But, of course,' he dabbed at his mouth again, 'anything would be better than … what is it you do now, serve writs?'

Ferdy went very still in his chair.

So, Sir Terrence knew how Ferdy earned the bulk of his money. He made it sound pathetic, disreputable. Annabel was furious on Ferdy's behalf. Sir Terrence should have seen Ferdy coming back on some of the days, still with that light in his eyes, even when sometimes holding himself stiffly, as though he'd been in a fight.

'I still pay your allowance,' said Sir Terrence quietly. 'Every month, into your account.'

'You should stop. I don't want it.'

'Keep it to pay for school fees,' said Sir Terrence flippantly.

There was a tense silence.

'Would you like more salad?' Sarah asked Annabel.

'Anyway, here we are now,' said Sir Terrence. 'We need to discuss the arrangements.'

'I presume that it's just the four of us who know the whole situation?' asked Ferdy, his tone crisp and business like.

Sir Terrence raised his eyebrows but responded, 'That is correct. Our guests this weekend are Gerald Harcourt, his wife Violet and their daughter Lucy –'

'They're bringing their daughter?' It was the first time Annabel had spoken and her voice expressed her surprise. Surely, if Gerald Harcourt was planning to steal anything he wouldn't bring his wife *and* daughter?

Sir Terrence turned to her, it seemed, reluctantly. She had reminded him of her presence. 'Yes, it is a surprise. A last minute arrangement, they telephoned yesterday. On the face of it, it does make it less likely that he is our spy. Then there is Alexi Galkin who I gather you know?' He had turned back to Ferdy.

'Yes.' Ferdy didn't elaborate.

'When you were out in Germany,' Sir Terrence continued, his voice suddenly hard.

Annabel realised she was missing something here. What was Ferdy doing in Germany and why wasn't his father happy about it?

'It was national service,' said Ferdy in the tone of voice that suggested they'd had this conversation before.

Ferdy had been in national service? Of course, he would have been! It was so easy to forget all that. That would explain why his time in college was put back. She hadn't done the maths before, but if he was twenty-seven now he must have done something between leaving school and starting college. She wondered why he hadn't mentioned it.

'Yes, which for most people is two years but you stayed on, when you knew I–'

'Oh, for God's sake! Let's not go over all that again!' Ferdy burst out. 'Yes, I stayed. I liked the work. And I came back, went to college like you wanted,' he shot a bitter glance at Sarah, 'and see what came of that!'

He had met Sarah at college. She, presumably, had come straight from school. But what work was he doing out in Germany that he liked so much? And it sounded as though it was his father's wish, rather than his own that he went to college to become a lawyer. He had told her, she remembered, that he hadn't felt cut out to be a solicitor.

Sarah had turned a shade of white.

'That's enough!' said Sir Terrence.

'It's all right,' Sarah said. She turned to Ferdy. 'How well do you know Alexi Galkin? Do you think it could be him?'

Ferdy took a few moments to calm himself down. 'Yes, I do know him well. We worked together. And, no, I don't think he would ever work for the Russians. Who else is invited?'

'Professor Humphrey Calder, my old friend from college days. You remember him?' asked Sir Terrence. 'He often visits, as you know –'

'I don't know,' Ferdy interrupted.

Sir Terrence paused, 'Ah, of course. Well, he *continues* to visit me every six weeks or so. This will be one of those visits. It will help having someone neutral here. And Dorothy and Matt will be here.' He made it sound like an afterthought.

Getting engaged.

'Dorothy said they're going to announce their engagement,' said Ferdy.

'So I gather.' Sir Terrence smiled. 'The perfect cover don't you think?'

Annabel looked at him almost with hatred.

'I know why *we* want Alexi and this Harcourt man here but why do *they* want to be here?' asked Ferdy. 'That is, if they're not after the documents?'

'I don't normally have people turning down invitations to my house,' said Sir Terrence stiffly, then he grinned as though realising how that sounded. Suddenly, he looked very like Ferdy. 'But, that aside, Harcourt collects snuffboxes – we often come up against each other in auction houses. He's been wanting to see my collection for a long time. And Alexi has expressed a desire to see my art collection.' He pushed his chair back and stood up. 'But now we'd better show you around.'

They followed him into the hall where they saw a small boy of about two years old being led slowly and carefully down the stairs by a young woman. The boy saw Sarah and cried out, 'Mummy!'

Sarah's face softened, she opened her arms and the child, who had reached the bottom of the stairs by then, ran towards her. She swept him up in her arms and turned to Ferdy.

'This is Jonny. Jonny, this is your brother Ferdy.'

Looking between the two of them Annabel was hard pressed to know who looked the more confounded: Ferdy at meeting his new brother or the child seeing an adult described as his brother.

'Half-brother,' Ferdy corrected.

Jonny looked at Ferdy, taking in his height, puzzlement clear in his eyes.

'Your father is my father.'

Now Jonny was more confused than ever. He hid his face in Sarah's shoulder. She unclasped his arms from behind her neck and set him down on the floor holding him there with her hands on his shoulders.

Ferdy stepped forward and squatted down. 'Hello little man,' he said. He held out his hand.

Sarah pushed her son gently forward. 'Shake hands, Jonny.'

Annabel watched the three of them with something approaching pain. They might have been husband and wife. Jonny might be their child. Then she glanced at Sir Terrence who stood in the background watching on. His face wore an expression that she was unable, at first, to place. Then she realised that the expression was fear. She wondered if her own face wore a similar expression.

'I've tried to explain it to him,' Sarah said, 'but I think he was still thinking you'd be … younger.'

'Yes,' said Ferdy. He withdrew his unshaken hand and stood once more.

'This is Ruby who looks after Jonny for us, and this is Sir Terrence's other son Ferdy and his partner Annabel Staple.' Sarah introduced them to each other.

Ruby nodded in a friendly way. 'We're just going out for a walk, aren't we Jonny!' She opened the door to the right of the front door. Annabel and Ferdy looked into a sizeable cloakroom which contained coats, hats, boots, walking sticks and umbrellas. This explained the lack of such things in the hall. They existed. They were just out of sight.

They followed Sir Terrence and Sarah round the rest of the house. The intimate nature of the room in which they'd eaten their lunch was explained when they entered a huge room to the left of the front door containing a dining table that must be able to seat up to twenty-four people and still leave room for more. The polished ash table reflected back the silver birch trees visible through four floor-to-ceiling windows. This must be where the formal meals took place.

A door to the rear of the hall and beneath the ascending stairs led through to the staff area and they were shown round the kitchen area which appeared to Annabel's eyes to be state-of-the-art, all gleaming metal and scrupulously clean. A tall rangy man wearing a full length apron and a black and white bandanna – presumably to keep his long hair out of his eyes and the food – was busy at the central table rolling out pastry. He flicked them a glance, nodded to acknowledge their presence but said nothing. He looked capable of catching and killing wild meat with his bare hands but no doubt he used the shops like everyone else. Beyond the kitchen were offices for the housekeeper and the butler, a staff dining room, a staff living room and several store rooms. A door at the end of the corridor led out to the back yard and garage area.

Upstairs the two wings curved away to the east and

west of the central gallery. They went to the east first. Beyond their bedrooms was the bedroom allocated to Professor Humphrey Calder, whilst opposite them were the bedrooms allocated to Gerald and Violet Harcourt and to Lucy Harcourt with a further bedroom that would remain empty. There was a door at the end of that section of the corridor.

'Where does that lead?' Ferdy asked.

'The staff bedrooms are beyond together with stairs down to the kitchen quarters,' Sarah said.

Turning in the other direction and entering the wing running westward they were shown Dorothy's bedroom and next to it Matt's bedroom. The room that Alexi would occupy was opposite. Three further bedrooms remained unoccupied on this side of the house whilst a doorway led through to the area occupied by Sir Terrence and Sarah, together with Jonny, the nursery quarters and Ruby's bedroom.

Twelve guest bedrooms: it was like a hotel! Now that Ferdy had pointed it out, they did all seem rather characterless and uniform but she was still hugely impressed. Annabel and Ferdy were in the 'east wing', apparently. Annabel might have expected Sarah to sound grand as she said this but Sarah used the term matter-of-factly and maybe if you lived in a house this big you had to have terms for the different areas so that people knew where things were.

'I presume there are locks on all these doors,' said Ferdy. 'Will we be provided with copies of the keys?'

'There is a master key which you can both have,' said Sir Terrence. 'It will open staff and guest rooms alike. You will, of course, use it with discretion.'

Downstairs a corridor to the west of the hall led to a library and the room in which they'd eaten their lunch which Sarah called the morning room. Beyond were offices for Sir Terrence and Sarah and their respective secretaries. Annabel was surprised that Sarah had an office and a secretary. Looking into Sarah's office Annabel saw shelves full of files, a large desk with two telephones and three clocks on the walls set to different time zones. There was a large board on the wall with what appeared to be an itinerary for the second half of the year mapped out. Annabel saw Paris written across the previous week and New York written across the following week. Their weekend had been shoe-horned into a busy schedule. It looked as though Sarah had a hands-on role in running … what? The company? The house? The two secretaries also had bedrooms on this level but neither of them were to be there this weekend.

They finished up in the library and it was immediately apparent that this was where Sir Terrence and Sarah spent most of their time. The colours were warm and rich, there were books and pictures and low lamps and cushions of different colours and shapes. Two deep, high-backed armchairs stood either side of the fireplace and it was clear from the reading lamps and the two side tables that they were used.

Further down the room was a desk. Annabel wandered

over. On it there were three framed photographs. One was of Sarah with Jonny on her lap. From the expression in her eyes, Annabel was sure that Sir Terrence had been the one behind the lens. One was of Dorothy looking much younger and trouble free. Annabel suspected it had been taken in her teens before her parents divorced. It was the third photograph that caught Annabel's attention. A younger fresher faced Ferdy looked fearlessly out at the viewer with an expression in which a laugh was just building. There was little else on the desk apart from a telephone, a rather lethal looking paper knife and a glass paperweight.

Annabel glanced across at Ferdy. She wondered if he had seen his photograph. Did he know that his father still treasured his image, held it before him where he could see it every day?

'What about the staff?' Ferdy asked.

'Reduced for the weekend,' his father replied. 'You've seen the chef, John. He's been with us for at least two years. Ruby you've also met. Then there's Mrs Fry our housekeeper, who's been with us since we moved here, Alice the maid – she brought in the cake and biscuits – and Thomas who is new. He is here to act as butler-cum-waiter. They've all been vetted.'

Five staff was 'reduced'? That was more staff than family! And vetted by whom, Annabel wondered … MI5 presumably?

'And how will this all work?' Ferdy asked. 'Where will the "bait" be held and what do you expect us to do?'

'The "bait" as you call it will be here in this safe.' Sir Terrence pulled back the middle one of three pictures on the wall behind the desk to reveal a solid metal door with a handle and dial. He opened the safe and took out a single document. Annabel looked at it in fascination. Rosemary had referred to it as a blueprint and it really was blue! It looked like a technical drawing with lots of intercrossing lines and tiny detailed writing.

'This is the entry code.' He handed Ferdy a slip of paper. 'Please memorise it and destroy the paper.'

Not eat it? Nerves were making Annabel flippant. She strove to be serious.

'Your job is to keep a watch and notice if anyone attempts to steal it.'

Annabel looked around her at the open room. 'Watch from where?' she asked. Sir Terrence threw her a look in which she read irritation. She had reminded him of her presence again.

'Come and see.' He led the way through a door at that end of the room out into the corridor and away from the hall before turning left into a small passageway lined with what appeared to be cupboards. He opened the middle door and they found themselves in a small dark room with a raised platform on which stood a comfortable chair. 'Come and see,' he repeated and his voice betrayed a measure of pride. Annabel stepped onto the platform and sat in the chair. There was a screen in front of her and through it she had a one hundred and eighty degree view of the entire library.

Ferdy joined her on the platform and studied the screen. 'Ingenious! a system of mirrors leading to … the convex mirror?'

Annabel vaguely recalled seeing such a mirror on the wall above the safe.

'Correct,' said Sir Terrence.

'How many of these *things* are there around the house?' Ferdy asked.

Sir Terrence paused then replied evenly. 'Just this one. I have no desire to *spy* on my guests. And this will be removed after this weekend. I thought it would keep you safe whilst allowing you to do your job.'

The room must have been sound-proofed because when they emerged a few minutes later, sounds of arrival were coming from the hall. Dorothy and Matt had arrived and a young man – Annabel assumed it must be Thomas – was carrying a quantity of matching leather luggage into the hall from outside. From past experience of Dorothy's travel arrangements, Annabel knew that the suitcases would be numerous and heavy but Thomas, tall and heavily built, managed them with ease.

Dorothy was wearing a blush pink coat with a high collar and her black handbag exactly matched the large buttons on her coat, her shoes and her gloves. Her brunette hair was glossy with health. She looked, as ever, gorgeous. Annabel couldn't help comparing Dorothy's appearance, which was young and trendy, with that of Sarah whose clothes, though evidently expensive and smart, were those of an older woman. She wondered if Sarah dressed older than her age deliberately because she was married to an older man or if she was naturally conservative.

Unlike Ferdy, it was clear that Dorothy would have welcomed an embrace from her father but Sir Terrence's reaction was perfunctory, hands on her upper arms keeping her at bay and a brief kiss on the cheek.

'Good to see you, sir.' Matt stepped forward and Sir Terrence released Dorothy, without apparent regret, to shake his hand. Matt then turned to Sarah and said, 'I understand congratulations are in order. When is the baby due?'

'In November.'

'I hope you won't find this weekend too much. It's very kind of you to allow us to come.'

Sarah coloured and Annabel, having seen the Baxter's itinerary, wondered if this classed as one of their lighter weekends.

CHAPTER FIVE

'Which of these will you wear tonight?' Annabel asked. She was sitting on Dorothy's bed watching as Dorothy hung her dresses in the wardrobe.

'Well, not this one.' Dorothy waved a beautiful pale pink dress in the air as she lifted it from its suitcase and slotted it onto the rail. 'Not now I know Lucy is going to be here,' she added.

Annabel had opened her mouth to ask why not but closed it again. She had watched her friend go very still as her father had announced casually over tea that other guests were expected. Dorothy's face had set. She had said very little after that. But that didn't explain why Dorothy wouldn't want to wear the lovely pink dress or what this Lucy girl might have to do with it. Annabel opened her mouth again.

'You'll understand when you see her,' Dorothy said.

Oh, all right.

'You must wear your yellow dress,' Dorothy pronounced.

Annabel had intended to wear the blue one. She wasn't looking forward to wearing either. She just knew that something would get spilled on it.

'You know Lucy, then?'

'Oh, yes! We were at school together. She's nice.'

'I could tell it was a … surprise … to you that other guests were invited.' Annabel felt she ought to give her friend an opportunity to talk about it if she wanted.

Dorothy's face set again. 'Oh!' she shrugged, 'I'm used to it, you know, not being …'

Annabel understood.

'I think I remind him of Mum.' Dorothy hung up the final dress. 'Well, that's done.'

'I presume your dad is happy with you marrying Matt?'

'He hasn't said that he isn't. Matt's with him now.'

Annabel wondered what they would do if Sir Terrence said no. She assumed that was not on the cards. It seemed ridiculous to her that Matt wanted to jump through these outmoded hoops. Surely what mattered was that Dorothy wanted to marry him. But perhaps he hoped for some sort of monetary settlement?

Annabel didn't meet the other guests until just before dinner time when they gathered in the sitting room for drinks. She had decided to wear the yellow dress as directed and as she met Ferdy in the corridor outside their bedroom she was rewarded by a widening of his eyes.

'You're looking nice,' he said as he leant in to kiss her on the cheek.

As she carefully descended the stairs in her low-heeled sling-back shoes, she felt she needed every bit of encouragement to see her through the evening ahead. Ferdy's appreciative look was nothing though to the look that the young man in the hallway gave her. He was dressed in what Annabel recognised as pure Carnaby Street, with tight black trousers and a velvet jacket in a shade of blue that matched his eyes. A cream linen shirt with the collar raised and a paisley cravat completed the look. Annabel regarded the ensemble with distrust.

'Enchanted!' To Annabel's astonishment he took her hand and kissed it. His voice had an exotic accent. This must be Ferdy's Russian friend. 'Alexi Galkin at your service.'

He then turned to Ferdy and said something in, she supposed, Russian? Rather pointless, and a bit rude.

'This is Annabel Staple, Alec Stanhope's daughter,' Ferdy replied in repressive tones. It sounded as though he had understood what Alexi was saying and had not approved. Ferdy understood Russian? And what was it that Alexi had said?

Alexi raised his eyebrows and gave a low whistle.

'You speak Russian?' Annabel asked Ferdy, unable to keep the surprise out of her voice.

'Hardly at all.'

'I knew your father.' Alexi drew her hand through his arm and they walked towards the drawing room. The velvet felt soft under her fingers. 'You must tell me all about yourself.'

This was a social gambit that Annabel had not met before. She looked rather desperately back over her shoulder at Ferdy but he merely raised his gaze to the ceiling and followed them.

The sitting room in the early evening light looked stark and cold. Clouds obscured the sun which might otherwise have warmed the room, but Annabel was only briefly aware of her surroundings before Sir Terrence welcomed them and introduced Gerald and Violet Harcourt and their daughter Lucy and Professor Humphrey Calder.

Gerald Harcourt stood before the fire. Tall and well-built, he was a solid, assured presence. He was holding a half-drunk gin and tonic in one hand and an expensive brand of cigarette in the other. If he had indeed been shut out of the weekend house party circuit, Annabel imagined that he would be relieved to have been invited, especially to the house of someone as noted as Sir Terrence. Perhaps he was not feeling quite as assured as he looked.

His wife, Violet, sat in the armchair to the left of the fireplace. Petite and elegantly dressed, she looked less at ease than her husband, her smile a touch brittle. Did she miss the habitual weekend house parties and wish to have them resume? Was she afraid of a recurrence of whatever had happened before? She had a large bag by her feet and every now and then her hand twitched towards it. An almost untouched drink stood on the table beside her chair together with an ashtray on which a lipstick stained cigarette with half an inch of ash rested. She offered Annabel the tips of her fingers by way of acknowledgment and smiled, but the smile did not reach her eyes.

One look at Lucy gave the answer to Dorothy's decision not to wear pink.

Tall with powerful looking shoulders and slim hips, Lucy took after her father rather than her mother. Straight fair hair fell either side of a face that was characterised by a strong jaw line and a pair of fine eyes with a direct gaze. She looked like an Amazon or an athlete but the effect of upright, fearless, health was spoilt by a dress of bright pink. The colour did not suit her. She clutched Annabel's hand in a grip that made Annabel wince but smiled in a friendly way.

Professor Calder was sitting on the armchair to the right of the fireplace but he rose at their entrance, with some difficulty Annabel noted, favouring his right leg, and shook hands.

'A pleasure to meet Alec's daughter,' he said.

'Thank you, but please do sit down again.' Annabel was concerned about his leg.

'Humphrey likes to make nothing of his injury, don't you, my friend?' Sir Terrence said from the side table where he was preparing drinks. 'But I can assure you it is not.'

'Nonsense, nonsense,' said the professor but he seemed glad to sit once more. He was of medium height and sturdily built. He looked to be much the same age as Sir Terrence. Like everyone else there he had made an effort to dress up for the evening but his dinner jacket had seen better days and his tie was too wide to be fashionable. His shoes were polished but looked old.

Annabel's attention was drawn to his face which was intelligent looking with heavy frown marks hinting at extensive reading or maybe a prolonged association with pain. Sir Terrence had said that he was a scholar of some repute in the field of early civilisations and he looked just that.

Sarah handed Annabel her sherry. She was wearing a dress of an elegance and simplicity that could only have come from the most expensive shops. The diamond necklace round her neck looked real. Dorothy had been right. A dress from Annabel's normal high street shop would not have done here.

There were sounds in the hall and Dorothy and Matt made their entrance. For a moment there was silence. Dorothy stood there magnificent in a three-quarter length dress of the palest blue, her hair piled upon her head, her face glowing with health.

'I can see who got the looks in your family,' Annabel heard Alexi mutter to Ferdy before surging forward to greet Dorothy. More hand kissing, Annabel noted. Dorothy appeared to take it as her due, she was probably used to having her hand kissed. Let's face it, looking like that she *deserved* to have her hand kissed.

Matt stood slightly behind Dorothy no doubt recognising that this was not his time for the limelight. His stance was proprietorial. He must have got what he wanted from Sir Terrence – consent to the engagement at the very least. Matt's eyes swept over the rest of the guests and Annabel saw him flinch as he took in Lucy's pinkness. He rested his gaze once more on Dorothy where the scenery was more to his taste.

Matt had not been subtle. Annabel saw a flush rise up Lucy's neck. She was about to move across to speak to Lucy when Ferdy got there first. She saw Lucy smile, heard her laugh. Annabel was torn between appreciating Ferdy's no doubt well-meant kindness and a feeling of pique. Did he have to make such a bee line for the Amazonian queen? She was trying to overhear what Ferdy was saying to Lucy when Alexi spoke in her ear.

'The man does not approve.' He too was looking at Lucy and Ferdy but he cocked his head at Matt as he spoke. He had observed Matt's behaviour as well. It was hard to know if he agreed with Matt or not. He drew in on what looked like a foreign cigarette. It smelt nicer than the usual brands. Annabel resigned herself to a weekend amongst smokers. 'But perhaps he is what you would call a … stuffed shirt?'

She couldn't help smiling. There was a lot of truth in the expression as far as it related to Matt. But conservative or not, he loved Dorothy and Annabel had to like him for that.

She was rewarded with a puckish grin. 'There, I knew the daughter of Alec Stanhope would be all right.'

Annabel wasn't sure if what had just passed between them allowed him to make that judgement and didn't much appreciate the sense of collusion against Matt that Alexi's words implied. There was a faint frown on his face as he looked across at Ferdy. Was he surprised to see

Ferdy there? She was about to ask how he knew her father when Sir Terrence tapped his glass and silence fell.

Sir Terrence held the stage as one accustomed to such attention.

'I have,' he smiled upon them all, 'a special announcement to make. One that gives me great pleasure …'

Here it is, and so far so good.

Dorothy put down her martini glass with hands that weren't entirely steady.

'My daughter is to be married and I wish her, and Matthew, every happiness.'

Mrs Fry was walking round with a tray full of glasses filled with champagne. Sir Terrence took one and raised his glass: 'To Dorothy and Matthew!'

'To Dorothy and Matthew!' everyone intoned.

'May they live a long and happy life together.'

It was the first time that Annabel had tasted champagne. She wasn't sure that she liked it. She glanced at Alexi's face. The look of speculation had gone. Ferdy had been right to think that Dorothy's engagement would give them a reason to be there.

'Unlike her father's first marriage,' said Alexi sotto voce with a wicked lift of the eyebrow at Annabel.

Matt then stepped forward. It took a moment for everyone to realise that he was going to speak.

'Dorothy you have made me the happiest man on earth.' He reached into his jacket pocket and withdrew – a colossal diamond ring.

Annabel wasn't the only person to stare. She looked

around the room, interested to see the reaction of the others. Sir Terrence's eyebrows rose and his lips twitched. Lucy flushed and looked at the floor. Violet Harcourt appeared to have frozen, eyes wide, face drained of colour. Gerald Harcourt's face bore a look of dismay. He so rapidly resumed his expression of general benevolence that Annabel doubted her initial reading of his expression. The professor looked faintly scornful as though he disliked such overt display of wealth. Why, on earth, would the sight of Dorothy's engagement ring trigger such reactions? And what, if anything, had they to do with the business of spying?

Matt slid the ring onto Dorothy's finger. The diamond was set in rococo style twirls of gold that threatened to eclipse the stone within. She looked down at her hand in some bemusement, then up at his face. He bent down and kissed her on the lips.

'Christ, that's some rock!' Alexi muttered.

Annabel moved forward to congratulate Dorothy.

'It's been in my family for generations …' Matt was saying to Sir Terrence.

'Congratulations Dodo!' said Ferdy, giving his sister a huge hug. 'Happy?'

Dorothy nodded, flushed and radiant.

They stepped back to allow others to come forward.

Annabel saw Alexi move over to speak to Lucy. He seemed to be asking Lucy a question and Annabel saw her shake her head. Violet had extracted some needlework rather jerkily from her bag and was watching them too. Surely she couldn't be about to start sewing now?

'Lucy,' Violet called out, 'come and adjust my light for me. I can't see to do my sewing.'

Sarah moved across. 'I can do that for you.'

'No.' Violet held up her hand. 'Thank you, but Lucy knows how I like to have my work lit.'

Lucy came over willingly. It seemed to Annabel that Alexi watched with disapproval but he followed and sat down next to Violet.

'My grandmother used to do embroidery,' he said. 'May I see?'

Violet looked at him with suspicion and somewhat reluctantly angled the embroidery frame towards him.

'Ah yes.' He studied the work closely. 'Drawn fabric work; very intricate, very skilled, most beautiful. Sadly my grandmother's eyesight became too poor in later life but she used to do just such sewing when she was younger. I have some of it still.'

This was lavish praise, both of Violet's skill and her eyesight, especially since she did not appear to wear glasses. Violet must surely respond favourably. She did indeed seem to unbend sufficiently enough to nod her head.

'My eyesight is very good,' she said complacently. 'I am fortunate.'

Lucy had moved round to stand behind Alexi.

Violet drew back sharply, 'Lucy! Don't hover!'

Lucy walked away to the other side of the fireplace

and started to talk in a low voice to her father. Alexi observed this with an expression that was as unreadable as most of Ferdy's expressions. He turned back to Violet.

'You would have loved to see the tapestries in my grandparent's house. Late medieval.'

Violet cast him a look in which disbelief was mixed with pity. 'Such items,' she said, 'are very rare and valuable. I am sure you will find that what you have are Victorian.'

Alexi raised his eyebrows. A small smile played across his lips. 'I can assure you it is true. My grandparents managed to escape with them when they fled Russia during the revolution, along with other precious items.'

Annabel admired his charm but wondered why he was wasting it where it wasn't appreciated. He didn't have to persist for long because Thomas soon entered the room and announced that dinner was ready.

Annabel regarded the table settings with misgiving. The cutlery stretched on for ever each side of the place settings. Goodness only knew which piece she was supposed to use when! At least there was plenty of elbow room, the places were spaced well apart. Sir Terrence and Sarah took the places at each end of the table. Annabel found that she had Alexi to her left and Humphrey Calder to her right whilst Dorothy sat between Alexi and her father. Ferdy was opposite with Lucy on his right and Violet to his left. Too far away to be any help. There were five on his side of the table with Gerald and Matt. Wasn't that supposed to be a no-no? But, of course, Lucy had not been expected.

There was a large linen napkin by her place which she unwrapped and laid across her lap. She wished it was a full length apron. Thomas placed a bowl of soup in front of her. Clear, with bits floating in it, Annabel regarded it with suspicion. A small bowl with tiny squares of what looked like toast was placed nearby. The professor shovelled some of them into his soup. Annabel followed suit.

Sarah lifted the spoon on the extreme right of her place setting. Annabel did likewise. So far so good. She began to eat and was surprised to taste onion. It really wasn't too bad.

'Perfect croutons,' said Humphrey.

So that's what they were.

'What is this soup?' she asked.

He looked at her properly for the first time, a slight smile in his eyes. 'French onion. You've not had it before?'

Annabel shook her head. 'It's tasty.'

He leant in and lowered his voice. 'Makes you windy.'

Annabel bit her lip on a laugh.

'You remind me very much of your father,' he said. 'We last met in Helsinki, must have been two years ago. I was there on the invitation of the state museum. They'd just acquired some interesting religious icons. I think Alec was there to buy art?'

'He was an art collector, so that's quite likely. I don't know, I'm afraid. He died before I could get to know him.'

He raised his eyebrows in surprise and looked as though he would have said more but his attention was claimed by Sarah.

The soup plates were removed and replaced by what looked like ice cream sundae glasses but they had shredded lettuce and pink things in them. Looked like it was the turn of the funny little spoon and fork. She speared one of the pink things and discovered it was a prawn. She was just transferring this tasty morsel from dish to mouth when Thomas leant in from behind. 'White wine?'

'Yes please.'

As his gloved hand stretched forward, his sleeve drew back revealing strong, hairy arms. Annabel's hand shook in surprise, the prawn fell, she looked down in dismay and saw that it had landed just beyond the edge of the napkin. It nestled on her expensive dress as though it belonged there.

'Allow me.' Alexi shot in with a spoon and scooped it up.

Scarlet faced, Annabel looked around to see if anyone had noticed. Ferdy was looking at her. She wished, not for the first time, that his face was easier to read. 'Prawn!' she mouthed at him. He frowned.

The meal progressed slowly and with far too many courses, in Annabel's opinion. It was over the meat course – small, round, melt-in-the-mouth fillet steaks with French beans and a sauce that Annabel had never tasted before but was delicious – that the conversation turned to stolen art work. Annabel's ears pricked up. She'd had first hand experience of that.

Matt who worked at Christie's was talking about the difficulty experienced when art work appeared in the show rooms without the proper provenance, the paperwork, all too often, lost in the war through bomb damage or fire.

'Or the art work itself stolen. The paperwork conveniently "lost",' Alexi chipped in, his voice deeper, more strongly accented than Annabel had heard up to now.

'Indeed yes, that too.'

'It happened a lot during both wars,' said Alexi.

'Yes, it did,' agreed Matt. 'The Nazis, in particular. We do what we can to authenticate the seller but the painting might have changed hands many times and identifying the correct provenance can be near impossible.'

'Well,' said Sir Terrence leaning back in his chair, 'whilst my sympathies might be with the original owner, speaking as a purchaser, and having paid good money for a work of art I should take a dim view of someone coming up and telling me it was theirs, especially if they had no proof.'

'And therein lies the difficulty,' said Matt.

'So you would say to some person who came to you and said, you have my picture and I want it back …?' Alexi's voice was light once more.

'I would say,' said Sir Terrence, 'I paid – whatever I paid – for it. Give me that amount and you can have it.'

'Sounds fair to me.' Gerald gave a rumbling laugh.

The conversation moved on once more to a well-worn subject that, since Churchill's death at the start of the year, the country was going to the dogs.

A concoction of peaches and whipped cream appeared in front of Annabel. She lost interest in the conversation.

'I am ready!' Alexi waggled his spoon and his eyebrows.

'That won't be necessary,' she replied with dignity. She hoped.

With the meal finally over, Annabel was heartily relieved when Sarah got up. It was only as Annabel followed her to the door that she realised only the women were leaving. This struck her as archaic to the point of gothic. She wished that, like Violet, she'd brought her handbag. It could have hung over the stain like a sporran. Sarah led the way to the sitting room where the housekeeper was waiting to serve drinks.

Annabel made an excuse, went upstairs to her room and changed into her blue dress. Just as well that she had brought two with her! It was as she was leaving her room to go back downstairs that she heard a door opening further down the corridor. Instinctively she stepped back out of sight into her doorway. Someone was coming out of the room that was allocated to Lucy. She heard footsteps turning away from her towards the door through to the staff quarters and chanced a look. It was Thomas. He opened the door at the end of the passage with his gloved hands and went through closing it softly behind him.

Whatever was he doing in Lucy's room?

Back in the sitting room Dorothy was showing Lucy and Violet her ring.

'Is it real?' asked Violet.

'Of course it is! It's a family heirloom.'

'I can't understand why girls are so desperate to get married,' Violet said in a complaining tone.

Dorothy stiffened.

'Oh, Mum didn't mean you, Dot!' said Lucy. 'It's obvious you and Matt are in love.'

'Lucy has no plans to be married,' said Violet comfortably.

She took her embroidery out of her hand bag and started to sew. Tiny stitches, white on white. So that was what drawn fabric work was. It looked as though she'd been working on it for a while.

Lucy looked at her in affectionate exasperation and went over to one of the two window seats where she sat looking moodily out into the darkness.

Dorothy and Annabel joined her there.

'Don't you, Lucy?' Dorothy sounded puzzled. 'I thought –'

Lucy raised a warning hand and Dorothy was silenced.

'Are you still doing all that rowing?' Dorothy asked.

'Couldn't give it up. It's the best part of my day; up at four, out on the river, nobody else around, just me and the sound of the oars.'

No wonder she looked so athletic.

Dorothy looked horrified. Then she noticed Annabel's dress. 'You've changed! Why?'

Not everyone had noticed the prawn incident.

'I spilled something.'

Dorothy looked momentarily sympathetic. 'Oh well, it doesn't matter now.'

'Why doesn't it matter now?' Annabel demanded, aggrieved.

'I've made my entrance. If we'd both worn blue it would have looked odd.'

Sarah helped the housekeeper hand round chocolates.

'Chocolate mints?' said Violet. 'Now if you had some cherry liqueurs I might be tempted.'

Annabel took one. 'Do you always leave the men after a meal?' she couldn't help asking Sarah.

Sarah flushed. 'Not always. But with more formal meals like this, yes. It's when Terry likes to do … business.'

Perhaps they would be talking about industrial innovations. Ferdy would be able to tell her, of course, but Annabel felt the frustration of exclusion.

Shortly after that the men entered the room and the talk became general.

Gerald lost no time making his way over to the display case containing the snuff boxes. Sir Terrence joined him there, the case lid was opened and the two men regarded the contents in concentrated silence.

'Quite a nice collection,' said Gerald finally.

Sir Terrence nodded his head. He knew this.

Gerald pulled a pair of white cotton gloves from his

pocket and put them on. 'May I?' He picked up one that was round and looked as though it was made of gold. 'Had my eye on that one in the Bonham catalogue. Withdrawn before the sale, always wondered who'd got in ahead.'

Sir Terrence permitted himself a smile of acknowledgment.

Humphrey had joined them. He observed Gerald's use of the gloves with obvious professional approval. This, his expression said, was how you treated precious objects.

'This is my favourite.' Sarah lifted out the one she liked.

'Ah yes,' said Gerald. 'Gold and porcelain, late 18th century Fabergé, very pretty.'

'May I see it?' Violet called out.

Sarah placed it carefully in Violet's hands.

Violet turned it this way and that. 'I have to say it's not to my taste. A little bit gaudy, don't you think?'

'Perhaps,' said Sarah quietly, 'but I like it.'

Ferdy soon found an opportunity to speak to Annabel. 'We need to talk.'

'How about the library?'

As they left the room Annabel heard Sarah draw the housekeeper aside and ask her to get some cherry liqueurs couriered up by lunchtime the next day from Fortnum & Mason.

CHAPTER SIX

Ferdy closed the door of the library behind them and Annabel allowed herself to relax in the corresponding silence. The evening up to now had been stressful. Of all the rooms in the house, she liked this room the best.

'What was Alexi doing rooting about in your lap?' Ferdy demanded, startling Annabel.

'Removing a prawn – and he wasn't "rooting", he used a spoon. I *told* you, "prawn".' She mouthed the last word.

Ferdy stared at her as though she were mad, then he grinned. 'I did wonder. So that's why you've changed.' He lit a cigarette, drew the smoke in deeply and expelled it towards the ceiling.

'And anyway, why were you being so pally with Lucy?' As soon as the words were out of her mouth, Annabel regretted them.

Ferdy lowered his gaze from the ceiling. He looked surprised. Then he shrugged his shoulders. 'I felt sorry for her. She looks as though she wants to be here as little as I do.'

Annabel was getting fed up with his attitude. 'We're here because we have a job to do.'

He raised his eyebrows. 'Of course we do. All right, let's review where we are. Dad sowed the seeds nicely over the brandy. Without actually saying, "the secret documents are in the safe" he managed to give a strong indication that recent developments had been made. I must say, it was neatly done,' he admitted grudgingly.

'How did our two suspects react?'

'Can't say that either of them reacted as such. Gerald said something about how Dad must be involved in a great many innovations and wasn't it great for our country etcetera. Alexi didn't seem that interested at all.'

'Surely you must have noticed something!'

Ferdy looked at her and grinned. 'Felt left out, did you? Actually, I'm inclined to think this is a waste of time. Unless it is Gerald Harcourt and he's a very good actor.'

'He looked horrified when he saw Dorothy's ring,' put in Annabel.

'He wasn't the only one. It's hideous!'

'It is rather,' Annabel couldn't help agreeing.

'Also a responsibility, but nothing to do with espionage.'

It certainly seemed unlikely.

'When I was upstairs changing,' said Annabel, 'I saw Thomas coming out of Lucy's room.'

Ferdy whistled. 'Did you now! Well, either she reported a running tap which he was trying to fix or there is a bit of intrigue there.'

Annabel recalled Lucy's negative gesture to Dorothy earlier. Could she be having a relationship with Thomas? Perhaps that explained why she was here?

Annabel stifled a yawn. The day had caught up on her.

Ferdy glanced at her. 'I'll take the first watch. You try to get some sleep.'

Annabel opened her mouth to protest, but then closed it again. She really was very tired.

She had got her pyjamas on when there was a sharp tap on the door.

What now? She looked at her comfortable bed.

Dorothy was huddled in the hallway. 'Annabel, thank God! Help!' She slipped past Annabel into the room. It was then that Annabel noticed Dorothy's contorted stance. 'It's caught!' She was almost in tears.

'What is?'

'My ring – hurry up and help!'

Biting back a laugh, Annabel inspected the problem. The ring seemed to have got impossibly tangled in the zip at the side of the dress.

'Oh! It's ruined!' Dorothy wailed.

Join the club.

Annabel worked away at the entangled ring. There was a ripping sound.

'Be careful!'

'I am being careful. It was just the stitches. Keep still.' Eventually she had the ring extracted from the dress.

'Hateful ring!' said Dorothy. 'And I laddered my best stockings too.' She flumped down on Annabel's bed. They looked at one another. 'What am I going to do?'

'Can't you tell Matt you want another ring?'

'But it's an heirloom! Every bride in their family has worn it since … whenever.'

It can't have been easy to wear.

'But, doesn't it belong in a vault? Somewhere safe?' Annabel suggested.

Somewhere dark and out of sight?

'You don't understand. What will Matt think if the first thing I do is tell him I don't want to wear his beastly family ring? I want this marriage to work.'

Matt should pay heed to his fiancée's wishes but Annabel remembered his pride in the ring and maybe it was his way of saying, yes I might be marrying into a fabulously wealthy family but I can bring *something* of worth.

It was some time before Dorothy eventually took herself off to bed. Annabel wearily set her alarm for two-thirty in the morning, turned out the light and was asleep as her head hit the pillow.

The alarm went off a minute later – or so it seemed. Annabel got out of bed and staggered blearily into the bathroom. Minutes later she was in the corridor – where she almost bumped into Lucy.

Even Lucy's dressing gown was pink.

'Lucy! What are you doing up at this hour?'

'I might ask the same question.'

Good point. Annabel improvised. 'I want some milk. All that rich food …'

'Me too.'

Annabel looked at Lucy's empty hands.

'I drank it in the kitchen,' Lucy said.

'Good idea,' said Annabel. 'Well … I hope you get back to sleep.'

'You too.'

At the head of the stairs Annabel looked back. Lucy was watching her, a speculative look in her eyes. Annabel was pleased she'd just thrown on a dressing gown. It would have been difficult to explain being fully dressed.

She descended the stairs into the darkness of the hall. It was very quiet in the house and, she had to admit, a little creepy. Suddenly, the prospect of sitting in a small dark room on her own for several hours didn't seem very inviting. The corridor past the library was darker still and she almost missed the passage to the observation room. Looking around to see nobody was watching, she opened the door with her key and slipped inside, closing the door behind her. Ferdy's face was a pale oval in the gloom. As her eyes accustomed to the darkness Annabel could see that the viewing screen through the 'spy' mirror cast a weak light.

'Kill me now,' said Ferdy. 'I have never, and I mean *never* been so bored.'

'Nothing's happened?'

'Zilch, zero, ничего …'

'So Lucy hasn't been in there?'

'Nobody has been in there. Not even a mouse has been in there. I know, I would have seen it. Why Lucy?'

'I bumped into her in the corridor upstairs. She said she'd been down to get some milk.'

'She probably had.'

Maybe she had been with Thomas?

Ferdy yawned hugely. 'If you don't mind, I'll leave you to it.'

Annabel resisted the urge to ask him to stay. She could see he was dead tired.

'Don't forget, if anything does happen, you are just here to observe. Not go charging in – as you have a habit of doing.'

Annabel bristled but she knew he had a point. She had done so on a previous occasion and had almost been killed. He had been angry.

'Of course not.'

He put his hand on her shoulder and gave it a squeeze. 'I'll be back at seven. Don't forget to lock the door behind me.'

Left on her own, Annabel took stock of her surroundings. The room was small and a bit stuffy. The chair was surprisingly comfortable. Perhaps too comfortable; she'd better be careful not to fall asleep. She didn't like the fact that she had her back to the door and was glad that she had securely locked it.

She turned her attention to the viewing screen. The convex mirror gave a panorama of the entire room and from its height on the wall it gave a bird's eye view. The moon shining through the library windows was enough to light the scene so that the view was eerily clear. She was mesmerised, her face lit up by the screen, the darkness close around her.

Time passed. She drank some of the water that
Ferdy had left. Nothing happened. Her head jerked up.
Goodness! Had she nodded off? She began to wish that
the water was coffee. She looked at her watch. It was five
o'clock. Light started to seep into the room from the window. Two hours still to go! She wished Ferdy was with her
– at least they could talk.

Annabel yawned.

At five-thirty a young woman came in, Annabel recognised the maid, Alice. She went first to the two French
windows throwing them open, then emptied the ashtrays,
wiping them clean. Then she straightened up the papers
and magazines, plumped the cushions, tidied and dusted
the surfaces, inspected the flowers and evidently decided
they could do another day. Annabel was expecting her to
leave the room at this point but she laid down her cleaning things and suddenly transformed. Her chin raised,
she glided about the room, acting out the part of a grand
lady, accepting a 'glass' from someone, laughing over her
shoulder at someone else, angling her head to have her
cigarette lit. It was utterly convincing – and deeply pathetic. Annabel almost turned away in embarrassment
but knew she must keep watching. After a few moments
more, Alice closed the French windows, gathered up her
cleaning stuff and left the room. Alice could be in amateur dramatics but Annabel didn't think so. At any rate,
she had made no attempt to steal any documents.

There were some aspects of her new job that Annabel
didn't enjoy.

Ten minutes later Gerald entered the room. He was wearing his dressing gown, a rather fancy mulberry velour with frogging down the front. Annabel shot forward in her chair. Could this be it? But Gerald went nowhere near the picture on the wall below her. He moved over to the two chairs by the fireplace where he lifted the back cushions and felt down the sides of the seat. Evidently he found nothing because he stood and looked slowly round the room. Finally he left.

What was all that about?

At seven o'clock Ferdy came to relieve her. Boredom had frozen her features so that she found it impossible to smile.

'You look like I felt at two-thirty this morning,' he said.

'Is surveillance always this boring?' she asked.

'Pretty much. Anything happen?'

'Nobody went near the picture. Alice, the maid, came in and tidied up. It was rather sad. She play-acted being a rich socialite. Then Gerald came in and was looking for something down one of the armchairs.'

'Probably lost some change. Dad, Gerald, Alexi and Humphrey came in here after the rest of you had gone to bed.'

'Do you mean to say you watched them?' Annabel was shocked.

'Don't forget that Dad knew I was here. I think it amused him.'

'Could you hear them?'

'Yes, they were talking about espionage.'

'Wasn't that a bit dangerous?' Not to say, obvious.

'Dad started the subject. Gerald said it was an increasing problem. Alexi said it wasn't by any means one-way traffic. Humphrey said very few new inventions come out of the blue and that mostly it was just one person getting there first.'

'He's probably right,' said Annabel. She rubbed her eyes.

'Why don't you go upstairs, have a lie down, maybe a bath. Breakfast will be about nine.'

There was more kindness in his voice than she had heard in a while – and a bath sounded wonderful.

'I think during the day we can probably take two-hour shifts and we don't need to be in here necessarily,' Ferdy said. 'I suppose we need to play along but the sooner this charade is over, the better, in my opinion.'

Annabel climbed the stairs wearily and was just about to turn down the corridor to her room when she heard a hissed cry.

'Annabel!'

Heart sinking she turned round. Dorothy was beckoning to her from her room. She looked frantic.

'Whatever's wrong?'

Dorothy grabbed her arm and pulled her in shutting the door behind them.

'It's gone, Annabel!'

'What's gone?'

'My ring, of course. What do you think!'

'What do you mean, "it's gone"? Gone where?'

'Well, if I knew that ...'

'Ok. Sorry.' Annabel sat down on the bed and struggled to think clearly. 'I presume you took it off?'

Dorothy coloured. 'Well, Matt was here last night and we ... you know ... and anyway, he got scratched.'

Ouch! Annabel didn't want to know where.

'So, he told me to take it off.'

Annabel could imagine the conversation.

'And I put it *here*.' Dorothy stabbed her finger at the bedside table. 'Right here! And now it's gone!'

'I suppose you've looked on the floor? It could have been kicked.'

Dorothy looked at her. 'I've looked *everywhere*.'

'Do you mind if I look?'

'Go ahead!'

Annabel got down on her hands and knees and started to search. If the ring was there, she couldn't see it.

Dorothy sat down on the bed, pale and trembling. 'Oh, what am I going to do? It's a family heirloom.'

Annabel sat back on her heels. 'You don't suppose Matt took it with him? Maybe he realised it was too much of a responsibility for you?'

'He wouldn't do so without telling me. And I can't ask him, because then he'd know I've lost it.'

'Did you leave the room at any time?'

Dorothy looked struck. 'I did go downstairs to get a cup of tea. You don't think …?'

'Did you lock the door behind you?'

'Of course not!' Dorothy protested but then she turned even more pale as the implication of what Annabel was suggesting sank in.

'It would be very tempting to a would-be thief,' said Annabel.

'But who? It must be one of the staff.'

Annabel remembered that Lucy had been out and about during the night. And the previous evening she had seen Thomas coming out of Lucy's room. But if it had been stolen it could really be anyone.

'Are you going to tell your father?'

Dorothy recoiled. 'Absolutely not!'

'He needs to know, surely?'

'Can't you help me find it?' Dorothy turned to Annabel pleadingly. 'I'd much rather nobody but us knew. You're good at finding things aren't you?'

Where did she get that unwarranted and unsought reputation? 'I can tell Ferdy, can't I?'

'Oh, yes, of course you can tell Ferdy!'

That was good.

'What are you going to do in the meantime?' Annabel asked.

Dorothy looked blank.

'If you'd cut your finger,' Annabel considered, 'you wouldn't be able to wear the ring, would you?'

Dorothy caught on quickly. 'Do I have to *actually* cut my finger?'

'A bandage should cover it,' in more ways than one. 'Don't worry,' she said to her friend, 'I am sure it will turn up.' But, what if it didn't?

Annabel returned to her room. Too tired to bother with a bath she lay down on her bed. They now had two people to look for: a spy, who may or may not exist, and a jewel thief, who probably did exist because otherwise where was the ring? But who would be mad enough to steal such a prominent piece of jewellery when the cast of suspects was so limited?

CHAPTER SEVEN

Annabel must have slept because the alarm woke her for the second time that Saturday morning with its shrill bell. Struggling to remember where she was, she enjoyed a brief moment of blissful ignorance before reality emerged. With a feeling of *déjà vu* she staggered into the bathroom. There was no time for a bath. She washed and dressed and made her way along to Dorothy's room. They had agreed to go down together so that Annabel could watch the faces of the other guests as Dorothy's 'cut finger' and lack of ring became apparent.

Dorothy had rather overdone the bandage. Nobody was going to miss seeing the thick bundle of wadding strapped around her fourth finger. She lifted it wearily at Annabel in greeting.

They went downstairs and entered the dining room together but the immediate reaction was underwhelming. Thomas was standing to one side of the room ready to help if needed and didn't appear to take any particular notice of Dorothy or her finger. Violet was leafing through a copy of *The Lady* and Lucy was engrossed in a heaped plate of what looked like a sample of everything on offer. Gerald had a folded up copy of the *Times* by his plate but seemed to be absorbed in his own thoughts. Sarah was reading a letter. She laid it down as they entered the room and invited them to help themselves adding a polite enquiry as to how they had slept.

'Really well, thank you,' Annabel lied.

'Me too,' said Dorothy.

Annabel inspected the dishes on the sideboard. The day was definitely looking up. She helped herself liberally to eggs, bacon, fried bread, mushrooms and fried tomatoes. Dorothy took a slice of toast. Alexi followed them in with Matt just behind him. Was it Annabel's imagination or was Matt walking just a *trifle* gingerly?

'Dorothy, darling!' he cried, 'What have you done to your finger?'

'Oh! It's nothing – just a scratch.' Dorothy blushed and continued rather woodenly, 'But, obviously, I couldn't wear the ring.'

Gerald blanched and looked at his wife. Annabel had rarely seen anyone look more ill at ease. Violet returned his look coldly and returned to her reading. Lucy looked concerned.

Alexi inspected the bandage with a fascinated eye. 'Is there some finger left under there?'

'But how did you do it?' Matt asked, concern evident in his voice.

Annabel held her breath. In all their planning she and Dorothy had failed to consider this.

Matt lowered his voice. Annabel edged closer. 'Was it … the ring?'

An infinitesimal pause, then Dorothy raised her head. 'I'm afraid it was.'

Annabel sat down and began eating as fast as she could. She wanted to relieve Ferdy so that he could eat and they needed to talk. As she left, Dorothy was resolutely refusing Sarah and Matt's offers to have a look at the cut finger.

She found Ferdy in the library. He was sitting in one of the chairs that Gerald had investigated earlier that morning and was reading the *Guardian*. Annabel would have put him down as a *Telegraph* man but from the pile of sullied papers beside him, he'd probably already read that.

'We need to talk,' she said imperatively and would have continued had he not lowered the corner of his paper to reveal a face of caution. She then saw that Professor Calder was occupying the chair with its back to her. Due to its high-winged back and deep seat he had been completely invisible from the door.

'Is it breakfast time already?' he said and heaved himself to his feet. He smiled at them both. 'I presume I'm not required for this "talk"?'

Annabel stammered an apology.

'Then I'll take myself off. Leave you to it.' He left the room, his stick tapping on the floor as he walked.

'Subtle,' said Ferdy.

'Sorry. I didn't see him. What's wrong with his leg?'

'It's an old war wound. Dad could tell you more.' He folded his paper and put it on the table with the rest.

'And before you ask, no, nothing has happened, except that I have read more news than I have ever read or ever want to read again.'

'Why are there so many newspapers?'

'Dad gets them all. Always has. He likes a "rounded" view of events.'

Annabel waited but as no question was forthcoming, she spoke. 'And, before *you* ask, yes, something *has* happened.'

'Oh yes?' Ferdy didn't sound too interested.

Annabel told him in a hushed voice about Dorothy and her ring and Gerald's reaction. 'Last night I wondered if Thomas might be a thief but there's definitely something not quite right about Gerald Harcourt. And here he is again at a weekend house party where something has gone missing. Maybe his bad reputation comes from the fact that he's a thief, not a – you know what.'

Ferdy heard her out in silence. 'A thief?' He sounded disappointed and it certainly was a bit of a let down to catching a spy. 'Well, all we can do is keep watching and listening. Poor Dodo, I'll have a word with her.' He stood up. 'I'll go and eat now. Are you OK to take over here until eleven?'

Annabel walked restlessly round the room. The weekend wasn't going at all to plan. It looked as though the espionage was a red herring; Ferdy seemed no nearer to making things up with his father; the 'tag' arrangement with Ferdy meant that she and he did not get any time together and now, to top it all, Dorothy had lost her ring. It was frustrating being stuck here in the library when she could be searching for the ring.

She found an *Evening Standard* in the pile and sat down in the seat recently vacated by the professor.

Someone entered the room behind her. Whoever it was stopped, then walked over to the window. Annabel peered round the back of her chair. It was Lucy. Today she was wearing pink cigarette trousers, previously hidden beneath the breakfast table. They revealed excellent legs and looked good. The effect was spoiled by a pink georgette top. Lucy paced impatiently up and down. It seemed she was waiting for someone.

Annabel was in a quandary. Should she make her presence known? If she didn't and was then discovered it would be terribly awkward. But then, wasn't she there for exactly this – to watch and overhear? And what if Lucy and Thomas were the thieves?

Annabel heard someone else came in.

'Here you are.' It was Sarah's voice. 'Matt is going to show some of the others round Terry's paintings. I wondered if you needed anything? Perhaps you might like to go for a walk? Or maybe a game of tennis with someone?'

'Oh! Perhaps later. Yes, later would be nice. I have … a letter to write.'

Annabel stole another look round the chair. Lucy was looking at her watch. After a few more minutes Annabel heard a sigh and then footsteps as Lucy left the room.

Annabel had almost finished the *Evening Standard* crossword when Ferdy put in an appearance.

'Anything?' he asked.

'Lucy was in here. It looked like she was waiting for someone who didn't turn up.'

'Oh?' Ferdy didn't sound particularly interested. 'Her dad maybe?'

Annabel didn't think so. Lucy's behaviour had more the feel of an assignation. She wished Ferdy would show more interest.

'You don't think,' she said, 'that the spying might be two people working together?'

'What? Gerald and his daughter? Unlikely. Spying is usually a lonely job.'

'But possible?' Annabel pressed.

'Oh,' Ferdy shrugged, 'anything is possible.'

Annabel remembered Thomas coming out of Lucy's room.

'How sure are we that it is just Gerald or Alexi in the loop?' she asked.

Ferdy grinned at her. 'Two suspects not enough for you? And anyway, how would anyone else know about the documents?'

'Thomas has strong hairy arms,' she paused. That sounded a bit silly. 'I mean, it struck me as strange for a butler.'

But Ferdy nodded his head. 'And he wears a sea diver watch.'

Annabel hadn't noticed that. She didn't see why a

butler couldn't wear such a watch but it did seem a bit unusual.

'I can take over again,' he said.

'It's not eleven yet.'

That's OK. I spoke to Dorothy. There's not a lot we can do at the moment.'

Annabel gratefully took herself off. As she passed the sitting room she saw Gerald Harcourt. He had his back to her and was head down in one of the armchairs. It looked as though he was looking for something down the seat cushions again. He glanced up, saw her and straightened up.

'I'm looking for my reading glasses,' he said. 'You haven't seen them have you?'

She shook her head. She wondered if that was what he was looking for during the night. If so, it looked as though he was another who had not slept well the previous night.

She went on upstairs and saw Matt with Sir Terrence and Alexi standing in front of a painting. It looked rather gloomy to Annabel's eyes, a portrait of a sallow faced man in dark tones against a black background. For some reason she got the impression that the figure was Russian. Sir Terrence was saying it was a fairly recent acquisition.

'Not one of ours,' said Matt, meaning Christie's.

'No,' said Sir Terrence. He offered no further explanation.

Alexi had already moved on to the next painting

which was more modern looking, lots of colour and much more pleasing, in Annabel's opinion. 'Very nice; A. J. Peploe if I'm not mistaken? Scottish colourist.'

Annabel left them to it. She entered her room and closed the door behind her with a sigh. She was definitely going to have a bath now.

The water was blissfully hot and as she lowered her body inch by inch into its embrace she regretted that Ferdy was not doing likewise in the bathroom next door. They could have practised the scene from one of her favourite movies *Pillow Talk* where Doris Day and Rock Hudson, both in their baths, touch feet on the screen. The scene was both erotic and romantic. She had been to see the film every week for the six weeks that it had been on at the local Palladium – five times with her friend Helen who now lived in Australia, and once with Jack, her ex-boyfriend. Once had been enough for him.

Acclimatised enough now to lie down fully, Annabel tried it out. She raised her foot, reached, stretched – there was no way that she could touch the wall behind the bath. So much for erotic illusions.

She had emerged from the bathroom in her dressing gown when there was a knock on the door. Mrs Fry stood outside holding what Annabel recognised as her yellow dress. Annabel flushed in embarrassed surprise. Her accident had not gone unnoticed.

'I've done the best I can,' said Mrs Fry handing it over, 'but that pink sauce …' She disclaimed all thanks. It was Lady Sarah who had asked her to see what she could do.

Sarah seemed to be prepared to go above and beyond to ensure that everything ran smoothly in the Baxter household. The stain, on closer inspection, was considerably faded but still apparent.

Refreshed from her bath, Annabel made her way along to the stairs then paused. She hadn't had an opportunity to look at the paintings in the gallery. Her father's extensive collection had given her an interest in works of art. It wouldn't take a minute. She started to move around the walls. Sir Terrence had eclectic tastes which ranged from heavy religious through impressionist and Pre-Raphaelite to the most modern. The only common denominator appeared to be cost. They all looked expensive. She liked the light on the water in the Monet. She wished she had hair like the woman in the Rossetti. She stood for some time before the portrait that looked Russian. She still couldn't exactly pinpoint why she had thought it was Russian. The man appeared severe, but as she looked more closely she saw that the artist had caught a glint in his eyes. It changed her whole perception of the portrait.

Once back downstairs, she went first to the library. To her surprise Ferdy wasn't there. The room appeared empty. She was about to go and look in the observation room when she heard a faint groan coming from behind the desk.

CHAPTER EIGHT

With a cry of fear Annabel ran forward. She saw a pair of men's shoes first and her heart almost stopped. But as she rounded the desk she could see that it wasn't Ferdy lying there; it was Sir Terrence. He was lying face down, head tilted to one side. He groaned again as she threw herself down on her knees beside him. If he was groaning he wasn't dead. That was something to be thankful for. The hair on the side of his head looked sticky. She reached forward and touched what was already a sizeable bump; her finger came away red. She fought down a feeling of nausea.

'Sir Terrence!' she cried. 'It's Annabel. Can you hear me?'

Where was Ferdy? He should be here. Was he hurt too? She wanted to go and find help but didn't want to leave Sir Terrence alone.

She heard someone enter the room and sticking her head above the desk saw Ferdy.

'Oh Ferdy! Thank goodness! It's your father!'

'Dad?' Ferdy came forward and as he saw his father he staggered and went pale.

'It's OK, he's alive. He's been groaning.' Annabel hastened to reassure him.

Ferdy knelt down and took his father's hand at the wrist. He then carried out an efficient investigation of his father's body. His face cleared somewhat.

'Looks like it's just a bash on the head.'

Sir Terrence's eyes flickered open and slowly focussed on his son's face. His hand tightened on Ferdy's. His eyes softened.

'"*Just* a bash on the head"!' he repeated with a grimace.

Ferdy nodded tightly. 'You'll live.'

'Good to know. Can you turn me over?'

'Can you feel your toes?' Ferdy asked.

Sir Terrence flexed his toes.

'OK.' Ferdy carefully turned his father. Annabel fetched a cushion which they placed under Sir Terrence's head.

'What happened?' asked Ferdy.

'I was just getting something out of the safe when someone hit me on the head. I don't remember anything after that.'

It was then that Annabel, with a sense of suddenly waking up, realised that the safe on the wall behind them was open and it was empty.

'Look again,' Ferdy said to her. There was a strange light in his eyes.

Annabel did so and gasped. It was the *left* hand picture that was pulled away from the wall, not the middle picture. But that didn't make sense! Sir Terrence had definitely said the safe was behind the *middle* picture. Were there *two* safes?

'So the documents …?' she asked.

'There was nothing of importance in there,' said Sir Terrence.

There was a cry from behind them and Sarah ran forward. Annabel got up to make room. Sarah cast herself down on the opposite side of Sir Terrence to Ferdy and grasped his hand.

'Terry!'

'Sal.'

'Oh! What happened? Are you hurt?' Sarah's accent was strongly evident. She raised his hand to her cheek.

'I'll be all right in a minute,' he said.

It looked to Annabel as though Sir Terrence was exactly where he wanted to be – between his wife and his son, both of them leaning over him with concern and in Sarah's case, love.

'Someone knocked Dad on the head but he is all right and the documents are safe,' Ferdy explained.

Sarah looked appalled.

'You mustn't worry,' Sir Terrence assured her.

Ferdy had settled back on his heels and was looking at his father and Sarah with an expression of stunned enlightenment on his face.

'I think you should go and lie down,' said Sir Terrence. He and Sarah could have been alone in the room.

'You think *I* should go and lie down?' said Sarah with a twisted smile on her lips.

'I think you should both go and lie down,' Ferdy spoke with decision. 'But first we need to agree on our story.' It was not the first time Annabel had seen Ferdy react to a difficult situation. It was as though he shifted smoothly into a higher gear. 'Dad, you fell, banged your head on the desk. Nobody else was involved.'

Sir Terrence regarded him with a glimmering smile. Annabel wondered if he had met this Ferdy before. 'All right,' he said. 'How did I fall?'

'The rug!' said Sarah. 'Haven't I been saying for ages it's slippery?'

'I slipped on the rug,' agreed Sir Terrence. 'But whoever bashed me on the head will know that I know he did so. Won't it be odd if I say I slipped?'

Ferdy considered this. 'No, I think we'll be all right. You can say that you don't remember what happened and *think* you must have slipped. A bang on the head like that can cause short-term memory loss. And why should our spy be on his guard? We know that we are setting a trap for him but as far as he knows, it's just another job.'

Yes, if it were the work of the 'spy', but couldn't it be the work of whoever stole Dorothy's ring? The whole thing smacked of opportunism and that was exactly how Dorothy's ring had been stolen – a chance opportunity seized. But she couldn't mention that now without giving Dorothy away. She'd wait until she and Ferdy were alone.

'Yes, but what *was* used as the weapon?' she asked.

Ferdy looked around. 'Good question. Nothing obvious.'

She heard the soft tapping of a stick approaching.

'I think the professor's coming,' she alerted the others in a low voice.

Humphrey Calder entered the room from the French windows, the tail end of a cigar between his fingers. He stopped short when he saw the interesting tableau before him.

'Good God, what's happened?'

'It's nothing Humphrey,' said Sir Terrence, his voice tired and slow. 'I fell … hit my head, that's all. Nothing to worry about.'

'Good gracious! How did that happen?'

'I don't know. I must have slipped on the rug. Stupid.'

Gerald and Violet came in from the hallway. Another exchange of exclamations and explanation. Sir Terrence's simulated tiredness was now becoming genuine.

Violet, looked at Sir Terrence as though he was a specimen on an operating table. 'Is he badly hurt?'

'I don't think so, my dear,' said Gerald.

'If he's feeling better, why doesn't he get up?' she asked.

Sir Terrence withdrew his gaze from Sarah's concerned and loving face and surveyed the surrounding faces. It struck Annabel that, such was the presence of the man, even lying flat on the floor, he commanded attention.

'"He,"' he said, 'is quite comfortable where he is, thank you. Just for the moment.'

'There you are, you see, he'll be all right in a flash,' said Gerald. 'But, don't you think we should call a doctor?'

'Yes, please call a doctor,' said Sir Terrence.

'Yes, we must,' said Sarah.

'I want him to take a look at you,' he said to Sarah.

'That's not what I meant,' said Sarah, but she smiled.

'Of course, of course,' Gerald hurried out almost colliding with Alexi and Matt in the doorway.

More explanations ensued.

Where's Dorothy?' asked Matt looking round the room.

Nobody knew.

'I think she might have gone for a walk,' said Annabel. Nobody had asked where Lucy was. She studied Alexi's face but all it displayed was the normal concern and interest. Someone had struck Sir Terrence a brutal blow on the head but who?

Ferdy cut through what was becoming a general conversation conducted over Sir Terrence's prone body by asking Matt to help Sarah up to her room.

'She's had a shock,' he said.

'My goodness, yes,' said the professor. 'Of course, she should rest. What are we thinking standing around talking!'

Gerald came back into the room with Mrs Fry and Thomas. He announced that the doctor had been called. Mrs Fry stood taking in the scene with calm authority before stepping forward to help Matt assist Sarah to her feet.

'I'm really all right,' she protested.

'The doctor must see my wife first,' said Sir Terrence.

'I'll see to it,' said Mrs Fry.

Before they left the room Sarah turned to Ferdy. 'You'll help your father?'

'Yes.'

Annabel held the door open for them. As they passed through the hall the door leading through to the kitchen area opened. John, the chef, stood in the opening. His expression as he watched Sarah being helped across the hallway to the stairs was dark. Then he caught Annabel observing him and gave a curt nod before disappearing back to the kitchen.

Ten or so minutes later, Annabel was alone in the library. Ferdy and Thomas had helped Sir Terrence upstairs. Violet and Gerald had gone back to the sitting room. Matt had come back from helping Sarah upstairs and announced that he was going to look for Dorothy. Alexi had gone in search of coffee.

Ferdy entered the room. He closed the door behind him. His whole demeanour had acquired urgency.

It was just what Annabel wanted to see.

'I'm so sorry about your father,' she said. 'Is he going to be all right?'

'His head's going to be sore for a while, but I think he's OK. Anyway, the doctor will take a look at him.' He crossed to the French windows and looked outside before closing them. Then he came back and lowered his voice. 'You see what this means, don't you? We have a live case!'

Ferdy stepped over to the three pictures on the wall and pulled away the third picture to reveal – a third safe.

'Who needs *three* safes?' Annabel couldn't believe it.

'At least three,' said Ferdy. 'He probably has safes built in all over the house. It's just luck that "our spy" got the wrong safe.'

'But why weren't you here?' Annabel didn't want to criticise.

'My mistake. Dad was in here. Lucy came and asked me to help her get down the tennis rackets in the cloak-room and Dad said he'd be OK.'

Lucy again.

As if he had read her thoughts, Ferdy said, 'Yes, you were right – we do need to keep an eye on her.'

'I suppose the documents *are* still there?'

Ferdy looked at her, opened his mouth, then shut it again. Then he opened the middle safe. 'Yes, they are.' He stood looking at them for a few moments and then took them out and slipped them into the inside pocket of his jacket. 'We need to find out who has an alibi for the time that Dad was alone in here and we can do that best together. But we can't leave the documents here if we're not here to watch.'

Annabel agreed. 'But isn't it dangerous carrying them around? If our spy realises that you've got them, what's to stop him … them … having another go?'

'How will they know? And anyway, I suspect that they may be regretting their "gung ho" approach. My guess is they'll have another go tonight when there is less risk and more time.'

'So we'll replace them in the safe later?'

Ferdy nodded.

'There was a glass paperweight on the desk on Friday when we arrived,' said Annabel. 'It's not here now. It could be the weapon.'

'Was there indeed?'

They both looked under the desk and found it rolled into the corner. Ferdy pulled a handkerchief from his pocket and picked it up.

'Fingerprints?' said Annabel.

Ferdy nodded. 'Of course, Dad could have knocked it off as he fell.'

'Gerald has gloves in his pocket,' Annabel was thinking aloud. 'And Thomas was wearing gloves last night at dinner.'

'And Humphrey always carries gloves in case he wants to look at a valuable book or something. But,' he put the paperweight carefully in his pocket 'it's worth a try.'

'I presume it *is* our spy that hit your father on the head? After all, someone stole Dorothy's ring and that was most likely an opportunist theft. Couldn't it have been them?'

Ferdy frowned. 'Yes, you're right,' he said reluctantly. Then he grinned. 'But *something* is definitely going on – and we're going to find out what.'

'And also find Dorothy's ring,' said Annabel.

'Yes. Come on, let's go outside. I think we could both do with some fresh air.'

CHAPTER NINE

Annabel hadn't yet been outside the house at the back. As they stepped through the French windows she had an immediate impression of space. A wide stone-flagged terrace stretched along the entire rear wall of the house curving away in both directions from where they stood. Several of the rooms on the ground floor opened out onto this space and could have given access – or an escape route – for their spy. A low wall ran round the edge of the terrace and in two or three places gaps allowed for steps onto the lawn which was extensive, stretching down to the lake. Ferdy led the way to the left and down the nearest steps which were shallow and wide.

A deep flower bed lay along the lawn side of the terrace wall. The colour scheme, to Annabel's eyes, was disappointingly green and seeming to consist of pampas grasses and large established shrubs, some of which were being fashioned into topiary. An embryo cockerel had still to grow its head and tail, a chess pawn had half a top circle. It gave a strange sense of incompletion, of time halted. But it wasn't all green; on either side of the steps was a splash of pink and orange almost shocking in its comparative intensity. Annabel recognised

Busy Lizzies – one of her stepfather Frank's favourite flowers. She approved. They added some much needed colour.

'Whoever put those there?' said Ferdy in disgust.

'Don't you like them?'

'Don't tell me you do.' Ferdy looked appalled.

'They're colourful,' said Annabel.

'Exactly.' He regarded her with suspicion. 'You're winding me up aren't you?'

No, Annabel wasn't winding him up, but now she began to doubt her own taste. Perhaps the Busy Lizzies did jar. But maybe it was that she didn't like such a plain and simple garden in the first place. She preferred her garden at Haddens with its mix of herbaceous plants and flowering shrubs.

Humphrey was sitting on one of three benches placed on the grass in front of the shrub border. It struck Annabel that he was a very self-contained man, one who preferred his own company. He was reading a book but smiled as he saw them. They walked across.

'How's the invalid?' he asked.

'All right,' said Ferdy 'He's resting.'

'Taking a tumble at our age,' the professor shook his head. 'Never good. He slipped on a rug, you said?'

'Apparently.'

'He'll need a stick, like me, if he's not careful.'

He had rested his stick up against the arm of the bench. It was, Annabel noted, an unremarkable object, the shaft made of lacquered metal with a worn rubber ferrule and a grey resin handle, designed for strength and safety rather than appearance.

'You were outside at the time. Did you hear it happen?' asked Ferdy.

'I was down here and didn't hear anything. Poor Terry! Do you think he cried out?'

'I expect so. You'd think someone would have heard him,' said Ferdy.

'I haven't seen anybody around.' said Humphrey. 'Except Thomas. He walked along the terrace a while back.' His hand strayed to the book on his lap. It was *Ice Station Zebra* by Alastair Maclean. Annabel was surprised. She'd expected him to read something considerably more high brow. She must have revealed her thoughts because he smiled ruefully and patted the book. 'Not my usual fare but I found it on the shelves. We all need some release from work now and then.' As she hadn't expected anything otherwise at a country house weekend party, Annabel kept silent. 'Beautiful weather now,' he continued. 'I expect you're catching some fresh air?'

They took their cue and set off across the lawn. The sky was a deep blue above their heads. Birds were singing. Annabel breathed in deeply and felt her spirits lift. They started to walk around the lawn.

'So,' said Ferdy, 'we have an opportunist jewel thief and an opportunist spy who could be one and the same person or two people acting independently of one another with different objectives. Unlikely, but possible.'

'Or,' said Annabel, 'the attack on your father could

just be the thief trying again and there is no spy. The thief could be Gerald.'

'Who could also be the spy,' said Ferdy.

Were all spy cases this complicated?

'Or, you could be right,' Ferdy continued, 'and perhaps we should widen the search to include others, although there's still the problem of how they could have known about the documents.'

'Lucy has been acting strangely and Thomas too,' said Annabel.

Ferdy was silent for a few moments. 'OK, we widen the search. Where does that leave us?'

'Whoever knocked your father on the head must have sneaked up very silently behind him. Your dad isn't hard of hearing. That must rule out the professor surely? His stick gives him away.'

'But the stick would make an ideal weapon, ready to hand. Then all he had to do was exit via the French window, hang around a bit and re-enter from the terrace, feigning surprise.'

'He's an old friend of your father!'

'He is. And he's not on the list of suspects.'

'As a spy, but he could be the thief,' said Annabel.

'Hmm, well, it wasn't Lucy. She was with me all the time I was away from the room.'

'Unless she is working with someone else – to draw you away.'

'True. The most obvious suspects remain Gerald and Alexi. They are the reason we are here. We shouldn't lose sight of that. We need to find out where they were at the critical time.'

'If we do widen the search that will mean including the staff,' said Annabel.

'Which takes us back to Thomas, who, according to Humphrey, was on the terrace at about the right time.'

'That chef, John, looked like he could knock someone on the head easily,' said Annabel.

'Yes, he does look a cool customer.'

'But how are we going to find out where everyone was? We can't ask straight out without giving the game away.'

'We're going to have to be subtle.' Ferdy grinned at her.

That rules me out.

They had walked some way down the left side of the lawn and could hear the sound of tennis balls being firmly hit.

'Let's start here,' said Ferdy.

They followed the sound through an archway in a high hedge and came upon a rectangular area surrounded by eight foot high chain link fencing and containing what looked like a brand new tarmac tennis court. Dorothy and Lucy were playing with concentration and determination, each hitting the ball with a ferocity that was impressive. Annabel could understand Dorothy wanting to take out her troubles on a tennis ball but what was driving Lucy? But then, perhaps she always played like this. As they watched, Lucy served an ace down the centre line with a force that lodged the ball in the end fence. Dorothy fielded the next serve with a magnificently timed return down the line.

Annabel and Ferdy watched as the game went to deuce and then went Lucy's way. Annabel was interested to note that both women were wearing tennis whites. She hardly recognised Lucy; off-white suited her complexion and she looked so much better in the simply styled dress.

'Three games all,' called Lucy. 'Decider?'

Three games all? Dorothy must be a good player. She remembered Dorothy talking about going to tennis parties when she was younger.

They were spotted as the women went to change ends. Dorothy came over to them, a pathetic look of hope in her eyes. Lucy was collecting balls at the end of the court.

'Have you found it?'

'I'm afraid not,' said Annabel.

Dorothy drooped.

'Good match?' said Ferdy.

Dorothy nodded. 'Lucy's a good player.' Then, as though responding to some unspoken criticism, she added, 'I know I should be looking for the ring but, honestly, I've looked everywhere.'

'I'm afraid I have some bad news,' said Ferdy. 'Dad's had a fall. He's fine but he hit his head and we've called the doctor.'

'Dad's hurt?' Dorothy paled. 'I must go and see him.'

'He's gone to lie down in his bedroom,' Ferdy warned.

Annabel was glad that he stopped short of adding,

'and shouldn't be disturbed,' but the implication was there and Dorothy sagged a bit.

'Of course you must go,' said Lucy who had joined them. 'We can stop the game now.'

They hurried back to the house together.

'I didn't know you were planning on playing tennis this morning,' Ferdy said to Dorothy.

'I wasn't, but then Lucy asked me. Alexi was going to play but didn't turn up.'

Lucy looked annoyed. 'He must have forgotten.'

Dorothy ran up the stairs to see her father. Annabel hoped she would be allowed to do so. Lucy followed more slowly saying she needed to get changed and Annabel was just saying, 'Where first?' to Ferdy, when Mrs Fry came down the stairs and saw them.

'Lady Sarah would like to speak to you – if you are free to come now?' she asked Annabel.

Surprised, Annabel followed her up the stairs and along to the suite of rooms occupied by Sir Terrence and Lady Sarah. Mrs Fry knocked on a door and upon Sarah calling out, opened it and Annabel walked in. Her first reaction was one of relief. Sarah was alone in the bed. The prospect of walking in and finding Sir Terrence in bed with her had been a worry. The second reaction was one of surprise. The bedroom was overwhelmingly floral, a bower of green leaves and yellow roses. There was a floral counterpane and matching curtains. There was a kidney-shaped dressing table with a flounce of similar fabric hanging down to the carpet and a *chaise longue* over by the window with a pale green waffle-weave blanket hanging over the back. Botanical pictures of roses hung, overwhelmed and defeated, against a rose-patterned wallpaper.

It was not the sort of decor that Annabel would have expected someone of Sarah's age to choose, but everything was unmistakably brand new. In the midst of all this floral opulence, Sarah looked pinched and ill at ease.

'How pretty!' Annabel exclaimed, since politeness called for a reaction.

Sarah's face crinkled in pleased surprise. 'Do you think so? My mother chose it all.' She looked rather dubiously round at the walls. 'Please draw up a chair,' she invited. 'Thank you for coming up, I just wanted to find out how everyone was and how you're getting on.'

Annabel pulled over the stool from under the dressing table. 'How are you feeling?'

'Oh, fine! Just a little tired. But the doctor doesn't think there's anything to worry about.'

'I'm sure Sir Terrence had no idea something like this would happen when he arranged the weekend.'

Sarah gave a twisted smile. 'No he didn't. But he wasn't sure about the weekend. It was I who persuaded him.'

'*You* persuaded him?'

'Yes. I felt we should be doing anything we could to help. All these innovations getting stolen is crippling our country's future. But I never imagined that Terry would get hurt.'

The first part of this reply sounded a little pat but there was no denying the truth in the last part. Annabel had to reassess her ideas. She had been imagining Sir Terrence as the somewhat thoughtless instigator of a situation that could harm his pregnant and vulnerable wife. She looked at Sarah with reluctant respect.

Sarah looked down at her hands. 'There's another reason why I wanted this weekend to happen.' She looked up. 'My marriage to Terry is … almost perfect, but there is one thing in particular that I regret hugely.'

Annabel thought she saw a calculating look in Sarah's eyes. She believed she knew what Sarah was talking about but she wasn't going to help her.

Sarah had paused, then as though realising that this was a subject she would have to take forward unaided, she continued, 'It's Ferdy. I know I hurt him terribly, but worse than that, I have caused a rift between him and his father. And that has hurt Terry. So, I was hoping that this weekend might see them mend their differences. Or, at least start talking again. It would mean so much to Terry.'

Annabel believed this reason far more readily than the first reason. But if it was hurting Sir Terrence so much, why hadn't he made more of a push to get in touch with Ferdy himself? And Sarah's concern seemed to be mainly for her husband, not for Ferdy. However, Annabel knew that she wanted exactly what Sarah wanted. She had just as much invested in reconciling Ferdy with his father. She recalled Ferdy's face as he had watched Sarah's concern over her husband's body.

'I think we might be part of the way there already,' she said. She used the word 'we' deliberately and saw from Sarah's expression that she understood.

'Do you think so?'

Annabel nodded. 'Is Sir Terrence with the doctor?'

'He's in his bedroom. The doctor must be still with him because he said he'd let me know what they said.'

They had separate bedrooms? Annabel had read that this wasn't unusual in well-to-do family homes but it still struck her as odd.

As though Sarah had read her thoughts, she said, 'Terry often takes calls in the middle of the night and then when Jonny was a baby I was up and down breast feeding. I couldn't bring myself to bottle feed. Anyway, it just makes sense to have separate bedrooms. But tell me please how things are going regarding the operation.'

'The documents are safe but Ferdy now has them in his jacket.'

Sarah looked alarmed. 'Is that safe? For Ferdy I mean?'

Perhaps there was *some* concern about Ferdy.

'Ferdy thinks so. It frees us both up to investigate the attack on Sir Terrence. We'll put them back tonight. We're thinking of widening the list of suspects beyond just Gerald and Alexi.'

'Widening it? But didn't they spend quite a bit of time and effort making sure that only the two of them knew of the documents? How could anyone else have found out about them?'

'We're not sure. But we think it might be possible. We are going to speak to everyone and see if anyone has an alibi. It would be good to rule people out, if possible.'

Sarah still looked worried. 'You will be careful won't you?'

'Of course. We wondered about the staff. What about Thomas?'

'Thomas? Well, he's new but he came highly recommended.'

'Do you know who gave that recommendation?'

Sarah wrinkled her brow. 'I think it was Rosemary Hutton?'

'And your chef, John?'

'John! Oh no, I don't think so! He's always so kind.' Sarah picked at her floral counterpane. 'So, we are all going to be under suspicion,' she said.

'Not everyone,' said Annabel. 'Not you or Sir Terrence, or Dorothy or Matt.'

'I can see I didn't fully think it through,' said Sarah. 'But it's too late to stop it now.' She raised her head as though to say something else when there was a knock on the door and Mrs Fry entered. Annabel suspected that her visit had been monitored for time so as not to exhaust Sarah. It was good that Sarah's staff seemed to be watching out for her.

'The cherry liqueurs have arrived,' Mrs Fry said. Her tone suggested that a lot of bother had been taken to please an unworthy guest.

Annabel agreed: she hadn't taken to Violet.

'Oh, thank you so much, Mrs Fry. Please have them taken up to Mrs Harcourt's room. And could you ask Ruby to come in?'

'Thank you for asking Mrs Fry to look at my dress,' Annabel said to Sarah when Mrs Fry had left.

'Has it come out all right?'

Annabel assured her it had – now was not the time for honesty – but she could see that Sarah was no longer paying attention. She had the impression that the business she'd been called up to discuss had been completed. It was time to leave.

Annabel found Ferdy in the library. When he saw her, he laid aside the book that he was reading. Annabel saw that it was *The Spy Who Came in from the Cold* by John Le Carré.

'Is that any good?' she asked.

'Yes, I've read it before. The guy seems to know his stuff.'

Again, a suggestion that Ferdy knew about such things, but perhaps Alec had talked about that sort of life.

'How is Sarah?' Ferdy asked.

'She's all right. The doctor has seen her and he's with your father now. I told her what we planned.' She paused. 'Did your father ever apologise for – you know – running off with Sarah?'

Ferdy raised his eyebrow at her. 'Talked about me, did you?'

'A little. I just wondered.'

'The words "I'm sorry" aren't in his vocabulary. What he wants, he takes. It's the secret of his success. You have to admire it, in some ways. I suppose I'd just never been on the sharp end before. Anyway,' he stood up and stubbed out the cigarette he was smoking, 'let's go and find someone to grill.'

'Sarah said she thinks Rosemary approved Thomas. But if that's so, why didn't Rosemary tell us?'

'Good point. We definitely need to talk to Thomas. But Gerald first.'

They found Gerald and Violet once more in the sitting room. Gerald was thumbing through a copy of *The Field* and Violet had her embroidery out. Annabel wondered if she ever got bored with it. They both looked up when Ferdy and Annabel walked in.

'How are the invalids?' asked Gerald.

'Both resting,' said Ferdy 'but otherwise all right.'

'Good, good. I was sure it would be nothing serious.'

'How can you possibly know that?' said Violet languidly. 'Head wounds can be dangerous. He could get compression and die.' She sounded as though this might at least be of interest.

'Well,' said Ferdy, 'it doesn't seem so.' He walked over to the fireplace and stood in front of it. 'I suppose you must have heard it happen?'

Violet raised her eyebrows, 'I don't think we heard anything, until Sarah cried out and Gerald said to me, "Did you hear that?"'

'Yes, that's what I said,' Gerald corroborated.

'And we thought we might as well go and see. I must say it's not what one expects. I hope there aren't too many loose rugs lying around. I suppose it'll be lunch time soon.' She said this last with no change of pace or tone.

Annabel began to wonder if she was quite right in the head. It would appear, from Ferdy's expression, that he was thinking the same.

'Well, you seem to have found a nice quiet spot here,' he pressed on.

'Can't think where everyone has gone,' Gerald agreed. 'We've been here all morning, haven't we, my dear?'

'You went upstairs to get my book.'

'Yes, that, but not the sight of a soul.'

'Until we went into the library.'

'Until we went into the library,' agreed Gerald.

Annabel and Ferdy came back out into the hall and moved over towards the front door out of earshot of the surrounding rooms. The late morning sun had created a transformation of this cold space. Annabel knew that all the walls were painted a uniform white but the way that the light hit the walls made every angle and facet appear a different shade. The effect was subtle and interesting.

'Have we entered a madhouse,' Ferdy demanded in a lowered voice, 'or is it just me?'

'Violet doesn't seem to care one iota about your poor father. I think she's a bit gone in the head.'

'A bit?'

'But if Gerald went upstairs for a few moments, it doesn't look as though we can rule either of them out.'

'No,' Ferdy agreed.

Matt came down the stairs and joined them.

'Dorothy's in with her father,' he said. 'What a strange weekend! First Dorothy's finger and now this!'

'Did you hear it happen?' asked Ferdy.

'No. I was upstairs in my room, too far away to hear anything.'

'Don't suppose you saw anyone whilst you were up there?' asked Ferdy.

Matt grew still and peered at them both. 'Why?' he said. Then he held his hand up. 'On second thoughts, don't answer that. I'd rather not know. Strikes me things seem to happen around you two that I'm better off not knowing.'

'Question still stands,' said Ferdy.

Matt sighed. 'I saw Alexi go into his room but I don't think he stayed there long. And I think Gerald popped up about ten minutes before it all kicked off. Heard him cough – distinctive cough.' From the expression on his face, curiosity was fighting his wiser instincts. Curiosity won. 'I thought it was an accident.'

Ferdy opened his mouth but was forestalled by Matt who raised his hand again. 'Don't want to know,' he muttered as though to himself. '*Don't* want to know.' He turned to go but then looked back. 'You haven't seen my bookmark have you? It's a little thing, like a clip, silver with my initials on it.'

They disclaimed all knowledge.

'OK,' said Ferdy as they watched Matt amble away on his long legs into the sitting room. 'That was interesting.'

Annabel agreed. 'It supports what Gerald told us.'

'Also Alexi was out of his room at the critical time. And if he wasn't available to play tennis with Lucy, what was he doing?'

'In fact, we haven't managed to eliminate anyone yet. Do you think Matt knows why we're here?'

'No,' said Ferdy, 'but he's a lot brighter than he looks so it wouldn't surprise me if he suspects that something's going on.'

'Bright enough to not want to get involved?' suggested Annabel.

'Precisely,' grinned Ferdy.

CHAPTER TEN

There was a commotion at the top of the stairs and Ruby and Jonny came down, the latter in a high state of excitement. They were dressed in shorts and sun hats. Thomas followed them down with suitcases and beach bags whilst Sarah took up the rear. John appeared from the kitchen with two large picnic baskets. Sir Terrence and his wife were taking no chances where their son was concerned.

'Where are they going?' Annabel asked.

'Dunwich,' said Sarah. 'We have a house there.'

'You're not going as well?' asked Ferdy.

'Terry wanted me to but I can't leave him to deal with all this on his own.'

A Daimler drew up at the front door and two men in lightweight trousers, polo shirts and linen jackets started to load everything into the boot. As one of them leant forward, his jacket fell open and Annabel saw the butt of a revolver under one arm. Was Jonny accompanied by security guards everywhere he went? She glanced at Ferdy. He was looking at Jonny with an expression approaching pity but then he met Annabel's eyes and shrugged.

Having waved them off, Sarah gave her apologies and said she needed to do things in her office.

'What does she do?' Annabel asked Ferdy when she'd gone.

'I imagine, if it's anything like when Dad was with my mother, there are all the houses to manage, plus the social calendar to organise, plus all the family arrangements. My mother wasn't very good at it. There was usually some domestic drama or other going on. It used to drive Dad mad. I suspect that Sarah is better.'

Sarah's office was so neat and well-organised: Annabel could quite imagine that to be the case. No doubt Sir Terrence valued and was grateful for the calm that Sarah contrived. Loving Sir Terrence as it was clear that she did, might that have become Sarah's primary aim; to maintain a calm and trouble-free household? If so, this weekend was a gamble.

'"All the houses"?' she asked. 'How many do they have?'

'Well there's the one in London and the apartment in New York and I imagine he still has the place in Paris. Mum got the house in the Bahamas but I can't see Dad managing for long without a bolt hole there. And it sounds as though they now have somewhere in Suffolk. Makes sense – it's where Sarah grew up and her parents still live there.'

Annabel stared. It did look as though Sarah would be kept busy.

'Let's go and speak to Thomas,' said Ferdy. He led the way through to the staff quarters and knocked on the door of the butler's room. They waited a while and Ferdy was about to knock again when the door opened and Thomas stood there in a white apron holding a lint cloth. He looked at them both and for a moment Annabel thought he would say something as though he were addressing a friend or colleague. Then the mask of the servant was resumed.

'Can I help you?'

'May we come in?' asked Ferdy.

Thomas hesitated then stepped back. 'Of course.'

They followed him into a reasonably sized room with a glass door and window looking out onto the back yard and containing a comfortable armchair, a desk, some bookcases and a square wooden table. It seemed that they had disturbed him as he had been cleaning the silver teapot, milk jug and sugar bowl. Annabel looked with interest at the progress made. There was a definite shine to one side of the teapot. It looked good, but what a lot of effort to keep it clean!

Thomas was now facing the window and, in the better light, Annabel could see that his eyes were an unusual toffee colour with long dark lashes. They looked like eyes that could laugh but just at the moment they held a wooden expression.

'Is there something I can help you with?' he repeated his question.

'We're just trying to understand how my father came to fall and wondering if anyone heard anything, or saw anything.' said Ferdy.

Was it Annabel's imagination, or did Thomas look relieved?

'I thought that Sir Terrence slipped on the rug?' said Thomas.

'That is what he thought must have happened but he can't remember fully.'

'I'm afraid I saw nothing. I was elsewhere at the time.' Thomas passed the lint cloth from one hand to the other. 'Surely, if someone had been there they would have helped him?'

A good point.

'It's just that Professor Calder saw you walk along the terrace at about that time,' Ferdy continued.

Thomas frowned. 'Perhaps I did. Yes, I think I did. But,' his frown cleared, 'I'm afraid I didn't see anything or anyone who might be able to help. I hope Sir Terrence is feeling better?'

'Yes, I think so,' said Ferdy.

Annabel stepped in, 'Were you able to fix whatever was wrong in Lucy Harcourt's room? I saw you last night.'

For a moment she thought she saw an exasperated expression in his eyes but then the wooden look was back. 'Thank you, yes. Alice reported a stiff window. I was able to loosen it. Will that be all?'

Ferdy nodded towards the teapot. 'You're getting a good finish on that.'

Thomas raised his brows. 'Thank you.' He picked it up and turned it this way and that. 'Lovely, isn't it? Like a mirror.'

Back in the front hall Annabel asked Ferdy, 'What was all that about the teapot?'

'There's something definitely wrong about that man. He's never polished silver before in his life.'

'It looked like he was doing a good job,' said Annabel.

'I've watched Benson, my mother's butler, polishing silver enough times. He wears protective sleeves over his shirt and gloves on his hands. And he's done it long enough not to get excited about the finish.'

Annabel had been rather touched by Thomas' delight at the mirror like finish but she could see the point that Ferdy was making. 'He could just be new at the job.'

'And he could have been the one who knocked my father on the head.'

Annabel recalled the relieved expression. 'I think he's hiding something.'

'Agreed. And not only because …'

'Because what?' asked Annabel.

'Well. I might be wrong but I think he's ex-forces.'

John, the chef, appeared from the door to the kitchen area and gave the gong in his hands a hefty wallop.

A *gong?* But then, in such a large house, Annabel supposed it made sense if you wanted everyone to know that lunch was ready. The sound would be audible throughout the house and beyond. She suddenly realised that she was ravenous.

John tipped his thumb towards the dining room and said, 'In there.' He paused, 'Has Lady Sarah gone back upstairs?'

'She's in her office,' said Ferdy.

John frowned. 'She should be resting.'

It struck Annabel that he moved like Ferdy. No wasted movements and a contained energy. His bandana today bore the Union Jack. Perhaps he was on their side.

Alice stood in the dining room ready to help serve if needed, but apart from her they were the first to arrive. After the previous night when Annabel had seen her act the part of a society lady in the library, Annabel regarded her with interest. She appeared the perfect maid, silent and self effacing, but Annabel had seen what lay below this outward appearance. It was a salutary lesson to never take anyone at face value.

Annabel turned her attention to the well-stocked sideboard. There was a soup tureen which contained, on inspection, some home-made mushroom soup. Beside it stood a covered dish containing tiny, cubed croutons. Both stood on warming plates. In addition to this there was an assortment of cold meats and cheeses, a variety of fruits, a lemon jelly and some scones with jam and whipped cream. There was a freshly baked loaf ready for people to cut their own slices. Annabel approved. Other people never seemed to cut the bread quite right. It was always just too thin or just too thick. Annabel cut herself a slice of the perfect thickness, helped herself liberally to soup and croutons and looked around for the butter. Perhaps it was in one of the dishes on the table? It was. And it was softened ready for spreading – no gouging away at the bread here with lumps of solid butter!

Ferdy sat down next to her.

'I presume we just start?' she said.

'Absolutely.'

Matt appeared at the door, saw that it was just the two of them and almost turned to escape but behind him Gerald and Violet entered. The three of them addressed the sideboard.

'Mushroom soup,' Violet said. 'I'd have preferred tomato.'

'Looks delicious,' said Gerald. 'Try some.'

Violet hesitated. 'No. I'll just have some cold meat.'

Matt sat down opposite Annabel and Ferdy. He had taken ham and cheese with two slices of bread and proceeded to assemble a sandwich. 'Mushrooms don't agree with me,' he said. His face brightened as Dorothy entered the room. She had changed into a pair of black and cream checked slacks and a short-sleeved cream top. Her hair was pinned back in a chignon. It was quite restrained for Dorothy but perhaps she had chosen the outfit out of respect for her father. Matt regarded her with ill-concealed pride. His brows creased as Lucy entered the room. She too had changed – back into her pink trousers and georgette top.

Alexi was next into the room. 'Lovely morning to be under the bonnet!' he announced brightly.

'Problem?' asked Ferdy.

'Just didn't sound quite right yesterday.'

Matt perked up. 'Carburettor?' he suggested.

Annabel zoned out of the conversation. She liked the

fact that cars got you to places and that was the extent of her interest. However, it did explain Alexi forgetting about the tennis. Apparently Lucy realised this too because she raised her gaze to the ceiling.

Dorothy sat down beside Matt with a bowl of soup and a half slice of bread. Annabel passed her the butter. Dorothy eyed it with regret and waved it away.

'How was your father?' Annabel asked.

'Oh, OK. But he did look shaken. He's been advised to stay in bed for the rest of the day, but he wasn't resting. He took three phone calls whilst I was there.' She nibbled at her bread.

Annabel didn't know what to say. She hoped he had been kind to his daughter.

Sarah and Humphrey entered the room together. Ferdy pushed his chair back and got up to draw out Sarah's chair. She looked at him in surprise and gave an uncertain smile. Alice fetched her a bowl of soup and slice of bread. The window was open and the sound of a lawnmower at work was audible.

The professor sat down beside Annabel. She noticed that he ate a substantial meal with several returns to the side table. There was general discussion about what people would be doing in the afternoon. Gerald had been going to play golf with Sir Terrence but that was not now possible. He suggested to Violet that they might take a walk. She agreed reluctantly. Annabel suspected that she would prefer to sit indoors and pursue her endless embroidery. There was a general atmosphere of despondency in the room. No doubt in a praiseworthy attempt to lighten the mood, Matt suggested a game of croquet but nobody responded.

Annabel leant in to whisper to Dorothy. 'If you could get Alexi and Lucy outside, Ferdy and I would be free to search the rooms for your ring.'

Dorothy caught on quickly. She turned to Matt. 'Great idea!' The delay between Matt's suggestion and this enthusiastic response was marked. Alexi looked from Matt to Dorothy, his eyebrows raised.

'You'll play, won't you, Lucy?' Dorothy said.

'Oh! I suppose so. Yes, all right.'

Alexi shrugged his shoulders and agreed to play.

'And I know that you and Ferdy can't play because ...' Dorothy realised she hadn't thought through their possible excuse and ground to a halt.

She really wasn't good at subterfuge.

'Dad wants us to look at some papers,' said Ferdy.

'That's right!' Dorothy beamed at them.

Nobody asked Humphrey if he wanted to play.

'I won't either,' he said, with only a touch of dryness, 'Terrence has a book I've been wanting to look at ...'

They all looked at him with faces that displayed varying degrees of embarrassment at their omission.

'... on the Etruscan civilisation.'

'Oh ... ah ... yes, of course,' said Matt.

Sarah suddenly let out a cry. 'Oh! Jasper!' She jumped up from the table.

Jasper?

The professor's spoon clattered onto the table hitting his bowl on the way and spilling soup on the table.

Everyone stared at Sarah who was waving her hands around. 'Oh! Get it away! Get it away!'

'Oh,' said Matt as they all heard the buzzing sound, 'it's only a wasp. Don't you like them?'

A redundant question.

Gerald leapt up and swiped at the insect with his napkin. It easily evaded his attempts to swat it.

Alice stepped forward and mopped up the spilt soup.

Annabel looked with concern at Professor Calder. All the colour had left his face which bore a stunned expression.

'Are you all right?' she asked quietly.

It was as though she was dragging him back from some far off place of horror but eventually he focussed on her face.

'Yes, thank you. Yes. Bit of a thing about wasps.'

Annabel sympathised. She had a 'bit of a thing' about spiders.

Ferdy picked up his empty glass and a card from the mantlepiece and walked over to the window where the wasp had settled. He trapped it with the glass, slid the card behind the glass and released the wasp outside. It was all done with the minimum of fuss.

'Oh, thank you!' Sarah gasped in relief. 'I'm so glad you didn't kill it. It wasn't its fault. I'm so stupid.'

'I know you don't like them killed,' said Ferdy quietly.

'I saw someone die after being stung by a wasp,'

Violet's clear, unemotional voice cut in. 'Their throat swelled up, they couldn't breathe. It took ... no time at all.'

Alexi stared at her expressionlessly. Then he turned back to Sarah. 'Why "jasper"?'

'Oh,' Sarah gave a shaky laugh, 'in Suffolk we've always called them that. I'm so sorry ... such a fuss!'

They waited until everyone had gone outside before Ferdy led the way upstairs.

'Well done back there,' he said, 'getting Dorothy to go along with the game. We should have a clear field for our search.'

Annabel was upset about his protective attitude to Sarah but was determined not to show it. However, the words worked themselves out, despite her wishes. 'So, Sarah doesn't like wasps to be killed.'

Ferdy stopped half way up the stairs and looked at her. 'She's always been afraid of wasps,'

'Really?' *You don't say.*

'Yes, *really.*' He took two more steps and stopped again. 'I get rid of spiders for you.'

He seemed to feel that this ended the matter and it was true that he did remove spiders for her. Annabel realised that she preferred it when Ferdy was not so protective of Sarah; when, in fact, his main feeling was one of bitter disillusionment.

'Right,' said Ferdy, 'let's look for that ring. And whilst we're at it, anything else incriminating.'

Annabel wasn't looking forward to this bit at all. They would be poking about amongst people's things, people they had come to know. 'Where shall we start?'

'Humphrey first, and work back from there. Lucy's room then her parents and finish up with Alexi.'

It would be a lot worse for Ferdy; Alexi was a friend.

They climbed the stairs and turned left, going past their own rooms and on to Humphrey's room. He had not locked his door. The room overlooked the front of the house and, facing north-east, no longer received any sunshine. The air was stuffy and smelt of cigar smoke. Annabel was tempted to open the window but was afraid she might forget to close it again. The professor was not a tidy man. His clothes lay strewn across bed and chair and hung from the handles of the wardrobe. His bed-side table held a copy of Marcus Aurelius' *Meditations* and a bottle of indigestion medicine. The book was certainly more in line with what she had expected him to read but she understood his need for some light reading. He wore striped cotton pyjamas and his dressing gown was of a green and brown checked flannel, frayed at the wrists. In the bathroom they saw that the professor used a traditional brand of toiletry; a not very clean shaving brush stood in a shaving cream jar which bore the brand name, as well as a bottle of after shave lotion. They checked drawers and pockets. They felt under the pillows and looked in the bathroom cabinet. They checked inside shoes and in the suitcase. They didn't find the ring or anything else untoward. They exited the room carefully looking in both directions before re-entering the corridor.

Lucy had not locked her door either. Facing south, her room was filled with sunshine. She had left the window wide open and the room felt fresh. Her room was very tidy with pink bedroom slippers lined up together beside the bed, brush and comb neatly aligned on the dressing table and a minimum of beauty products – just a pot of face cream and a lipstick. Annabel didn't bother to check the colour.

They could hear the croquet game starting up out-doors – disembodied voices. Annabel hoped that the game would keep them occupied for a long time.

'Stay away from the windows,' Ferdy warned.

The wardrobe revealed an assault of pink but this was to be expected. They followed the same search pro-cedure as before but didn't find the ring.

Back out into the corridor and the next door down was the Harcourt's room. This too was unlocked but as they opened the door they heard sounds from within the room. The maid, Alice, appeared from out of the bath-room and saw them.

'Oh! Are you looking for the Harcourts?' she asked. 'I think they've gone out. Mrs Harcourt asked me to clean their bathroom, again.' There was the slightest inflexion on the word 'again' which suggested that in Alice's opin-ion, this was unnecessary. Her brow creased, 'I'm sorry, I'm afraid I didn't hear you knock.'

Ferdy and Annabel retreated.

'Next time we knock first, just in case,' he said. 'Now for Alexi's room.' They crossed back past the gallery and into the west wing.

Holding up his hand, Ferdy popped briefly into Dorothy's room and stole a glance out of the window. Apparently the game of croquet was still in progress because he then knocked on Alexi's door. No reply. They slipped in. Annabel was disturbed by how normal this had now become. Alexi appeared to be living out of his suitcase. It lay open on a rack specially provided for unpacking but he had not unpacked. The wardrobe was empty save for his velvet jacket which hung in solitary splendour. There was nothing on the dressing table. His toiletries in the bathroom were exotic looking with foreign writing on them – Italian possibly? On his bedside table was a copy of *The Pride of Miss Jean Brody* by Muriel Spark, cigarettes, an ashtray and a bottle of vodka. Ferdy raised his eyebrows at the book not, Annabel noted, at the vodka.

Annabel was about to start searching through the clothes in the suitcase when Ferdy stopped her. He then undertook the search taking great pains to not disarrange the clothes.

Unsuccessful, they returned with the usual care to the corridor. Annabel was relieved on Ferdy's behalf that they hadn't found the ring in his friend's rooms. But it was frustrating that it remained unfound.

'Come on,' said Ferdy. 'Let's see if that maid has finished.'

They retraced their steps back to their side of the house. Ferdy knocked on the door. No reply. The room was tidy and fresh smelling. The window was open and the sounds of the croquet match in motion were audible.

Annabel had hoped that Violet's handbag would be there but it would appear that she took it with her on walks. In any event, it wasn't in the room. The cherry liqueurs had been placed on the right hand bedside table. The box was exquisite; patterned in turquoise and silver with a silver ribbon. Beside it lay Anthony Burgess' *A Clockwork Orange*. The two didn't go together, on any level. On Gerald's bedside table was an edition of Churchill's *A History of The English Speaking Peoples volume 2*. The bookmark showed that he was making impressive progress.

They carried out their now practiced search, but the ring was not to be found. Ferdy opened the door a crack and peeped out.

'Shit!' he said withdrawing hurriedly and closing the door silently. 'Gerald and Violet are coming up the stairs.'

Annabel stared at him wild-eyed. The bed was a divan otherwise she would be under it already.

Ferdy had adopted what she was starting to think of as his Buddhist monk alter ego where time slows down and he has acres of space in which to think. Then he grabbed her wrist and pulled her into the window embrasure. The curtains were partly drawn. He pushed Annabel into one corner and positioned himself on the other side. Thank goodness the window was so deeply set! There was room enough to stand sideways on to the window; the floor length curtains would hide them from anyone in the room but only up to a point. However, Annabel couldn't think of anything better. She pressed herself back against the wall and fought to steady her breathing.

Ferdy lifted a finger to his lips. Annabel threw him a murderous look. Of course they needed to be quiet! Did he think she was an idiot? Ferdy grinned. He looked as though he was enjoying himself.

So much for staying away from the window. But, in fact, from where she was standing the view of the croquet game was only peripheral. Just one hoop visible and at present no players.

CHAPTER ELEVEN

The door opened and the Harcourts came in, or so Annabel supposed. There was no conversation. They heard the sound of shoes being kicked off and someone entered the bathroom. The bedsprings settled under the weight of a body. There was a sigh. It sounded female. The flush of a toilet and the bathroom door opened.

'I did say I didn't want to go for a walk,' Violet's voice sounded self-justifying.

A male sigh this time.

'But it's such a beautiful day. You can't want to be stuck indoors all day.'

'Actually, I can.'

The sound of Gerald, presumably, pacing up and down. Annabel cringed as the pacing brought Gerald near to the window. She felt acutely uncomfortable. This was far worse than the morning in the library where she had overheard Lucy and Sarah. At least she'd had a right to be there and she could, if discovered, pretend to be asleep or something. Unlikely, just after breakfast, but just about feasible. Here, there was no excuse. Discovery would be hugely embarrassing.

'I do wish you would just —'

'Just what? What do you wish I would do?' Violet demanded.

Another sigh. The sound of Gerald's foot scuffing the carpet. 'Enjoy yourself more.'

'How can I? How can I enjoy myself more.' A pause. 'This weekend is a disaster.'

'Yes,' Gerald sounded tired. 'Yes, I know. But if you'd just try.'

'Well I can't.' Violet moved abruptly causing the bed to creak. 'You should know that by now. Why can't you just understand?'

'Oh, I understand. You know I understand.'

'Oooh!' Violet cried in a completely different tone of voice, 'some chocolates have arrived! My favourite.' She paused, 'Sarah must have arranged it.'

'I like Sarah,' said Gerald.

'Do you? I find her a bit too perfect but, yes, I suppose this was kind.' The tone was grudging.

Annabel hadn't expected to find anything in common with Violet but she had to admit that she found Sarah just that little bit too perfect.

There was the sound of the box being opened. It made a sucking sound as the tight fitting lid was removed. Even from behind the curtain, Annabel detected an enticing waft of chocolate. She visualised an envelope of wrapping paper, possibly silver, perhaps patterned with the maker's name. Almost certainly with a silver paper seal holding the envelope together. After opening such a box, the contents might almost be said to be a let down.

'Darling!' Gerald burst out, then paused and continued in a more temperate tone. 'Darling, you know this has got to stop.'

The sound of a cherry liqueur being popped into the mouth and sucked with relish. Violet had wasted no time in appreciation of the wrapping.

'I really don't know what you are talking about,' she said. 'Oh, do stop pacing about! You're making me nervous! Sit down here.' – the sound of the bed being patted – 'We need to talk about Lucy.'

There was a pause, another pat and a louder creak as Gerald's body settled on the edge of the bed.

'If only she hadn't wanted to come,' Gerald complained.

'What do you mean? She likes doing everything with us.'

'You know that won't always be the case.'

'Of course it will.'

'She might want to get … married.' said Gerald.

The sound of fretful movement on the bed.

'You know that upsets me. How can you be so uncaring! Anyway, if there was going to be any danger of that it would have happened by now.'

'She's the same age as Dorothy.'

'Yes, I know. But Dorothy is pretty,' said Violet. 'In fact, I'm surprised it's taken her this long to get married.'

'I think Lucy is pretty.'

A scoffing sound. 'Gerald, Lucy is a carthorse.'

'Would you really say … carthorse? I think she's –'

'All right, Amazonian, if you prefer that. The fact is, men don't. Look at Matt. You can see he thinks she's a freak.' Her voice held a strange mix of pique and complacency.

'I found him thoughtlessly unkind,' said Gerald. 'Unlike Ferdy – he seems to be a nice lad.'

'Yes, but there's no danger there. You must know his history. In fact, I'm amazed he's swallowed his pride enough to be here, but I suppose he doesn't want to cut the purse strings. Anyway, I can't see him popping the question any time soon. It'll be a long time before he considers marriage again.'

Gerald didn't disagree.

'From what I've heard,' Violet continued, 'he's wasting his time in some sort of private eye nonsense. What a come down! That son of Sarah's will take over the business, inherit everything. No, I'm more worried about that playboy Alexi.'

'There's something a bit odd about that young man,' said Gerald. 'There's nothing wrong with his car. I heard him arrive. Engine sounded as sweet as a nut.'

'I don't know anything about that. It's his address. He can be charming.'

'He comes from Russian nobility,' said Gerald.

'Does he? Perhaps his tapestries are original?' Violet sounded genuinely interested. 'But anyway, Russian nobility means nothing now, except that he's exiled.'

'We're getting off the point,' said Gerald. 'You know how important this weekend is to me, to us.'

Silence.

'It's the first time we've been invited to a weekend party for months and I think we both know why the invitations stopped. You need to, *we* need to work together. I can't do it on my own.'

'I know! I know.' An impatient movement on the bed. 'Oh, do go away, Gerald! I want to rest.'

Silence.

'Yes, all right darling,' The sound of a kiss being delivered. 'Would you like me to close the window? Draw back the curtains?'

Annabel held her breath.

'No, leave them as they are. Don't fuss, Gerald.'

The sounds of movement.

'I'll let you know when tea is being served.'

Silence.

Gerald left the room, closing the door softly behind him.

A sigh. Then a book being opened up. Another chocolate popped in the mouth. The comfortable sound of Violet settling down for a long read.

Annabel looked at Ferdy in despair. When would they ever escape?

Ferdy made strangling movements with his hands.

Time passed … very slowly.

Every now and then Violet let out a deep sigh.

Every now and then she popped another chocolate into her mouth.

The sun had moved round and now shone fully on

Annabel. She could feel herself wilting. The open window was on Ferdy's side and he stood in the shade. He was looking at her with concern. The game of croquet came to a dramatic conclusion with much noise and theatrical self-congratulation and sour grapes. However reluctant the players had been at the start, it sounded as though the game had been a success. It sounded fun.

Annabel had been hard pressed not to leap out and whack Violet on the head when she talked so unpleasantly about Ferdy. She had also been unable to look at Ferdy, afraid of the pain that she might see in his face. Then she wondered if he might interpret that as her agreeing with Violet's assessment, so she had looked … and seen a very strange light in Ferdy's eyes. It was as though he'd just been struck with an idea that gave him hope. At any rate, he didn't look downcast.

Now he was looking at something outside, something obscured from her sight unless she stepped forward and looked to her left. She raised her eyebrows in question. Ferdy grinned reassuringly. With the minimum of movement he extracted from his jacket pocket a note pad and then from his handkerchief pocket a pen and proceeded to write. Then he turned the pad to her. Annabel read the word 'HELP'. She would have thought that was self-evident – they both needed help. But Ferdy was folding the paper into an aeroplane shape. He then launched it out of the window. It lurched and staggered before a chance breeze swept it out of sight behind Annabel. Ferdy watched its progress. He was already making another.

This one he aimed in a kamikaze-like plummet to the terrace below. It landed in full view of them both, a small white SOS on the pale flagstones.

Annabel heard the sound of approaching footsteps on the terrace below and Sarah came into view. She regarded the aeroplane with surprise then stooped and picked it up.

'How odd,' Sarah said, looking around, but not up. 'I wonder where that came from?' She didn't appear to notice the writing.

Ferdy abandoned finesse, took another sheet of paper, scrunched it into a tight ball and chucked it down with some force. It bounced on the terrace at Sarah's feet.

This time Sarah looked up. Ferdy put his finger to his lips. Sarah took in their faces which Annabel was sure, in her case, showed some distress, and then visibly counted the windows from the end of the house to theirs. An unholy smile swept across her face as she realised whose room they were in. She gave a nod which Annabel interpreted as an undertaking to help.

Annabel revived. The sun no longer felt unbearable and she no longer feared she might pitch forward from her hiding place. It can't have been much more than five minutes, ten at most, before there was a tap on the door.

'Who is it?' called Violet. Her voice didn't sound encouraging to any would-be visitor.

The door opened.

'Oh, Violet,' they heard Sarah say, 'I wonder if I could

possibly trouble you? I need some advice. It's a piece of embroidery and something has got spilt on it.'

'Embroidery? What has got spilt on it?'

'Cough medicine. It's sticky, you see, and as you know so much about embroidery I hoped you might be able to help.'

'Cough medicine! Bring it to me here and I'll have a look.'

'I'm afraid that would be impossible. It's on a chair you see, in the nursery. I really don't want the embroidery to be spoilt, but I don't know what's best to do.'

'Oh dear. Yes, I shall come.'

'Oh, thank you! Thank you so much.'

The sound of movement, then steps, then the door closing.

Ferdy and Annabel leapt from behind the curtain and over to the door. Ferdy opened it and peered out.

'Coast's clear,' he said.

Annabel detoured past the box of chocolates. It was everything she'd imagined and more. She looked for Violet's bag but couldn't see it.

'What are you doing?' Ferdy hissed. 'Come on!'

Annabel needed no second telling.

They went rapidly down the stairs and out through the library doors onto the terrace. From there they descended to the lawn and began to walk quickly away from the house.

'That was awful,' said Annabel. Her legs were trembling. 'Horrible, horrible woman!'

'She wouldn't score highly on the nicest woman of the year award,' Ferdy agreed.

'Unlike Sarah,' said Annabel. 'I do hope she hasn't ruined a chair, just to get us out of a jam.'

They'd reached the lake by now and Annabel paced up and down along the bank, her arms crossed, her movements jerky.

'How could she say *that* about her own daughter!'

Ferdy nodded. 'Not exactly a contestant for best mother award either.'

'And she kept on pigging away at those chocolates! I hope she's *sick*!'

Annabel became aware that Ferdy was standing looking at her. He appeared calm. The tension in her body drained away. There was a bench nearby. She went and sat down on it.

'I'm not sure I'm cut out for this sort of work,' she said.

He sat down beside her. 'You may not believe it,' he said, 'but working with you has brought back all my memories of working with Alec.'

Annabel stared at him. 'I *don't* believe it!'

'It's true. You share that mercurial quality that he had and you notice things, just like he did. It gets results.'

'You're the one who keeps rescuing us from scrapes,' said Annabel.

'Again, like me and Alec.'

Annabel remembered that Alec had written in his letter to her that she could trust Ferdy with her life as he had done on numerous occasions. Perhaps what Ferdy was saying was true. Annabel liked the thought of that.

'I was so bored last night,' she said 'and so scared this afternoon.'

'Oh, you get used to it – the highs and lows.'

'You're so calm!'

'I'm used to it … now. You should have seen me when I first started.'

Annabel stared at the lake. A duck paddled by, its progress disturbing the surface of the water. Sunshine glittered on the ripples. She wasn't sure that she entirely believed Ferdy. She'd seen that look in his eye when he faced danger. It was as though he lived for those moments.

'What did you think of their conversation?' she asked.

Ferdy shifted on the bench. It was clear he had been waiting for her to recover so that they could continue their work. The reason why they were there, Annabel reminded herself.

'Gerald wants to get back into the weekend party scene. That much is obvious,' said Ferdy.

'And he seemed to imply that Violet was not helping. He said, "This has got to stop". *What* has got to stop?'

'Is Violet our spy?' suggested Ferdy.

'I think she'd be capable of anything. But,' Annabel sighed, 'I can't see it, and it would mean that Gerald knows and disapproves. Or they could both be in it, and Gerald is having cold feet.'

'They could have been talking about something else entirely, nothing whatsoever to do with espionage. And why was Alexi working on a car that sounded "as sweet as a nut"?' said Ferdy.

'Sorting out a hiding place for the documents?'

'Wouldn't he have done that already?' said Ferdy. He kicked at the ground.

'It did seem that Lucy particularly wanted to be here.' Annabel felt sorry for Lucy and didn't want to think that she might be a spy or a thief. 'I wonder why?'

'Yes …'

'I can't understand a mother who doesn't want her daughter to marry,' said Annabel. She paused then continued with constraint, 'You mustn't pay any attention to what Violet said about you.'

Ferdy lifted his face to the sky. 'Actually, that was the one good thing about the whole episode. Who knew how grateful I'd be for Jonny's existence?'

Annabel stared. 'Do you mean that you are *happy* he might supplant you!'

Ferdy looked at her with a crooked smile. 'Can you really see me taking over from Dad, running a huge business empire? The prospect has terrified me since I was old enough to think about such things. Endless board meetings … I'd go mad. No, if Jonny is willing to take over …'

'You would be more than happy?' Annabel couldn't keep the wonder out of her voice. But she could see what Ferdy was saying. That sort of life wouldn't suit him at all.

'Put it this way,' he said, 'I shall use every opportunity I can get to persuade him that it is just the sort of life he would love. Let's face it, with Sarah as his mother and Dad as his father, he ought to be ideal.'

'Sarah's all right, isn't she?' Annabel couldn't help liking the woman who had treated Ferdy so badly.

'Yes. Yes, she is.'

Annabel wanted to ask him if he still loved Sarah. She opened her mouth to do so, but closed it again. It wouldn't be right and anyway it wasn't the question that she really wanted to ask.

They heard footsteps behind them and, turning round, saw Sarah walking towards them. They made room for her on the bench between them and she lowered herself carefully down.

'Goodness! What on earth were you doing in the Harcourt's room? Such a risk! What if you'd been caught?'

Ferdy grinned.

'We'd hoped to do them earlier but the maid was in there,' said Annabel. 'We thought they'd be gone for a long time. We're so sorry about your chair.'

'I'm sure it'll be fine. I had to spill the cough mixture over it. It's got one of those hand-embroidered head rests. It was the only embroidery I could think of. Ruby will think I'm mad. What do you mean, Alice was there? She should have finished long ago.'

'Violet called her back to clean the bathroom again, said it wasn't clean.'

'That woman …' Sarah shook her head. 'She annoys

Terry. I feel quite sorry for her. She doesn't seem very happy.'

'Huh,' said Ferdy.

That rather summed up Annabel's feelings too.

'Have you still got the documents?' Sarah asked Ferdy.

'Yes. We'll put them back in the safe later. If anything is going to happen, it will be tonight,' said Ferdy.

'You will take care won't you?' she said.

CHAPTER TWELVE

It was late afternoon and Ferdy suggested that they both go and try to catch some sleep since they would be staying awake much of the night. Annabel felt far too wound up to sleep but could see the sense of lying down for a bit. They went upstairs and into their rooms where Annabel kicked off her shoes and lay down on the bed. Despite her misgivings, she was starting to drift off when there was a light tap on the door. Thinking it must be Ferdy she called out to come in.

Dorothy popped her head round the door. 'Oh!' she said in surprise, 'Were you resting? Shall I go away?'

Annabel heaved herself up on her pillows. 'No. Come in.'

'Are you not feeling well?'

No. I was just up for most of last night. 'No. I'm fine,' she said. 'Just a little tired.'

'Me too,' said Dorothy. She settled on the edge of the bed. Annabel moved her legs to make room. 'I just wondered if my ring had …'

'I'm afraid not. We had a look in the Harcourt's rooms, Humphrey's room and Alexi's. We'll keep looking.'

Dorothy drooped. 'I can't keep it hidden from Matt

for much longer. He's already saying that I should get my finger looked at by a doctor.'

The 'field bandage' had been replaced by a fabric plaster.

'Sarah got it for me,' said Dorothy, seeing Annabel looking at it. 'I must say it's easier to manage but Matt is saying that you should give cuts air to heal.'

Bother Matt. But at least he cared. 'I'm sure it will turn up soon. Who won the croquet?' she asked, to change the subject.

'Lucy and Matt,' said Dorothy. 'But it was close.'

'You didn't pair up with Matt?' Annabel was surprised.

'I wanted to but Lucy didn't want to partner Alexi so …'

After what she had heard in the Harcourt's room Annabel was starting to feel concerned about Lucy. Her mother seemed to have allocated her the role of unpaid and unappreciated companion to her parents. She wondered if Dorothy knew anything about it all.

'Lucy's mother seems very clingy,' she said.

'Oh, I suppose so. A bit like my mum, to be honest.'

Annabel had encountered Lady Baxter, albeit only by way of a phone call. Lady Baxter had been autocratic and had accused Annabel of kidnapping Dorothy. It had not been a pleasant experience.

'But your mother would never stand in the way of your marriage would she?'

'Goodness no! But Lucy has always been very loyal and she loves her parents.'

Annabel was still trying to understand Lucy. 'I got the impression that she was happiest when she was out on the water rowing.'

'Oh, yes. She's always been mad about rowing. She once told me that her greatest ambition would be to row for her country in the Olympics. Her dad rowed for Oxford, you know. But, of course being a woman, that's not possible.' She paused, considered that statement. 'It does seem rather silly doesn't it? I mean why can't women row in the Olympics? They can row internationally.'

Annabel agreed that it did seem silly.

'Does she have a boyfriend, then?' Annabel asked, thinking about the previous evening when Lucy had closed down any discussion about wanting to get married. Having overheard Violet's views on the matter, Annabel could quite understand that Lucy wouldn't want such a matter to be discussed. But she couldn't say that to Dorothy.

Dorothy wrinkled her nose. 'Well, I *think* so. She's been keeping a bit of a low profile recently, but I've never met anyone.'

Annabel was intrigued. 'Perhaps a girlfriend?'

'Oh no, Lucy isn't that way.' Dorothy spoke with confidence.

Annabel changed tack.

'I don't understand why she doesn't buy herself better clothes. Can't she afford it?'

Dorothy stared. 'Lucy spends more than I do on clothes! She inherited a fortune from her aunt.' Her face took on an expression of puzzlement mingled with pity. 'I can't understand it. She just has *no* taste.'

Annabel couldn't help laughing. It was obvious that Dorothy considered this akin to a major failing.

'It's true!' Dorothy insisted. 'That pink georgette top she's wearing today – I was with her when she bought it. They had it in a blue-green. She looked lovely in it – but she bought the pink.' To Annabel's astonishment, Dorothy's eyes filled with tears at the memory.

Dorothy left and Annabel settled back down but she no longer wanted to drift off. She felt she'd let Dorothy down. The ring could be anywhere. It could be in someone's pocket. It could be hidden around the house somewhere. It could be in one of the member of staff's rooms or in one of their pockets. It was a shame they hadn't been able to have a look in Violet's bag up in the Harcourt's room. Annabel would quite like the thief to be Violet. She was plotting how she might get hold of Violet's bag when the gong sounded downstairs. More food? But perhaps it was tea. A cup of tea would go down nicely.

Following the sound of voices, Annabel entered the sitting room where she found everyone, including Sir Terrence, present. The coffee table was set out with two, well polished silver teapots, porcelain cups and saucers, a milk jug, a bowl of sugar, two delicious looking cakes and a plate of home-made ginger biscuits. Maybe, she could manage a bite to eat after all.

Sir Terrence had just accepted a cup of tea from

Sarah and was about to sit down in his armchair to the left of the fireplace when it was occupied by Violet. Sarah looked somewhat pointedly at Violet, clearly hoping that she got the message. Violet sat composedly. If she had picked up on the social signals, she was ignoring them. Sarah opened her mouth to say something but Sir Terrence put his hand on her shoulder, a signal to let it be. He sat down on the sofa. Nobody could have told from his face that he felt put out.

Annabel asked how he was feeling.

'Much better thank you, Annabel.' It was clear he'd answered this question already, several times, before she arrived.

At Sarah's request, Annabel helped herself to a slice of Victoria sponge and, with resignation, to a cake fork. As she was trying to encourage a piece onto the fork, Alexi sidled up.

'The king has been deposed,' he said, nodding towards Violet.

So, he had noticed. Annabel wondered how much he *did* notice.

Lucy helped herself to a generous slice of the other cake on offer. It was a fruit cake. She stabbed at it with her fork and transferred a sizeable piece to her mouth. *She* had no problem with the fork.

'Some people never seem to stop eating,' said Alexi to nobody in particular.

Lucy flinched and took her plate away to the window seat.

Annabel looked at Alexi in dislike and moved away. Ferdy moved over to talk to Lucy and she appeared to cheer up. Annabel watched them with mixed feelings.

Humphrey took a slice of Victoria sponge, eyed the fork with wry amusement, picked up the slice in his hand and took a bite with aggressive enjoyment. He caught Annabel watching and gave a wink. She couldn't help smiling in return.

Violet got out her embroidery and started to set her tiny precise stitches. Annabel left the coffee table and moved closer. She tried to see inside the bag but it was one of those floppy voluminous ones that collapse in on itself and all she could see was the tip of what looked like a note book.

'How beautiful!' she said to justify her presence. 'Have you been working on it long?'

Violet looked up. 'Thank you,' she said cooly. 'Not long.'

'Oh! Someone might trip over your bag,' said Annabel 'Let me move it.' She bent to pick it up but Violet's hand shot out and got to it first. She lifted it and put it down on the other side of her chair next to the wall.

'Is that better?'

Annabel had recoiled. 'Y – Yes. Much better.'

'Quite right. We wouldn't want any more accidents,' said Violet.

Sarah and Gerald had moved over to the display cabinet against the wall behind Violet's chair, the one containing Sir Terrence's snuffbox collection.

'Terry?' Sarah asked. 'Did you take out the snuffbox that I like?'

Sir Terrence lifted his head. 'No. Why?'

'Well, it's not there now.' Sarah sounded puzzled.

Annabel met Ferdy's eyes. He gave a little flick of the eyes to right and left. Annabel needed no encouragement to watch everyone in the room.

'The pretty one with the two figures?' Lucy asked.

'We were all looking at it last night,' said Alexi.

'Perhaps it got knocked on the floor,' said Gerald. He got down on his hands and knees and started to search.

'Oh, no. Alice would have found –' Sarah started to say.

'Yes!' Gerald interrupted. 'Here it is, under this chair.' He stood up with the ease of a much younger man, holding up the snuff box.

'Oh!' said Sarah. 'How odd … but thank you Gerald. Thank you very much. I should hate to have lost it.'

Violet had paused momentarily in her sewing, a tiny frown creasing her brows. Then she carried on as if nothing had happened.

Upstairs, Annabel almost dragged Ferdy into her bedroom.

'It was in Violet's bag!' she burst out as soon as the door was closed.

'Yes. I think it probably was. But it could have been in Gerald's pocket. The easiest thing in the world to take it out as he got down on his hands and knees and then pretend to "find" it under a chair. Gerald's the one who loves those things. Maybe Violet was just trying to put it back. It would explain her annoyance with him.'

Annabel paced the room. 'If only we could get into Violet's bag! I'm sure we'd find the ring there.'

Ferdy smiled. 'Nice try with the bag, by the way.'

'You noticed?'

'I was just thinking of trying something similar.'

'I wish we could be like the police and *demand* to see inside,' Annabel said.

'We'd need a body first … even the police can't just walk in and demand to see everything,' said Ferdy.

Annabel remembered the body that she had found at Haddens. She still shuddered at the memory. 'Don't even think of it!' she said. 'We'll just have to do what we can without the police.'

Annabel changed into her blue dress for dinner and, as Ferdy hadn't put in an appearance, knocked on his door. He opened it. He looked fresh and clean and he smelt wonderful – a sort of citrus, musky cologne.

'You look nice,' she said.

He grinned. 'Isn't that what *I'm* supposed to say?'

'Nobody's stopping you.'

'Annabel, my darling, you look …' He stopped, then continued after a moment. 'You look beautiful.'

Annabel blushed. 'No need to go overboard.' This was the trouble with fishing for compliments.

'Who said I was going overboard?'

Annabel gave an uncertain half laugh. She wished, not for the first time, that he wasn't so inscrutable. They turned to walk along to the stairs and met Dorothy and Matt coming from their end of the house. Now *there* was beauty. Dorothy was wearing her pale pink dress. It had some sort of outer layer that shimmered in the light.

'You decided to wear it,' said Annabel as they descended the stairs together, Matt and Ferdy following on behind.

Dorothy tilted her chin up. '*I* look good in pink,' she said.

This was self-evident.

'And I don't see why I should let Lucy put me off wearing my favourite dress.'

The scene in the sitting room resembled the previous evening. Annabel decided to throw caution to the winds and accepted a martini from Sir Terrence. The first sip almost made her cough. Lucy was wearing a sheath-like dress in a rich pink satin. She really did have a superb figure but was hampered by the restrictions imposed by the tight skirt. Her stride had of necessity become a shimmy. The skirt also drew attention to Lucy's feet which were large for a woman. As though aware of this, Lucy placed herself behind pieces of furniture. She looked, if it were possible, even less at ease than previously.

Looking around the room, Annabel didn't think that anyone present appeared very happy, with the possible exception of Alexi whose puckish smile rarely left his face and who, Annabel suspected, was generally amused by things concerning other people. He made his way over to her.

'Sir Terrence mixes a strong cocktail,' he said.

He had seen her reaction. 'Too strong for you?' Annabel raised her eyebrows. She took another sip, schooling her face not to react.

He smiled, declining to rise to the challenge.

'You knew my father.' Annabel continued the conversation from the previous day. 'Not during the war, surely?'

'I was thirteen when the war ended, so, no, not during the war. Some time afterwards, in Germany, he and I were, shall we say, working together.'

Annabel stared. Did he mean that he was involved in spying with Alec against Russia? If so, this was being honest. And could he have been – what was the expression – *turned*?

'Don't worry,' he said. 'We were both on the side of the angels.'

'Your English is good.'

'Of course.' His eyes settled on Ferdy who was trying to talk to Violet and not making much progress by the looks of it. 'As good as Ferdy's Russian.'

'What do you mean?'

'How do you think he and I got to be so … pally?'

Annabel was fed up with all this stepping around the issue. 'Was Ferdy involved in spying against Russia?'

Alexi raised his eyebrows and then smiled. 'Ferdy's a "decent chap", I think you would say. I would be …

distressed … to see him hurt again.' He looked meditatively at Annabel.

He hadn't answered her question.

'If that is directed at me,' said Annabel, 'I have no intention of letting him get "hurt" again.'

Alexi inclined his head. 'I am pleased to hear it. I was puzzled when I saw Ferdy here, knowing his feelings for his father but then his sister's engagement was announced. That would explain his presence here.' Was there the faintest of question marks in his voice?

'Dorothy wanted him here,' she said. 'Sir Terrence said that you were interested in seeing his art collection?'

'In as much as I need a reason to accept an invitation from Sir Terrence Baxter, yes. His collection is … interesting.'

Strange choice of words. 'Why interesting?'

'Don't you think it so?'

'Yes, a bit,' she agreed. 'It doesn't seem to have any particular … genre or area of interest.'

'Precisely. Except that all are valuable.'

Annabel was silent.

'I believe that Alec had an impressive art collection,' Alexi continued. 'I presume you still have it?'

'Pending estate duty, yes.'

Alexi nodded his head. 'Ah, yes – the tax man.'

Thomas came and spoke in Sarah's ear and she rose, 'I think dinner is ready.'

Annabel sat in the same place as before with Alexi to her left and Humphrey to her right. She settled her napkin high across her lap. There would be no more accidents at this meal!

'Did you manage to sort your car out?' Annabel asked Alexi. 'What was wrong with it?'

Alexi didn't reply immediately. 'Yes, I did,' he said.

'Sounded fine to me when you arrived,' said Gerald from the other side of the table.

Alexi looked from Gerald to Annabel and dabbed his mouth with his napkin. 'Well, you were right,' he smiled suddenly. 'There was nothing wrong with it, as it happened.'

Some time through the main course Sarah started to recount the wasp incident and the talk became general.

'Are you allergic to the sting?' Annabel asked Humphrey quietly. There had to be some explanation for his reaction and he had been very quiet all evening.

He looked at her, appreciating her concern.

'No, thankfully not. Just an incident in my youth.'

'I understand,' she said. 'I'm terrified of spiders. It's silly because they are so small. It's just the way they move.'

At the end of the meal, everyone moved through to the sitting room together. No business to discuss tonight, Annabel surmised. Thomas helped Alice serve drinks and coffee.

The talk had moved to crime and in particular the increase in street crime.

'There just aren't the bobbies on the beat any more,' Gerald complained.

'It's nothing new,' said Sir Terrence. 'There was a boy beaten up when we were at college, wasn't there, Humph?'

'I've never seen a crime actually committed.' Violet sounded regretful.

'You wouldn't have wanted to see that,' said Sir Terrence. 'He died, I believe.'

'Yes,' said Humphrey. 'He died.'

'Life can be full of surprises,' said Alexi. 'One minute you're swimming along in the sunshine and the next … poof! … it's all over.'

Thomas had been topping up Humphrey's coffee cup. Whether Humphrey moved, or Thomas' hand slipped wasn't clear but liquid was spilt in the saucer. With apologies Thomas took the cup away and brought another one.

'That's a silly thing to say,' said Lucy.

'But true,' said Alexi.

'I don't know why people need to hurt one another,' said Sarah. 'Life is difficult enough as it is.'

Sir Terrence lifted his glass to Sarah in a silent toast.

Violet opened her eyes wide and gave her surroundings an overt look. It was clear that in her view Sarah should not find life 'difficult'.

Annabel wondered if all weekend parties were like this.

Sarah and Sir Terrence both retired early to bed and although they urged everyone to remain up as long as they wanted there was a general feeling that people would be glad to have an early night.

Ferdy drew Annabel into the library and checked that they were alone in the room.

'Everyone seems so jittery,' said Annabel. 'Even Thomas.'

'Yes. I think that if anything is going to happen it will be tonight.'

'Do you think we should both stay up all night, together?'

Ferdy considered this. 'No. Don't forget that all we are doing is observing. There should be no danger. I'll take the first watch.'

'I don't mind taking the first watch,' she said.

Ferdy looked at her undecided. 'All right. But don't do anything stupid. We're just here to watch.'

'Of course I won't do anything stupid! But, what if the spy runs off with the negatives?'

'Escaping would be a bit of a give away. They are believed to have been operating for some time now and will want to continue.'

Annabel wasn't at all sure. It seemed very risky. What if the spy had decided to stop spying and planned an escape to Russia, or wherever? What if this was going to be their last job, a final secret that they could take with them. But presumably Rosemary and Sir Richard knew what they were doing.

Ferdy said he would relieve her at half past two and went off to bed.

They had collected water and biscuits from the kitchen. Annabel wasn't hungry now, but she would probably be glad of them in the early hours of the morning. She locked the door behind Ferdy and settled down for what would be a long Saturday night. The library was once more lit by the moon shining through the windows. It cast an eerie pale grey light washing out the rich tones of the books and furnishings. Annabel shivered. Ferdy had also provided a blanket. She wrapped it round her shoulders. Some half an hour later, she removed it – the warmth was making her head nod. Better to be uncomfortable and awake.

Annabel started to review what they had learnt so far. It didn't amount to much. Instead of getting answers they seemed to have found more questions. Instead of eliminating suspects they seemed to have discovered more. What if they didn't catch the spy? There was also the possibility that no one was a spy and they were wasting their time, although this seemed unlikely given that Rosemary, and presumably Sir Richard, had gone to a lot of trouble to set the weekend up.

She turned her mind to their two chief suspects Gerald and Alexi. On the face of it, she really couldn't see Gerald as a spy. But then, why had Lucy particularly wanted to come this weekend? It was obvious that she wasn't enjoying herself. Was it because she was helping her father steal the documents? Dorothy had said she was very loyal. Was she loyal to another country? What would motivate either of them to spy against their own country?

She turned her thoughts to Alexi. It seemed he had Ferdy's best interests at heart, which was good. But that didn't mean he couldn't be the spy. He had as good as said that he was a spy and of course, he was Russian albeit a white Russian. He must surely be at the top of the list of suspects. It occurred to her suddenly why she had thought the gloomy portrait in Sir Terrence's art collection was Russian: the man in the picture looked very like Alexi.

Annabel grappled with these puzzles, turning the details over and over in her mind.

Time passed.

She heard the door open. Ferdy was early! She looked at her watch. It wasn't yet a quarter to two.

'Ferdy?' she said.

There was a waft of something sweet-smelling – it smelt like cleaning fluid – and a cloth was clamped over her face. Annabel struggled but was quickly overcome. As she sank into unconsciousness, she knew that they had failed.

CHAPTER THIRTEEN

'Annabel! Annabel!'

Ferdy's voice, urgent, alarmed, slowly filtered through the mists clouding Annabel's brain. She struggled to open her eyes. They must have flickered because Ferdy's arms tightened around her.

'Oh, thank God!' he cried. 'I thought you'd …', his voice broke.

Annabel was trying to remember what had happened. She appeared to be lying down and Ferdy was holding her. It felt good. But as the mists began to clear, she felt less good. Her head was hammering and she felt nauseous. She lifted a trembling hand to her head. Ferdy took it in a warm, firm grasp.

'Don't try to move,' he said.

That sounded like good advice.

'Where are we?' she asked.

She could tell from the brief pause and from his stillness that he was getting worried again. 'In the observation room,' he said.

Suddenly memory returned. Annabel jerked in Ferdy's arms. 'The documents!' And with memory came an onrush of despair. 'Oh, Ferdy! The documents!'

'Steady,' he said. 'There's no one there now.' He was

speaking slowly. She realised he was trying to calm her down. 'Can you remember what happened?'

Annabel tried to think. 'I heard someone come in. I thought it was you but you were early.'

'What time was it, do you remember?'

'I think … just before two.'

'I came down at half past two. They will have had half an hour at least.'

Annabel nodded, then wished she hadn't. A stab of pain ran through her head. 'Then there was a cloth over my face and I blacked out. It smelt sweet.'

'Chloroform,' said Ferdy. His face hanging over hers looked grave.

That didn't sound so bad. 'I'll be all right won't I? In a minute?'

'Of course,' he said.

'Go and check on the documents,' she urged. 'Don't worry about me.'

'Do you think you can move? I don't want to leave you alone.'

'If you help me.'

Gently, he supported her into a sitting position. Her nausea returned, her head throbbed.

'Here. Drink this,' he said, handing her the glass of water.

Annabel drank. The water was welcome.

'Ready?' He helped her up to a standing position. Then, half supporting her and half carrying, they made it round to the library where Ferdy lowered her gently into an armchair.

'Now, let's have a look at this.' He pulled on a pair of light gloves and, moving over to the middle picture, he drew it away from the wall. The safe was closed. Ferdy looked searchingly all round the edges. He appeared to be looking for something. He opened the safe. The documents were there.

'Thank God!' she said.

'Premature, I'm afraid,' said Ferdy. 'I left "tell tales" both on the door to the safe and on the documents. The documents have been moved. And look,' he moved over to the desk, 'the lamp has been moved. I left it square on to the corner of the desk. Someone took the documents out, placed them on the desk and moved the lamp so that they could study them. I would guess that they photographed them, then put them back.' He placed the documents in a plastic bag and slipped them into his inside jacket pocket. Annabel recognised it as an evidence bag from their kit.

'What do you mean "tell tales"?'

Ferdy glanced at her. 'Hairs stuck across the safe door and across the documents. If they're dislodged, as these now are, it shows someone has been here.'

Annabel slumped down in her chair. 'Ferdy, I am so sorry.'

'No. I'm sorry. You were right. We should have stayed together tonight. The question is what should we do now?'

Annabel raised her head. If only it would stop throbbing. She forced herself to think. 'We should be looking for someone with a camera,' she said.

'We have the advantage over them in that respect. They don't know that we know they managed to open the safe.'

'But they know that we were trying to catch them in the act. They were way ahead of us there. They knew of the observation room. They probably knew it was just me in there,' said Annabel bitterly. 'But who has chloroform lying around?'

'A spy?'

'Wouldn't we have seen it when we checked the rooms yesterday?'

'Not necessarily. And it may be one of the staff.'

Annabel felt another wave of nausea. 'Should we wake up Sir Terrence?'

'There's something I think we should do first. I think it unlikely that they will have left – that would be giving the game away – but we should check if everyone is still here and in their rooms. If you feel up to it?'

'Of course.' Annabel grasped the arms of her chair and stood up. 'Why did you take the documents? Isn't that a bit like closing the door after the horse has bolted?'

'We can't risk there being a second spy.'

Two spies?

'Let's start with Alexi,' said Ferdy heading for the door. His face was grim.

They climbed the stairs and turning to the right, made their way to Alexi's door. The door was unlocked and opened silently. There were advantages to new buildings, floors were less likely to creak, doors were smoother on their hinges. Alexi was there. His slim form barely registered under the blankets and he slept like a cat with the faintest purr of a breath.

To Annabel's considerable surprise, Ferdy opened Dorothy's door. Surely that was unnecessary? He looked inside, came out and closed the door, then saw Annabel's face.

'I like a complete picture,' he said.

He didn't bother with Matt's room.

'What about Matt then?' Annabel asked with more than a tinge of sarcasm colouring her voice.

He looked at her and grinned. 'No need. He's in there.' He jerked his thumb towards Dorothy's room.

They returned to the east wing and went to the Harcourt's room. This door was locked. Ferdy opened it with the master key. There was a considerable amount of noise coming from Gerald. Violet was wearing ear plugs and an eye mask.

Next they entered Lucy's room which was unlocked. Lucy was asleep on her side, her breathing barely discernible. She appeared sound asleep.

'I feel … dirty,' said Annabel as they returned to the corridor.

Ferdy didn't misunderstand. 'It's not the sort of thing you can expect to *enjoy* exactly. It's just part of the job.'

Humphrey had burrowed into his pillows and was snoring audibly, though not as loudly as Gerald Harcourt. His stick was propped up against his bedside table. His door had been unlocked.

'Now for the staff.' They used the master key to go through the door to the staff quarters. Here the doors were closer to one another but in all other respects the corridor looked the same. They started on the left and moved down the corridor.

The first bedroom was occupied by Mrs Fry. She wore a frilly nightgown and snored gently. Annabel opened the next door as silently as possible and entered the room. The room was lit by the moonlight shafting through the partially closed curtains and Annabel was startled to see a pair of eyes staring at her. Alice had the bedclothes drawn up to her ears and was evidently terrified.

'Oh, it's you,' she said. 'What do you want?'

Annabel improvised rapidly. 'Oh, sorry. I was looking for Mrs Fry.'

'She's next door,' said Alice. 'You should knock!' Terror had given way to anger.

'Yes, sorry. Thank you, so sorry.'

Annabel withdrew and closed the door. They moved away from her door.

'She was awake!' Annabel whispered.

'Yes,' Ferdy whispered back. 'Could you see if she was dressed?'

'She had the bedclothes drawn up to her chin. She was terrified.'

'Well, you had just entered her room in the middle of the night. Either you woke her up or she was already awake. She could just have got back to her bedroom after photographing the documents.'

Annabel considered this. 'I don't think she was the one who chloroformed me. It felt like a man. Do you think we should go back in? Question her?'

Ferdy considered this. 'Let's carry on with the search. Get the whole picture first.'

Thomas' room was empty.

They went in and had a look around. His belongings, such as they were, appeared to be still there. Pyjamas under his pillow, toothbrush in the bathroom. Apart from a copy of Nevill Shute's *A Town Like Alice* on the bedside table, he didn't appear to have any personal items other than the basics.

'Well, well,' said Ferdy.

It was one thing setting a trap to find a spy. It was another matter entirely to put a face to their mystery person. And, in spite of his un-butler-like wrists and the fact that she'd seen him coming out of Lucy's room in a furtive manner, Thomas hadn't been top of Annabel's suspect list as a spy. A thief, maybe.

'I suppose he might just have been unable to sleep?' she said. 'Gone for a breath of fresh air?'

'Huh,' said Ferdy.

'Shall we look for the ring?' Annabel said.

'If he's gone, he'll have taken it with him,' said Ferdy. But they had a quick look. The ring wasn't there.

They tried John's door next. Ferdy indicated to Annabel to stand back before opening the door with extreme care. He need not have bothered. The room, like Thomas', was empty. It was surprisingly comfortable with afghan rugs, an embroidered coverlet that had some sort of African zig-zag pattern in tones of brown and grey, a small bookshelf containing a selection of what looked like wartime novels and cookbooks including Elizabeth David's *French Provincial Cooking*. Dorothy had raved about it so it must be good. A beaten metal saucer provided an ash tray on the bedside table but the tray was empty and the window open. The air in the room smelt fresh.

They exchanged raised eyebrows and looked for the ring with no success.

Three further staff bedrooms were in use but empty. Presumably for those staff who weren't there that weekend.

'Let's try downstairs,' said Ferdy.

Narrow, steeper stairs at the end of the corridor led down to the kitchen quarters and, as they descended, soft but unmistakable, they heard the sound of music. They looked at one another in surprise.

Ferdy mouthed in disbelieving recognition, 'The Yard Birds?'

The record stopped. There was a clicking sound as of a 45 falling into place, a hiss as the needle hit the track and then – Annabel recognised this one – it was Buddy Holly's 'That'll be The Day'. She loved this song. She almost started to hum along.

They entered the kitchen. The light was on. Standing by the central table, kneading a large ball of bread dough, was John. He turned his head, gave them a hard stare from under his brows, then looked back at the dough and gave it a jostle and a slap. It settled like an overweight walrus on the marble slab.

'Strange time to be up and about,' he said laconically.

He was wearing a stars and stripes bandana today. It suited him. Annabel wondered if he was American. He had a slight accent but Annabel would have placed it as antipodean rather than American. It was a fair comment. He had a reason to be up at this time of the morning. They did not.

'Have you seen Thomas this morning?' Ferdy asked.

John looked at them under his brows. 'Came down the back stairs did you? Now, how did you manage that?'

'We have a key,' said Ferdy. 'We're looking for Thomas.'

'You have a key.' John scooped the dough onto a plate, walked across to the second door on the left, opened it and popped the plate onto the shelf in what looked like a larder. 'Well,' he drawled as he walked back, 'that explains a lot. And no,' he added as Ferdy opened his mouth, 'I haven't seen Thomas. Not since yesterday evening. You'll have checked his room?' He said this with an edge to his voice and Annabel could tell that he realised they had probably also been in his room.

'His pyjamas are still there,' said Ferdy. 'Does he have a car?'

'Motorbike,' said John. 'This wouldn't have anything to do with yesterday's incident would it?'

'Possibly,' said Ferdy.

'Don't like things that upset Lady Sarah,' he said. 'I'll show you where he keeps his bike.'

He strapped a purposeful looking knife onto his belt and led the way along the passage to the door at the end and out into the back yard. Ferdy raised an eyebrow at Annabel. They followed on behind. The coolness of the outside air was a shock.

'Don't suppose you want to tell me what's going on?' John said as he led them to a row of garages and covered outdoor storage areas.

Annabel left it for Ferdy to answer.

'There's a possibility that Thomas might have run off with something of value.'

John cocked his head. He looked sceptical. 'Wouldn't have figured him for that. Ex-marines, I'd guess.'

'Yes,' said Ferdy.

Ex-marines? So Ferdy was right. How did they know these things?

'Well,' John said, 'his bike's still here.' They all looked at the bike. It was huge and had two large panniers either side of the seat.

Ferdy had a quick look inside the panniers. They were empty. 'Can we find out if anyone has left through the front gate tonight?' he asked.

'Yep.' John led the way back to the kitchen and consulted a control panel. 'No one's been in or out all night. Of course there's the wall. It's high with security wire, but not impossible. And he may have a chum.'

'Yes,' said Ferdy.

A thought occurred to Annabel. 'Were you here in the kitchen yesterday at this time?'

'Always.' He looked at her curiously. 'Why?'

'I just wondered. Did anyone come into the kitchen?'

'No. Why?' He waited but when Annabel said no more he looked sardonic. 'OK, I've got things to do. Let me know if you need any *more* help.' It seemed he recognised that information was going to be a one way street.

They retraced their steps back to the hall and started to climb the stairs.

'What was all that about?' asked Ferdy.

'Lucy said she went to the kitchen to get milk but she can't have done or John would have seen her.'

'Hmph,' said Ferdy. 'The case against that girl is building. You find allies in the strangest of places.'

'John? But, how do you know he's an ally?'

'Don't you think he is?'

Well, yes, Annabel did think they could probably trust the knife-wielding, bandana-wearing chef but she couldn't have said why exactly.

'The guy's got seriously good taste in music,' said Ferdy.

'That's why you think he's OK?'

Ferdy grinned.

'Do you really think it could be Thomas?' Annabel asked.

'I think he's got the skills to do it. I think he could

have done it. My gut feeling is he didn't do it, but then …
where is he?'

All good points.

'Now, we wake up Dad.'

CHAPTER FOURTEEN

Ferdy knocked gently on his father's door and then opened it a crack. A soft faint light showed: Sir Terrence was awake. Annabel followed Ferdy into the room and they stood rather awkwardly at the entrance.

Sir Terrence was in bed and on the telephone. He motioned to them to come further in. The room was simply furnished with a walnut bed and dressing table. Almost monastic, the colour scheme was in tones of slate grey and teal blue. The only picture on the wall was an oil painting of Sarah, fresh and modern; she wore a pale blue summer dress and looked very young.

'Hmph …' He continued his telephone conversation. 'What's your view?'

Sir Terrence listened. The other person talked at length.

'Leave them to stew for a bit,' he said.

More talk, barely audible.

'Maybe, but I don't think so.'

More rumbles.

'Call me tomorrow. If we lose it, we lose it. I'm not paying that price.'

He put the telephone down and turned to face them. A small action but Annabel had the impression that he had shut the subject of his telephone conversation out of his mind and that his full attention was now directed upon themselves.

'Developments?' he said.

'Yes,' said Ferdy.

'Pull up a chair,' said Sir Terrence.

There was only one chair. Ferdy pulled it up for Annabel and stood beside her.

'Annabel was chloroformed. The documents were accessed, most likely photographed, and then replaced. Everyone is accounted for with the exception of Thomas who is missing but his belongings are still in his room and his motorbike is in the car park.'

Sir Terrence didn't waste time on unnecessary exclamations.

'Are you all right?' he asked Annabel.

'Yes. I …'

Sir Terrence silenced her with a raised hand. 'Thomas, eh?'

'What's his background?' Ferdy asked.

'He was recommended to me by Sir Richard. I took his word for it that he'd be useful.'

So Sarah was wrong in thinking it was Rosemary who had recommended him. It seemed strange that Sarah, who was in charge of running the household, should have got this wrong.

'Your chef thinks he's ex-marines.'

'That's quite likely then. John should know. I think this is where I start to rattle a few cages.' He picked up the telephone again and dialled a number. The call was answered quickly which was surprising considering it was still the middle of the night.

'Is Sir Richard available?' He raised his eyes to the ceiling. 'Yes, it's important.'

They waited. Annabel admired Sir Terrence's pyjamas which were of dark blue silk with pale blue piping. Monastic simplicity apparently stopped short of his night clothes. Sir Richard, presumably, came to the phone and Ferdy and Annabel listened.

'Yes, it's Terrence.'

'Three twenty.' This was said with no inflection and Annabel could only assume was in response to a demand if he knew what time it was.

'We've had a bite. Yes. Looks like the documents have been photographed. Our man Thomas is missing.'

'Yes. Thomas.'

'Less than an hour ago.' Sir Terrence raised his eyebrows at Ferdy as he said this and Ferdy nodded.

Sir Richard then talked for some time whilst Sir Terrence listened, his face darkening.

'This is not impressive,' he said at the end.

More talk.

'All right, keep me informed.' He replaced the receiver, looked at it for a few moments, then turned to Ferdy and Annabel.

'Thomas is Special Branch,' he said.

'Special Branch!' said Ferdy. 'And you weren't told?'

'No.' Sir Terrence sounded less than happy.

'Unlikely that he'd be our spy. If he'd been MI6 it might have been a different matter,' said Ferdy.

Sir Terrence smiled wryly. 'There'll be a full alert put out on all sea and airports.'

'But all he has to do is put the negatives in the post,' said Annabel.

'Yes. The information in the documents is gone. But we may still catch Thomas,' said Sir Terrence.

'If we're lucky,' said Ferdy. 'We probably ought to keep people out of the library for the time being. What about the maid, Alice?'

Of course! Alice would be going in there at about five thirty as usual to clean. In her befuddled state, Annabel had forgotten that.

Sir Terrence pulled open the top drawer of his bedside table and extracted two 'Do Not Disturb' signs. 'Lock the doors and put these on the handles. That should do it.'

Back in the corridor, Annabel was aware of Ferdy looking at her with concern. Her head still thumped and she felt unsteady on her feet.

'You go off to bed,' he said.

'But there are still things to do.'

'Nothing I can't handle on my own. And I want to see if there are any fingerprints in the library. He probably wore gloves but it would be stupid not to try.'

At the top of the stairs, he turned and put his arms round her, holding her close. She could feel tears pricking her eyes.

'You're doing really well,' he said. 'Now, go and get some sleep.'

Annabel didn't expect to sleep – she was afraid that her brain was too fired up to allow her to settle – but sleep she did, as soon as her head hit the pillow. She awoke to the alarm at half past six and lay for some moments assessing how she felt. Her headache had stopped – a blessed relief that took some time to register – so had her feelings of nausea. It was Sunday morning and normally she would be enjoying a lie-in but that was the last thing on her mind today; there was far too much going on.

Washing and dressing herself quickly, she went and tapped on Ferdy's door. He opened it almost immediately, not yet fully dressed, in socks, trousers and an open necked shirt. He looked tired.

'I don't know about you,' he said, 'but the world will look a whole lot better once I've had coffee and something to eat.'

Annabel smiled. 'Breakfast!'

He slipped on some loafers, grabbed a light-weight navy jersey and joined her in the corridor.

'Will it be ready yet?' said Annabel. 'We're very early.'

'We can always raid the kitchen.'

That proved to be necessary. There was nobody else up and although the dining room had been set up for breakfast there was no food laid out.

They found John, propped up against the open

kitchen door, cigarette in hand, blowing smoke out into the fresh morning air.

He looked them over. 'Up with the larks.'

'Any chance of some coffee?' Ferdy asked.

'Help yourselves.' He waved to a coffee pot on the range. 'Thomas hasn't turned up. I looked.'

'That was going to be my next question.'

John stubbed out his cigarette in a nearby pail filled with sand. 'Eggs?'

'Lovely,' said Ferdy.

'Me too,' said Annabel, 'and do you have any cereal?'

Annabel ended up eating cereal followed by two fried eggs on toast with mushrooms and grilled tomatoes and finishing off with two more slices of toast with marmalade. After which, she began to feel almost human. Being rendered unconscious, it seemed, gave one an appetite. Ferdy didn't disgrace himself either.

John raised his eyebrows but didn't comment. He had the body of a whippet. It must be strange to spend your life preparing food for other people and not eating much yourself. But perhaps that was why.

Ferdy followed John's example and smoked a cigarette at the open door.

Their meal over, Annabel and Ferdy stepped outside and started walking around the house. The early morning sun lit up the dark greens of the foliage and sent long shadows across the clipped lawns that still held the soft sheen of morning dew. It looked peaceful. Curtains were still drawn across many windows. There was the pleasant sensation of being a step ahead of the rest of the world, up and about whilst others slept.

'Did you manage to get any finger prints?'

'Lots. No idea if any of them will be useful.'

Something had been bothering Annabel, something that, in her anaesthetised state, hadn't occurred to her earlier.

'Why didn't you tell me about the "tell tales"?'

He looked at her blankly. 'Sorry, I didn't think. Alec would have known.'

Alec would have known. The morning light suddenly seemed grey.

He continued to stare at her. 'Annabel, I'm really sorry. You're quite right to be angry. Of course, why should you know?'

'Is that why you stopped me from looking through Alexi's suitcase? You were afraid he might have left "tell-tales"?'

'Well, I thought he might have arranged his things … in a particular way.' He reached for his cigarettes and lit one up. 'You know, in a way, it shows what I've been saying, that working with you is like working with Alec.'

'Oh, *really*?' said Annabel.

'Yes, really. And I am sorry, it won't happen again.' He sounded now like a naughty schoolboy. Annabel looked at him suspiciously and saw that he was grinning.

Her mother used to say, 'Take a deep breath and move on.' Annabel looked up at the clear blue morning

sky, took a deep breath and moved on. There was another thing puzzling her. 'How did the spy get into the
observation room?' she said. 'Aren't there just the three
keys? You have one, I have one and your father the third.'

'Good point,' said Ferdy. 'They could have obtained
a copy.'

'How could they have done that?'

'Or they could have picked the lock,' suggested Ferdy.

'But, wouldn't I have heard them doing that?'

'We could do a test. You sit in there and I'll have a go
at opening the door from the outside.'

Annabel didn't fancy going back into the room but
it was a good plan. She knew Ferdy was good at picking
locks.

They had reached the terrace. The shrubs and grasses
in the bed below the terrace wall created a rounded,
hummocky architectural effect, like so many moss covered rocks, all the more dramatic with the shadows cast
by the morning sun.

'I wonder where Thomas is now?' she said. Aware of
the open bedroom windows above them, she kept her
voice lowered.

'Long gone,' said Ferdy bitterly. He had also lowered
his voice. 'They'll have ways to get him out of the country
that don't involve ports or airports.'

'So it's a waste of time covering them?'

'Probably, but necessary.'

'The whole thing feels wrong,' Annabel said. 'Why
would Thomas take the photographs and then leave?

Why would he leave his motorbike behind and all his things in his room? And why was Alice terrified when I went into her room last night?'

There was something white on one of the larger shrubs. As they drew nearer, she saw that it was one of Ferdy's paper aeroplanes; the one that flew off mark. She remembered that it had the word 'Help!' written on it. They probably ought to remove it. She leant across the terrace wall but the aeroplane was further out than she'd thought. She stretched, almost losing her balance, and managed to grab the paper plane, but in doing so, fell into the top of the shrub. Ferdy steadied her, grabbing at her waist. He was laughing but she wasn't paying any attention for below on the dark, leaf-strewn soil something glinted. It was a diver's watch – and it was still on a wrist.

'Ferdy,' she said, 'I don't think Thomas has gone anywhere. I think he's here.'

CHAPTER FIFTEEN

Ferdy was still laughing and it took a moment for her words to sink in.

'What do you mean "here"?'

'Here. Down there, beneath the shrubs.'

Ferdy pulled her back without ceremony and himself leant over the wall. He pushed aside the shrubs and took a long look.

'Oh, Christ!' he said.

'Is he dead?'

'From the looks of that knife in his chest, I'd say yes.'

'Dead …' Annabel gripped the terrace wall. He had been so alive. 'Don't you think we should check?'

Ferdy was already on his way to the nearest steps down to the lawn.

'Won't you disturb any footprints if you look?' Annabel asked once he was opposite her on the lawn below.

'I expect he was pushed over the wall but, yes, I'll be careful.' He looked thoroughly at the ground. 'No one's come across from this direction.' He edged his way into the shrubs and past a huge pampas grass. Squatting down by Thomas, he put his fingers on the man's neck. He looked at, but didn't touch the knife. Then he extracted himself backwards from the shrubs and stood upright on the lawn. 'Yes,' he said, 'he's dead. Has been, I'd say, for some hours.'

'Dead … Thomas … the poor man!' Somehow their suspicions of espionage seemed the final insult. 'We were wrong about him.'

'Looks like it.' Ferdy marked the spot with three small stones on the edge of the lawn and rejoined Annabel. 'Are you OK to stay here whilst I go and get Dad?'

'Yes, of course.'

'Don't let anyone near.'

'Go,' she said.

Annabel was left alone on the terrace. Birds were singing as they flew back and forth finding their breakfast, a bee buzzed by intent on its goal of pollen. Life continued, but for Thomas, life had ended long before it should, with a knife in the chest. She recalled the innocent pleasure he had shown in cleaning the silver teapot and the mirror like finish that he was so proud to have achieved. She wondered if he had a family, wife, children, sisters or brothers? Were his parents still alive? How many people would wake to this terrible news and grieve?

It didn't feel right to consider the implications of this discovery yet, so she deliberately shut them from her mind. Just for a few moments she would honour the passing of a young man.

It was longer than she had expected before Ferdy and

Sir Terrence reappeared. One or two curtains had been drawn back but nobody else had appeared. Annabel tried to imagine the consternation that the news would generate amongst the other guests, family members and staff. Of course, to *one* person, the news would not come as a surprise.

'Dad has spoken to Sir Richard,' said Ferdy. 'The police will be here as soon as they can.'

'If they're not here within the hour, there will be hell to pay,' said Sir Terrence. 'Is that where he is?' He leant over the wall and peered into the bushes. 'That's my paper knife!' he exclaimed.

'Your paper knife? Where do you keep it normally?' Ferdy asked.

'On the desk in the library.'

'Must be sharp,' said Ferdy.

'Of course it's sharp! No use otherwise. Actually, it's a stiletto – a memento of an Italian deal that went south.'

Annabel would love to have asked for more details but now was not the time.

'My guess,' said Ferdy, 'would be that Thomas surprised "our spy" as they were photographing the documents, got stabbed for his pains, dragged out onto the terrace and dropped over the wall.'

'Wouldn't he have bled?' asked Annabel.

'Not necessarily, if the knife remained in place, which it looks as though it did.'

'Thomas was a large man, difficult to shift,' said Sir Terrence.

'Yes,' said Ferdy. 'We're looking for someone strong, or possibly two people working together.'

'And that person is still in the house, and presumably they still have the negatives. But, *who are they?*' said Annabel.

They both looked at her.

'That,' said Ferdy, 'is the sixty-four thousand dollar question.'

Within the hour Mrs Fry announced that the police had arrived.

'Hmph,' said Sir Terrence.

Annabel was relieved that the police hadn't already blotted their copybook by arriving late. She imagined that Sir Terrence could be difficult enough without being needlessly antagonised. She and Ferdy moved through to the hall and watched through the window as two unmarked black Cortinas drew up in front of the door. She recognised the two men who got out of the nearest car as she opened the front door.

'Detective Inspector Grange!' she exclaimed with a smile. It was not clear whether her delight was reciprocated but he responded politely.

'Miss Staple and Mr Baxter. I was told you'd be here. It's Detective Chief Inspector now,' he added. 'And you know Detective Sergeant Idle.'

Promoted. Annabel was pleased for them both – they deserved it. She wondered quite how extensive their briefing had been in so short a time.

'Sir Terrence is inside,' she said.

DCI Grange took a moment to look over the front of the house then followed them inside.

Ferdy led the way into the sitting room. Sir Terrence was standing over by the window and stepped forward to meet them. Annabel was surprised at his manner. She had found him formidable and somewhat distant from the outset but she saw now that the persona he presented to his family and friends was subtly different to that which he presented to officialdom. Here, despite his recent bang on the head, was a definite message of power and control.

DCI Grange appeared equally in control. They were evenly matched.

'How much do you know?' asked Sir Terrence after the introductions were completed.

'Sir Richard has briefed me. I understand that this whole weekend has been set up to catch someone assumed to be spying for the Russians and I know the names of the two suspects. I understand that blueprint documents are the ... er ... bait and that you are hoping to catch the spy in action. I do not suppose that the plan allowed for murder?' His voice was flat and unemotional with just the faintest hint to suggest that he found the whole enterprise far-fetched.

Sir Terrence caught the undertone. He stiffened. 'You are not wrong. The murder was unforeseen. How do you wish to proceed?'

'The body first and then I'd like to hear your side of things.'

'We've closed off the library, which is where we think it all happened, said Ferdy.

'I'd like that to continue, at least until we've had a chance to look around. After that, we'll want to talk to everyone and whilst that is going on it would be best if they were all gathered together.'

'In here?' said Sir Terrence.

'That would be ideal. And if we could have a room for our interviews?'

'I'll see that the morning room is made available. What about the staff?'

'We'll speak to them first and then they can get on.'

'If you are going to be looking in the library, we need to check something first,' said Ferdy.

Sir Terrence and Grange looked at him.

'The observation room,' he said.

'Ah yes,' said Sir Terrence.

'And what is "the observation room"?' asked Grange. The briefing hadn't extended to that.

Ferdy led the way. Idle put on gloves to open the door and they watched as he and Grange looked around. As with previous experience of watching them at work, Annabel didn't think they missed much.

'They know the room exists,' said Annabel. 'I was in here when I was chloroformed.'

'There's a lock,' said Idle looking at the door.

'I had three keys cut,' said Sir Terrence. 'I gave one each to Ferdy and Annabel and I retained one.'

'And you all still have your keys?' asked Grange.

They nodded.

'We were going to check if the lock could have been picked without my hearing it,' said Annabel, 'but then we found Thomas and other things took over.'

'Lock picking,' said Grange. He turned to Ferdy. 'That would be one of your skills, no doubt?' His tone did not indicate that congratulations were in order. Annabel wished she'd kept quiet.

Ferdy was silent.

'Let's try it now,' said Grange.

'Now?' said Ferdy.

'Yes, now. We'll stay in here.'

Ferdy left the room and at a sign from Grange, Annabel locked the door then sat in the seat. There was complete silence in the room, then, her ears straining, Annabel heard the faintest of scratching sounds and the door opened.

'Not too dusty,' said Idle under his breath.

Sir Terrence was looking at his son, his eyebrows raised. Annabel couldn't tell if he was unsettled or pleasantly surprised.

'Well, Miss Staple?' Grange said.

'I don't think I'd have heard that. Or, I would have thought, as I did, that it was Ferdy using his key.'

'I'll get John to secure the door,' said Sir Terrence.

Grange didn't ask who John was. 'Now if we could see the body.'

Sir Terrence excused himself and went off to talk to Sarah. Ferdy and Annabel led the way out onto the terrace.

Outside, the sun was already climbing the sky, the shadows on the lawn not as long as before and further delineated by the receding dew. The bed of shrubs and grasses was losing its magic. Grange and Idle peered over the wall. They took their time.

'What made you look over the wall just here?' said Grange straightening up. 'The body is not visible from the terrace.'

Good question. *I was trying to get back a failed SOS paper aeroplane.*

'We were playing paper aeroplanes with Jonny on Friday,' Ferdy improvised. 'One flew off course and we were just trying to get it back.'

'Jonny being?'

'My half brother.'

'He's two,' Annabel explained. 'Anyhow, I overbalanced and fell into the shrub and saw ...'

Grange looked at them. Annabel felt like a fly under a microscope. 'This is becoming quite a habit for you, finding dead bodies,' he said. His tone was non-committal but Annabel read disapproval. She was horribly conscious that, for the second time that year, she had been the one to find a dead body.

'I don't go looking for them! We thought he'd be long gone.'

'Have you been anywhere near the body?'

'I did get to him from the lawn,' Ferdy said. 'Felt his neck for a pulse but it was obvious he'd been dead for a while. I didn't touch anything else. And there was no evidence of anyone else walking in from the lawn.'

'We wanted to be sure he wasn't still alive,' said Annabel.

Grange spoke to Idle. 'Get a man here to guard the body and let me know when the doctor arrives.' He looked up at the house where more curtains were starting to stir. 'And get him to stand out of sight of the windows. There's no need to advertise our presence. Now the library.'

They went back into the house via the sitting room and entered the library which had an air of calm. It was extraordinary to think that only a few hours ago Thomas had probably been brutally stabbed to death in this room. The calm was then disturbed by the soft sound of a drill – John presumably, securing the door to the observation room. Ferdy went to check and reappeared a few moments later.

'We're secure. The documents were in here,' Ferdy drew back the middle picture.

'Where are they now?'

'In my pocket.' Ferdy drew them out in their sealed plastic bag. 'I left "tell tales" so we know that the safe was opened and that the documents were moved. We know that the light on the desk was moved. We assume that the documents were taken out, photographed and replaced. I took fingerprints of the safe, the documents, the lamp and the table. Also of the handle to the observation room.'

Grange raised his eyebrows and opened his mouth to speak.

'We didn't know then that a death was involved,' Ferdy added.

Grange considered this for a few moments then gave a brief nod. 'I'll take any fingerprints you have.'

Whilst Ferdy handed these over, Annabel looked around the room. It was not a great distance from the desk to the French windows and out onto the terrace. But it would feel further if one were dragging the dead weight of a fully grown man. Now that the sun was shining obliquely through the south facing windows, she could see two parallel tracks drawn into the thick carpet. She indicated these to the men.

'We think Thomas must have chanced upon whoever was photographing the documents and was then stabbed before being dragged out onto the terrace and tipped over the wall,' she said. 'The knife is Sir Terrence's paper knife. He kept it on the desk.'

'Did you walk over this part of the carpet?' asked Grange.

Annabel considered this. She hadn't really been taking in much in her post-chloroformed state.

'No. I walked from the door to the armchair. I was still feeling sick. Then I walked to the desk and then back out. You didn't either, did you Ferdy?'

'Not over to the window, no,' said Ferdy.

'Well, that's something,' Grange muttered.

Ferdy raised his eyebrows but said nothing.

Annabel could see that Grange probably thought they'd messed up his crime scene, but as Ferdy said, they hadn't realised they were dealing with a murder.

'Perhaps you could tell me your side of things now.'

They related what had happened over the weekend up to that point, leaving out the loss of Dorothy's ring.

'So from about one-fifty when you were chloroformed to two-thirty when Mr Baxter found you, the documents were accessed and possibly photographed. Did you notice if the knife was on the desk when you came into the room at two-thirty?'

Annabel closed her eyes. 'I'm afraid I didn't notice.'

Ferdy shook his head. 'No.'

'No it wasn't or no you didn't notice?'

Ferdy looked Grange in the eyes. 'No, I didn't notice. I didn't know, until my father told me, that the knife was usually there.'

'It's a prominent looking knife – hard to miss.'

Ferdy took a steadying breath, 'I haven't been to this house before. I haven't seen my father since he left my mother three years ago. Prior to that, he was not in possession of that knife. You'll have to ask him where it came from.'

'It was on the desk on Friday when we arrived,' Annabel put in.

Grange considered this in silence.

'When did you take the fingerprints?'

'It was between three-thirty and four, after we'd

checked on everyone and found that Thomas was missing.'

'And the chef was up?'

'He was making bread,' said Annabel. 'And Alice was awake but we may have woken her when we checked her room.'

'My father phoned Sir Richard and that's when we discovered that Thomas was from Special Branch.'

'And you thought that he had stolen the documents?'

'Yes we did, although his motor bike was still here and nobody had left by the main gate,' said Annabel.

'But you didn't look for him?' It was a criticism.

Perhaps he might still have been alive if they'd found him then.

'We assumed he'd be long gone,' Ferdy fired back. 'Our remit was to discover the spy, if one existed, not to catch him. The documents had been photographed. Thomas was missing. We passed on the information. To be honest, when we did find out he was Special Branch it didn't exactly make us think of him as a potential victim. In fact, far from it.'

Ferdy was right. It was all very well judging their actions after the event and finding them wanting. At the time, their actions were correct.

'The point is,' she said, 'that unless someone came in from outside – which is unlikely – whoever photographed the documents and killed Thomas is still here and they will have a camera.'

'Find the camera, find the murderer,' Ferdy agreed.

'What are your thoughts on who might be responsible?' asked Grange.

'The only person to have an alibi for the attack on Sir Terrence was Lucy Harcourt. She'd asked Ferdy to help her get down the tennis rackets and was with him at the time,' said Annabel.

'But she did draw me away from the room. We have considered that two people might be working together,' said Ferdy.

'We searched the guests' rooms yesterday but then we weren't looking for a camera,' said Annabel.

'What were you looking for?'

A very reasonable question. But perhaps the police could help search for Dorothy's ring? Hadn't Ferdy said that they needed a body to involve the police?

'My sister's engagement ring has gone missing,' Ferdy had reached the same conclusion.

'And you suspected one of the guests?'

'Or one of the staff,' said Annabel. 'Please don't mention about the ring to Sir Terrence,' she added, 'Dorothy doesn't want him to know.'

Grange raised his eyebrows. 'Does anyone here, other than Sir Terrence and his wife, know of your role in this matter?'

'John knows we are involved in something but he doesn't know what,' said Ferdy. 'Otherwise, no one except the spy.'

'All right, let's leave it that way,' said Grange. 'I'll call you in for questioning the same as everyone else.

In the meantime, if you find out anything new, let me know.'

DS Idle poked his head round the door to announce that the doctor had arrived and Grange asked them to leave.

CHAPTER SIXTEEN

'Let's go back outside,' said Ferdy.

They made their way through the sitting room and out onto the terrace. A policeman was standing up against the wall of the house. He looked at them with suspicion. Ferdy ran down the nearest set of steps onto the grass and Annabel followed.

'A bit rich,' said Ferdy 'criticising us.' He lit up a cigarette, drawing the smoke in sharply.

'You don't think we might have been able to save Thomas if we'd found him earlier?'

'Not a chance, judging by where the knife went in.'

That was a relief. 'At least he seems willing to work with us,' she said.

'On *his* terms.'

'Well, that's fair enough,' Annabel said. 'He is in charge of the investigation.'

Ferdy shrugged his shoulders.

'A camera should be easy enough to find, shouldn't it?' she added, 'They're large enough.'

'Actually, they can be pretty small. Fit in a cigarette case, or a pen or powder compact. Anywhere really.'

'I bet it's in Violet's bag,' said Annabel.

Ferdy grinned. 'You really don't like her do you?'

'Horrible woman. Anyway, you wanted a body and now we have the police who can demand to look wherever they want.'

'I did not "want" a body! But I must say it's convenient.'

'Poor Thomas,' said Annabel.

They had reached the lake and turned back towards the house. The white curving frontage with many of its windows still curtained, now held a sinister air; a shrouded place of secrets where terrible events had occurred.

'Whoever took Dorothy's ring is going to get a shock when they see the police,' she said.

'That's a point. They'll probably think the police are there for them.'

'Perhaps the ring will make a miraculous reappearance?'

'It would be good for something to come out of all this,' agreed Ferdy. 'Well, we'd better get back indoors. People will be coming downstairs soon and we should be there, watching reactions.'

They entered the house and hung around in the hall. Annabel looked into the dining room.

'Breakfast is all laid out,' she said.

At that moment John emerged from the kitchen quarters with the gong which he banged with some force.

'Hungry again?' he said with a wry smile, his tone indicating that it wouldn't surprise him.

'No, but a coffee would go down well,' said Ferdy.

'It's all in there.'

'You know the police are here?' Ferdy asked.

John nodded.

'And you know about Thomas …?'

Of course he did. Annabel wasn't remotely surprised. She didn't entirely trust John. He had been awake and about at the time of the attack. He knew about knives and she was sure he had the skill to stab someone to death. Also, they were still looking for a suspect for the attack on Sir Terrence and that thing he used to bang the gong with would make a good cosh.

It wasn't long before people started to emerge. Alexi came down the stairs first. He looked tired, not his usual bright self. Dorothy and Matt came downstairs together. They too looked like they hadn't had the best night's sleep, but there may be an all too obvious explanation for that. Annabel was interested to note that, even with the ongoing worry of the missing ring, Dorothy still maintained her usual dedication to style. Today she was wearing an apple green dress with a cream bodice. Cream shoes on her feet and an apple green headband tying back her hair, completed the outfit. As Dorothy reached the bottom of the stairs, Annabel saw that the back of the dress was embellished with a fabric bow, also in apple green.

The usual morning greetings were exchanged and everyone professed to have slept, 'really well, thank you'. Annabel wondered why anyone bothered when nobody ever told the truth. One might just as well say: 'Still alive, as you can see.' It would mean about the same and would, at least, not be a lie.

But, of course, Thomas was not 'still alive'. And one of those now coming downstairs for breakfast had plunged a knife into his chest. It was hard not to let suspicion show on her face.

Violet and Gerald Harcourt came next. As they reached the bottom of the stairs one of the uniformed policemen opened the door of the library and looked out into the hall.

Violet slipped on the bottom step and fell headlong onto the marble floor, her handbag falling from her grasp, the contents spilling out over the floor.

'Violet!' cried Gerald, almost falling himself in his rush to help his wife.

'Oh, my goodness!' said Dorothy. 'Are you hurt?'

Something skittered across the smooth floor and ended up next to Annabel's foot. It was small, bright, made of metal. It was not Dorothy's ring, but Annabel saw that it had the initials 'MSL' engraved upon it. This must be Matt's lost bookmark. It didn't look like any bookmark Annabel had ever seen but hadn't he said that it looked like a metal clip? With everybody's attention on Violet, Annabel stooped and picked it up. As she straightened, she looked around. Gerald was watching her and the expression in his eyes was one of entreaty. It was so unexpected an expression that Annabel stared back in astonishment. Gerald then mouthed something that looked like 'please don't'. Annabel hesitated but said nothing and thrust the metal object into her skirt pocket. Gerald's eyes half closed in thanks and he turned his attention, once more, to his wife.

People were pulling the fallen items together and putting them back in the handbag. It was an extensive and various collection of items. As well as the embroidery, Annabel saw pens, a lip salve, a comb, a notepad, a handkerchief and a powder compact, a silver lighter and a packet of a cheap and very strong brand of cigarettes. No ring, but Annabel had hopes of something useful coming from a private chat with Gerald. She was sure he would seek her out very soon.

By now, Violet had recovered enough to realise what had happened and scrabbled for her bag and belongings, clutching them to her saying, 'I can manage! Don't touch anything! I can manage.'

'But, Darling, are you hurt?' Gerald asked.

'I … I'm not sure. I think my knee is hurt.'

The disturbance had attracted Mrs Fry from her quarters. She surveyed the scene calmly. Annabel wondered if anything flustered the woman.

'Perhaps someone could help Mrs Harcourt into the sitting room,' she suggested.

'An excellent idea,' said Gerald. 'Matt, will you help?'

'I don't want to go into the sitting room,' said Violet. 'I want coffee and something to eat.'

'The dining room then,' said Gerald equably.

As they bent to help Violet up, Dorothy said, 'But, what on earth are the police doing here?'

Everyone went silent. It was the question that they all wanted answered but nobody had liked to mention whilst Violet was the focus of attention.

Humphrey came down the stairs with Sarah who looked down on the scene with horror.

'Oh! What's happened?'

'Violet fell,' Ferdy explained.

'Not down these stairs?' cried Sarah.

'Just the last step but she's hurt her knee, she thinks.'

'She must sit down immediately.' Sarah said. 'Should we call a doctor?'

'I just want *coffee*,' said Violet with brittle emphasis.

'Of course you shall have some coffee,' Sarah said as she shepherded Gerald, Matt and Violet into the dining room. Violet seated herself at the dining table.

Everyone else followed. Sir Terrence appeared from the direction of the morning room and joined them. He closed the door behind him.

'I'm afraid,' he said, 'I have some bad news.'

He had definitely got their attention. Looking around the faces, Annabel wasn't sure who looked the most apprehensive. Alexi seemed to have frozen. Gerald looked white-faced and pugnacious. Violet was trembling pitifully but that might just be reaction from her fall. Dorothy was flushed and cast Annabel a reproachful look. Did she think that Annabel had told Sir Terrence about the missing ring and he had called in the police? Matt looked as though he wished he were somewhere else. Humphrey looked tired and withdrawn.

The door opened behind them and Lucy came in. Pink somehow seemed even more incongruous given the circumstances. This time it was a pink dress with white polka dots. They all stared at her.

'What's happened?' she asked. 'There are policemen outside.'

'We are about to hear,' said Alexi tersely.

Sir Terrence looked around at everyone, taking for granted his position of authority.

'Thomas has been murdered.'

'*Murder* ...', said Gerald.

Humphrey took his glasses off and polished them with hands that were not quite steady. Without them, his face looked vulnerable.

Alexi gripped the back of a dining chair, his knuckles showed white.

Violet stopped trembling and stared at Sir Terrence in surprise. 'But, who is Thomas?'

Everyone looked at her. It seemed a question in very poor taste.

'Thomas is ... was ... my butler.'

'But how? Why?' said Matt.

'I'm afraid I can't divulge any more information than that. As you can imagine, the police will want to speak to everyone. I must ask you to remain in here, together ... and then you can move over to the sitting room after you have finished eating.'

'But, I'll want to go to my room then!' Violet sounded querulous.

'I'm afraid that will not be possible. The police will want to search the rooms.'

'Search the rooms? This is intolerable!' Gerald cried.

'So, if I may say, is murder,' said Sir Terrence coldly.

'I have no objection to anyone searching my rooms,' said Alexi. 'One must help the police after all.'

'Yes indeed!' said Dorothy. 'Poor Thomas, I can't imagine why anyone would want to kill him.'

'Lucy,' said Violet, 'I need my coffee.'

Lucy went to fetch some coffee. Annabel and Alexi joined her at the side table.

'Who knew a weekend in the country could be so full of incident?' said Alexi.

'You seem to be taking the news very lightly,' said Annabel disapprovingly.

He looked at her. She read approval in his eyes. 'You are right, there is nothing "light" about murder.'

Matt was behind them. 'Things seem to happen around you and Ferdy that I don't like,' he muttered in her ear.

'Aha!' said Alexi overhearing. 'You have solved it already! It is Annabel and Ferdy who are the murderers. I should have known.'

'Don't be silly,' said Annabel. She was in no mood for this sort of talk.

'But who would want to murder Thomas?' asked Lucy as she loaded her plate with eggs, bacon, sausage and fried tomatoes. The news did not seem to have affected her appetite.

'Surely the more important question is "why"?' said Gerald. 'It wouldn't surprise me if we find out that there is a lot more to Thomas than meets the eye.'

So, Gerald had noticed him.

'The police are speaking to the other staff now,' said Sir Terrence.

'There you are,' said Gerald. 'I expect they'll have it all sorted out in no time. No need to go searching rooms.'

Annabel wondered if he was saying this for Violet's benefit. She did seem to be recovering her poise.

'This is a terrible thing to have happened,' said Sarah.

'Are you all right, my dear?' asked Sir Terrence.

'Yes, of course! It's just … *murder*. Should we be contacting his family?'

'The police have that in hand, but, yes, I will find out … speak to them.'

It wouldn't be long before the realisation sank in that if Thomas had been murdered, it could be one of those seated round the table. A degree of constraint settled over the group as they started to eat their breakfast. Annabel and Ferdy weren't the only ones watching their neighbours. When everyone finished, Sir Terrence led the way through to the sitting room. They trooped self-consciously behind him across the hallway under the watchful eye of the policeman.

Violet lost no time establishing herself in Sir Terrence's chair where she got out her embroidery and commenced stitching with hands that trembled.

Sir Terrence and Sarah exchanged looks but let her

be. 'Well, let's make ourselves comfortable,' he said. 'We don't know how long we might be here.'

'There are papers, if anyone would like them,' said Sarah in an attempt to act as hostess.

Annabel sympathised; the social etiquette of such a situation was probably not in any handbook. She realised that Gerald was trying to catch her eye. He nodded briefly to the far corner of the room before moving off in that direction. Annabel followed a moment later. Under cover of pretending to show her a picture on the wall, he spoke in a lowered tone.

'Thank you ... back there,' he said. 'I will explain, but not now.'

Annabel decided to cut to the chase. 'Does Violet have Dorothy's ring too?'

To her surprise, he looked immensely grateful, as though a huge weight had been lifted.

'I have it here! Can you take it? Give it back to Dorothy?' His hand was in his pocket and, out of sight of the rest of the room. He held it out to Annabel. She looked at him in astonishment. How had he happened to have it with him at that moment? But the important thing was that it was found.

'Yes, I will take it but you *must* explain later.' She slipped the ring into her skirt pocket where it landed on Matt's bookmark with an audible chink.

He looked half-relieved, half-mutinous and she could see that, having handed over the ring, he would like to put the whole thing behind him.

Annabel's thoughts were mixed. On the one hand it was wonderful to have the ring back safe and sound. On the other, she could quite see how embarrassing it would be for Gerald if the ring were found in his possession by the police. She wondered how ready he would have been to give it up if the police had not been there.

Business accomplished, Gerald lost no time in moving away. He was replaced by Ferdy.

'What just happened?'

Annabel showed him the ring. Ferdy's lips pursed in a silent whistle.

'And there's this too,' she said, showing him Matt's bookmark.

'Is that what you picked up in the hall?' he asked.

He hadn't missed much.

'Matt's bookmark,' he said looking at the initials. 'Funny looking thing.'

It was rather. Annabel liked her leather bookmark with its tassel strips. It was nice and tactile.

'We have a magpie,' said Ferdy. 'Violet?'

'I think so. Gerald is going to explain later.' She paused. 'Shall we give the ring to Dorothy now?'

Ferdy was silent. Annabel was sure he was thinking the same as herself – Dorothy was not good at covering things up.

'Best not,' he said. 'Later, when we're allowed out of this room. Anyway, she can't suddenly put it on now.'

CHAPTER SEVENTEEN

The door opened and DCI Grange entered the room. He stood for a moment looking round. He had no need to draw anyone's attention to his presence, they were all looking at him. He introduced himself and DS Idle.

'I have to thank you for your patience,' he said, his voice calm, unhurried. 'We will want to speak to you all and, in the meantime, would be grateful if you would stay in here until we allow you to leave.'

It was politely put but it was an order.

'When will we be "allowed" to leave?' Gerald demanded.

'As soon as we finish our investigations.'

'What about comfort breaks? Refreshments?' Violet asked, her voice querulous.

'They can, of course, be arranged. Perhaps, Mr Harcourt, you could be first?'

They watched as Gerald left the room. Annabel felt his relief at having been able to offload the incriminating ring. She doubted that he had any qualms about handing the potential hot potato to herself. She wished they could have got a message to Grange that the ring had now turned up.

'The iron fist wears kid gloves,' said Alexi lightly.

'He is doing his job,' said Lucy.

'Lucy!' Violet moaned, 'my knee hurts.'

Lucy hurried forward.

'Sit on the sofa,' Sarah suggested. 'I am sure that would be best. You can put your leg up.'

'Yes, that would be best,' agreed Lucy.

'Oh! What a fuss!' said Violet petulantly but she moved across.

Sir Terrence sat down in his chair with the air of someone coming home. Sarah threw him a glance in which understanding and amusement were nicely mixed.

There was a ring on the doorbell and shortly afterwards Mrs Fry entered the room with a telegram which she handed to Alexi. He took it, walked over to the window, opened it, read it and came back.

Violet broke the silence. 'Well, what was in it?'

The gall of the woman!

He looked at her meditatively, no doubt wondering whether to tell her to mind her own business.

'It was a message,' he said, 'from a friend.'

Well, that gave a lot away. But it was a private telegram, no reason at all why he should say more. Annabel tried to read the expression on his face but it was impossible to tell what he was thinking. Anger possibly? Fear? Or maybe, excitement?

Gerald returned and Violet was called in. The sitting room now felt like a dentist's waiting room. Gerald was questioned but said the barest minimum. He sank into an armchair and buried his face in the *Times*.

Violet returned. She was white-faced and trembling and reached blindly for her daughter. Lucy supported her back to the sofa.

Gerald looked on in rising wrath. 'This is intolerable! I refuse to allow that man in there to bully us!'

Sir Terrence sighed. 'I am sure he is just doing his job.'

The morning wore on. Humphrey was called and returned. He was leaning heavily on his stick.

The door opened and Mrs Fry came in with Alice who was carrying a tray with coffee and biscuits.

'Have the police spoken to you?' Lucy asked.

'Yes, they have,' said Mrs Fry. She didn't elaborate.

'What did they ask?' This time it was Alexi who spoke.

'What you'd expect, I suppose. Where were we? What did we notice? That sort of thing.'

'Of course,' said Alice, 'it's not always easy to know if what you've seen is relevant. You don't want to waste their time.'

That would be up to the police to decide, surely. It was an odd thing for Alice to say. Had she seen something last night?

'We must all do what we can to be helpful,' said Sarah.

Alexi was called next. He walked out of the room, his back straight, his face pale.

Mrs Fry started to hand round coffees.

'You know, we planned to be away after lunch,' Gerald said at some point.

Sir Terrence raised his eyebrows. Annabel was sure he was thinking, 'the sooner the better.'

'No doubt we will all be told as soon as we are at liberty to … disperse,' he said.

Annabel was the last to be called in, after Ferdy. She entered the room and found Grange at the small dining table with Idle alongside. There was the audible sound of a jiggling foot. Idle belied his name by being a fidget. Annabel wondered how Grange could stand it. Idle must be very good at his job to make up for his annoying physical habits.

'I understand you have the ring,' said Grange when Annabel had taken a seat.

Ferdy must have told him.

'Gerald Harcourt handed it to me when we were in the sitting room.'

'And why would he do that?'

Good question. She described the scene in the hall when Violet had her fall and she had picked up Matt's bookmark.

'So you think, since you kept quiet, he trusted you?'

'Well, that, and I think he was desperate to get rid of the ring.'

'As soon as was feasibly possible after learning of our presence?' Grange hazarded.

'Yes, but I don't think he stole it. Ferdy and I think he's covering up for his wife.'

'Other things have gone missing,' said Grange. 'Sir Terrence has lost a pencil sharpener. Matthew Lloyd has lost a sock.'

'Those are not items of value. They are more likely to cause annoyance than grief if lost. Dorothy's ring is different.' Annabel paused, 'Gerald wants to talk to me once we are allowed out of the sitting room. I'm hoping he will explain.'

Grange sat in silence for a few moments. Annabel liked the way that he considered things, didn't rush into a reply.

'Everyone claims to have slept through the night, with the exception of the chef, and the maid Alice who complained that you woke her up,' he said. 'The Harcourts slept together as did Dorothy Baxter and Matthew Lloyd but of course that is not an infallible alibi.'

'Alice may have seen something. She looked terrified until she saw it was me.'

'I think she was hiding something,' Grange agreed. 'I'll have another word with her.'

'Do people know that it was Ferdy and I who found … the body?'

'I haven't mentioned that to anyone. However, most of the bedroom windows look out onto the terrace and people sleep with their windows open … it's not beyond the bounds of possibility that someone saw you,' he paused. 'Or heard you when you discovered Thomas.'

'Have you found the camera?' she asked.

'Not yet. We are going to search the rooms next. After

that I suggest you and Mr Baxter join us for a review of where we are.'

Annabel was surprised and gratified. She wasn't going to turn down the offer to collaborate with Grange. It was a shame though that the camera hadn't turned up in Violet's bag.

She went back to the sitting room where she found that trays of sandwiches and cake had made an appearance. She realised that it was lunchtime and she was hungry. Sunday lunch usually meant a roast of some kind. John must have adapted to the circumstances. The sandwiches were paper thin and cut into triangles, their crusts removed. Further inspection revealed that some were ham, some were egg mayonnaise and some were ...

'Sandwich spread!' Annabel exclaimed in delight.

'My favourite too,' said Sarah, pleased.

That explained it. Annabel suspected that if Sarah expressed a preference for anything, John would move heaven and earth to provide it, including sandwich spread.

'I feel violated!' Violet's voice rose up from behind them on the sofa. 'They emptied my bag. Actually emptied my bag! Is there no privacy anymore?'

From everyone else's reaction, which was polite but bored, she had been carrying on in this vein for a while.

'We were all searched.' Sarah's tone suggested that even she was losing patience with Violet.

'But what were they looking for?' Violet cried.

'Something to do with Thomas's death, don't you think?' said Sarah.

'We still don't know how he died,' said Alexi.

'Or where,' said Humphrey.

'Or indeed, who found him,' said Gerald. 'Someone must have done.'

'Do you think he was murdered in his bed?' asked Dorothy in a hushed voice.

'I saw policemen out on the terrace before I came down,' said Lucy.

'On the terrace?' Alexi moved over to the window and looked out. 'Yes, in fact it looks like they are taking him away right now.'

Humphrey limped over. Everyone else followed at varying speeds and looked out. They saw the tail end of a procession making its way along the terrace, with four policemen carrying a stretcher on which a body covered in a sheet was placed.

'So it happened outside!' said Gerald. 'It could have been anybody then. Nothing to do with anyone in the house! I must insist that I and my wife be allowed to leave.'

'We will all be allowed to leave, just as soon as the police have concluded their investigations,' Sir Terrence replied somewhat wearily.

'Would anyone like more sandwiches?' asked Sarah.

The door opened again and DS Idle asked Alexi to

accompany him. Alexi paled then shrugged and followed Idle out of the room.

'Told you it would be the Russian,' Gerald said to Violet. 'Why else would they call him back for further questioning?'

'You're going to want to see this,' said Ferdy as soon as Alexi was gone.

'See what?' She followed him to the end of the room where he showed her his notepad on which was written the words 'El Greco Bariloche'.

'El Greco Bariloche? What does that mean?'

Ferdy's eyes gleamed. 'It was on the telegram that Alexi received this morning.'

The telegram! Of course!

'Grange asked Alexi and he apparently had no qualms about showing it.'

Suddenly Annabel remembered. 'Ferdy! It's just like the others that Rosemary told us about. The messages that Alexi received. The name of an artist and a place! And afterwards he visited the place. But is Bariloche a place? I've never heard of it.'

'We've got Scotland Yard's finest looking into that,' said Ferdy.

Annabel remembered how strangely Alexi had reacted when he read the telegram. 'What did he tell Grange it was about?'

'Said it was a message from a friend about an

El Greco he'd been trying to track down. Said he didn't know where Bariloche was, or even if it was a place.'

'But the security services thought it might be a code. That's why he was on their list of suspects.'

'Yes.' Ferdy looked grim. 'And this turning up right after what happened last night is not looking good for him. Grange is grilling him right now.'

'But, surely, they wouldn't send the contact details, if that is what they are, to him here?'

'Unlikely,' agreed Ferdy. 'But they wouldn't know that there had been a murder committed. Or that the police would be here.'

This was true. 'El Greco … it's a strange name.'

'Doménikos Theotokópoulos,' Ferdy nodded. 'People called him "the Greek"'

'I'm not surprised, with a name like that. Could it be a code?'

'That's what I'm going to try to work out,' he said.

'And as soon as we are allowed out of here I will speak to Gerald,' said Annabel. 'Unless you think I should give Dorothy her ring back first?'

'No, Gerald first. My feeling is he's already starting to regret his offer to divulge the truth.'

Gerald was certainly avoiding Annabel's eye as they were finally released out of the sitting room. He was also being very solicitous to his wife.

'Gerald,' said Annabel loudly and in a voice that she hoped carried authority.

He hunched into himself then turned with obvious reluctance.

'My wife needs to lie down.'

'And we,' said Annabel coming closer and lowering her voice, 'need to talk.'

'I really don't think ... can't it wait?'

'No it can't. It's either that or I shall have to inform DCI Grange.' The fact that Grange already knew was something she would keep to herself.

He looked horrified, then she saw defeat settle across his features.

'All right. I'll just see my wife up to our room and then we'll talk.'

'Are you going upstairs Violet?' said Sarah. 'Let me give you a hand.'

Violet looked anything but gratified but Sarah began to shepherd her upstairs. Gerald turned to Annabel with the look of a man who is adrift on the sea with no anchor.

'Let's step outside shall we?' she said.

They descended from the terrace to the lawn and, for a moment, the relief of being outdoors overtook everything else in Annabel's mind. She lifted her head and took a deep breath. Gerald threw her a look in which a shared sympathy momentarily replaced his despair. They started to walk down towards the lake. Annabel decided to let him begin.

'She is not well,' he said as they drew near to the water.

'Violet?'

'She can't help it. Things upset her and then it's a compulsion.'

'She takes things.'

'Yes.' he turned towards her eagerly. 'It's not stealing. You do see that? She can't help herself.'

'Something upset her here?'

'Yes. Dorothy and Matt's engagement. You see she doesn't want to lose Lucy. She thinks it will put ideas in Lucy's mind.'

'But she can't want Lucy to remain single forever!'

Gerald looked at her with a twisted smile. 'I can assure you she does.' He turned to look out over the lake. 'Anyway the ring was a no brainer. I knew what had happened as soon as Dorothy arrived at breakfast with that story of a cut finger. Although, I couldn't understand why Dorothy didn't shout about the theft to the rooftops. I was just grateful she didn't. But Violet can be cunning,' he sounded almost proud. 'I can usually find things – she tends to have favourite hiding places – but this time she'd hidden it well. I didn't find it until this morning and then the police arrived. I thought they were here for us.'

Annabel remembered seeing Gerald feeling down the sides of the chairs. Perhaps that was a nightly exercise for him when they were away from home, creeping downstairs to see if Violet had secreted anything away.

'And then you picked up that thing in the hall,' he continued.

'Matt's bookmark.'

'Is that what it was? Anyway, I could see that you sympathised. I was going to drop the ring under the sofa but I decided to give it to you.'

Yes, give the hot potato away to someone foolish enough to accept it.

'How did *you* know about the ring?' he asked, then answered his own question. 'But I suppose you're Dorothy's friend.'

He had shown no concern about Dorothy's feelings in all this. In his own way he was as blinkered as Violet.

'And the snuffbox?' she asked. 'That was Violet too?'

'Violet had it in her bag. I pretended to find it under the chair. I was almost angry with her then. Taking something that I am known to admire and collect, it was too close to home. But again, I suppose it was to be expected.'

'Why was it to be expected?'

'Sarah had admired it, said it was her favourite.'

'But Sarah has been nothing but kind to Violet!'

'Sarah is Lucy's age, and married.'

Annabel was speechless.

'As I say,' he continued, 'she is ill. Actually, I can't tell you what a relief it is to talk about it. I have been living with it, walking on eggshells, for so long.'

'Can't you get some help for her?'

'I'm trying. The doctors talk of kleptomania. It seems to fit, although I don't think they really understand much about it; seemed to be all theory and conjecture. And I've been putting off doing anything such as medication or hospitalisation hoping she'd get better.' He sighed. 'She wasn't always like this.'

Annabel looked out across the lake. A light breeze ruffled the surface.

'Does Lucy know?' she asked.

'I think she suspects. She loves her mother. I haven't liked to worry her with it.'

'Maybe she knows enough to make her wary of getting married or becoming close to someone?'

Gerald looked distressed. 'I don't think she has anyone in mind! Do you think she has? Oh dear …'

'I don't know but maybe you should talk to her – away from her mother?'

CHAPTER EIGHTEEN

Annabel went in search of Ferdy and found him in his room. The police were still occupying the library and the morning room.

'Any luck?' she asked.

'Nothing. To be honest, I would be surprised if I had. It could be anything. It could be that all his contacts have been given code names of artists and the message tells him to meet that person in the place listed. It could be a code that is dependent upon a specific book. You know – the fifth chapter 'E', the twelfth line 'L', the seventh word 'G', etcetera.'

'Do you think Alexi is the spy then?'

Ferdy shrugged unhappily. 'Or, it could be exactly as he says, and a friend has found an El Greco in a place called Bariloche and is letting him know. How did you get on with Gerald? Did he talk?'

'Yes he did. Actually, it was all rather sad. He thinks Violet suffers from kleptomania.'

'Kleptomania? I know that's a legitimate illness but I always thought it was a kooky way to cover up a nasty tendency to pinch stuff.'

'He said she wasn't always like that,' said Annabel. She had to agree that there was a spiteful element to

Violet's choice of victims but then most people don't react by stealing things. There must be more to it than that. 'He's going to try and get her some help.'

'I think we all wish him well with that.'

Annabel could see that Ferdy was not going to feel any sympathy for Violet, but he hadn't seen the concern and the desperation in Gerald's eyes. In fairness, she herself didn't have much sympathy for Violet. She did have considerable sympathy for Gerald, although he seemed to feel none for his wife's victims.

'Anyway, that explains why things have gone missing in country houses where Gerald and Violet have been guests,' said Annabel. 'I'm inclined to think that he isn't our spy after all.'

'I'm not sure we can let him off the hook just yet. He could be doing both, looking after his wife *and* stealing documents.'

True, but then, Ferdy didn't want it to be Alexi and would be looking for any other answer. 'Alexi could have hidden the film in his car. He might have been checking that the hiding place was all right, you know, when he was out working on his car yesterday morning. The car that Gerald said was "as sweet as a nut".'

'Way ahead of you there,' said Ferdy. 'Grange's men are giving it the fine tooth comb as we speak.'

That was good. 'Shall we give the ring back to Dorothy now?'

They found Dorothy in her room. She opened the door

to them and it was immediately apparent that she was in a bad way.

'Oh, it's you. Oh, this weekend is just going from bad to worse!'

'Yes, poor Thomas. It's terrible,' said Annabel.

'Oh … yes, Thomas,' said Dorothy. 'Of course, yes, that is terrible.' She paced up and down the room. Put her and Idle in a room together and they would create unhappy vibrations that could hang around for decades.

'Do stop pacing, Dodo,' Ferdy said. 'You'll wear the carpet out.'

Annabel threw him a look. Such comments were hardly likely to help. 'We have something that will cheer you up,' she said. She pulled the ring out of her pocket and held it out. The stone, released into the light, glowed and sparkled. The stone itself was quite pretty. It was the setting that was so ugly.

'Oh!' Dorothy leapt upon it, gathered it to her heart. 'You found it! Oh, thank Goodness! Where on earth did you find it?'

'Under the sofa,' Annabel lied.

'Under the sofa? But how on earth did it get there?' Dorothy was understandably bemused, given that she had last seen it on her bedside table.

'We don't know,' said Annabel.

'Oh, well. It's turned up. That's the main thing. But it is odd …'

'You'd better put it on,' said Ferdy. *And don't take it off again.*

'Oh dear … must I?' Dorothy slipped it onto her finger. She turned to them, 'I *said* you were good at finding things. Thank you so much.'

'We're pleased it's turned up.' Annabel was puzzled that Dorothy still looked worried.

'So, what else's eating you?' asked Ferdy.

Dorothy flumped down on the bed. Annabel noticed that she kept her ring hand well away from her dress. 'Oh, it's all a disaster,' she said.

'What is?' Annabel asked.

'Matt has told Dad I won't need my allowance any more.' Dorothy made it sound like the end of the world.

'What a chump,' said Ferdy.

Annabel reflected that Ferdy was a fine one to talk. He had been refusing his allowance for the last three years.

'But why?' Annabel had definitely got the wrong idea about Matt. He wasn't interested in settlements at all. But surely Dorothy's allowance was her own? Nothing to do with him.

'It's a matter of pride,' said Dorothy. 'He wants to be able to support me himself.'

'Well, isn't he rich?' Annabel had always thought so.

'Well, yes, but he's "*old* money" and they never spend it if they can help it. If they do, it's on their *buildings* or their *land*. He'd never dream of spending what I do on clothes.'

Annabel realised the full extent of the disaster. She may – in fact she did – think that spending vast amounts of money on clothes that could be ruined at-the-drop-of-a-prawn was less than sensible but she knew what buying clothes meant to Dorothy.

'But, he loves the way that you look!' she said.

'Yes, but he has no idea … *no idea* what it all costs.'

Ferdy was shaking with silent laughter. Annabel elbowed him angrily in the ribs. His laugh turned into a cough.

'Poor Dodo,' he said. 'You'll just have to get him to change his mind. Tell him how much that little number you wore last night cost.'

Dorothy paled. 'I couldn't.'

Annabel left a respectful pause then cleared her throat. 'We also found this.' She held out Matt's bookmark. 'We think he was looking for it.'

'Oh yes.' Dorothy took it absently. 'He hasn't been reading much this weekend but I'll give it back to him. He's got another anyway.'

Something stirred in the back of Annabel's brain, something she felt was important. She struggled to retrieve it but it sank back into her subconscious.

Annabel and Ferdy headed back downstairs. Annabel was getting the hang of the staircase now. The trick was to hug the outer edge. She felt that the stairs had earned their place in the house that morning.

'Now for Grange,' said Ferdy.

They walked through to the morning room and knocked on the door, entering on the invitation. Grange was standing by the window and turned at their entrance. Idle moved over to a chair at the table and sat down, it seemed, reluctantly. Sitting still must be torture for him. Annabel wondered if he danced in his spare time, something energetic like the highland fling?

'Thank you for coming back.' Grange took the chair next to Idle and motioned for Ferdy and Annabel to sit opposite. 'I think it would be helpful for us to pool our resources. You are in a unique position to notice things that would otherwise be hidden from us. If I may go first, I would like to know what the mood was in the sitting room this morning and if you noticed anything worth mentioning.'

'Sticky,' said Ferdy. 'Very sticky; nobody was saying anything much.'

'We all saw the body being removed,' said Annabel. 'When they realised it was outside, they thought that meant it could have been done by someone not staying in the house.'

'Who said that?'

'It was Gerald. He and his wife want to leave as soon as possible.' She paused. 'But Violet didn't know who Thomas was. I don't think it's her or Gerald.'

'*Said* she didn't know who Thomas was,' Ferdy corrected.

This was true. But there was such a thing as a gut feeling.

'Have you managed to speak to Mr Harcourt?' Grange asked.

'Yes. He thinks his wife suffers from kleptomania. He seems to spend his time covering up for her, replacing things she's taken. I think his mind is wholly taken up by that.' She didn't mention Lucy.

'Hmph. Kleptomania – that would fit.'

Idle gave a derisive snort. Ferdy looked at him with sympathy.

'Gerald wanted to know why Thomas might have been killed,' said Annabel, 'and Dorothy said she couldn't imagine why anyone would want to kill him.'

'Interesting,' said Grange. 'Yes, we were asked about the how, the when and where, but not the why.'

'Usually the most important question,' agreed Ferdy.

'Well, we think we know the answer to all of those,' said Annabel. 'It's just the "who" that we still don't know.'

'Which comes back to you,' said Ferdy. 'Any luck finding the camera?'

Grange steepled his fingers. 'We checked shoes, lighters and cigarette cases, belts, powder compacts. We checked the professor's walking stick and his leg – '

'You looked at his leg!' said Annabel.

Grange looked at her. 'This is a murder investigation, Miss Staple. We checked anything and everything that might conceivably hold a camera – and we haven't found one.'

'Does he wear a bandage?' asked Ferdy.

'No, there's a sizeable scar – he was injured in the war.'

'You've finished checking the cars?' Annabel asked.

'We have and nothing.'

Gerald had been checking down the sides of chairs. 'Someone could have secreted the camera in the sitting room before they came to see you and then collected it again afterwards.'

'Indeed they could. If needs be, a full search will be carried out again before anyone leaves …'

That'll please everyone.

'… and the sitting room is being searched as we speak.'

'Did you find any chloroform?' asked Ferdy.

'We did. A small bottle lying nearby Thomas under the shrubs. No fingerprints. We're checking where it came from but aren't hopeful. The chloroform was decanted into the sort of empty storage bottle that is sold in most chemists.'

'What about the telegram?' asked Annabel.

Idle sat forward in his seat. If anything, his resemblance to a terrier became even more pronounced. 'It took some digging, but we now know what Bariloche is.' He paused impressively.

DCI Grange shifted impatiently. He might just as well have said: 'Get on with it!' But Annabel also saw satisfaction written across his features. No doubt he valued his sergeant for his ability to ferret out facts.

'Bariloche is a ski resort in Argentina – believed to be a favourite haunt of ex-Nazis.'

Argentina and *Nazis?* Annabel made no attempt to hide her astonishment.

DS Idle looked pleased with himself, as well he might. 'And El Greco is –'

'I think they know who El Greco is,' Grange cut him off. Enough was enough.

'But surely former Nazis wouldn't be stealing documents?' Annabel exclaimed.

'Why not?' said Ferdy. 'I'm sure they are capable of anything. What did Alexi say?'

'He still professed to knowing nothing about Bariloche. Stuck to his story of a helpful friend. Thanked us for finding out what and where Bariloche was.' Grange's tone was non-committal.

'That sounds like Alexi,' said Ferdy.

'I gather he's a friend of yours?'

'Yes,' said Ferdy, 'he is. But that doesn't mean I don't think he could be involved.'

Grange looked at him for a few moments. 'Is that so?'

'Let's just say his morals are … flexible.'

'None of this explains the "El Greco",' said Annabel.

'We wondered if it might be a code,' said Ferdy.

Grange considered this. 'Come up with anything?'

'Not yet.'

'Leave it with me,' said Idle, already busy with paper and pen.

They heard a commotion out in the hall and there was a knock on the door. Without waiting for an invitation to enter, Mrs Fry opened the door and stood there, her mouth opening and closing. Annabel had thought her un-shockable, but Mrs Fry was exhibiting all the signs of extreme shock. Annabel pushed back her chair and went forward to support the housekeeper who looked in danger of fainting.

'What is it? What has happened?'

'It's Alice …' Mrs Fry took a gulp of air, 'someone has tried to strangle her.' She tottered over to Annabel's chair and sat down heavily.

'Alice? Strangled?' said Annabel.

'Where?' demanded Grange.

'Kitchen … store room.' Mrs Fry waved her hand vaguely in that direction.

Grange and Idle left the room.

'You go too,' said Annabel to Ferdy. 'I'll stay with Mrs Fry.'

A moment later Sarah entered the room. 'What's happened?' she asked. 'Mrs Fry! Are you unwell?'

'Alice has been attacked,' Annabel explained. 'Could you look after Mrs Fry? I'd like to …'

'Alice, attacked?' Sarah paled but, like her husband, wasted no time in unnecessary exclamations. 'Of course you must go,' she said and turned her attention to Mrs Fry.

Annabel caught up with Ferdy in the kitchen corridor. It was long and dark. At the far end they could just make out a small group of people gathered around the entrance to a room on the left hand side. As they drew nearer Annabel saw that Grange and Idle were with John. Grange glanced their way and Annabel could see from his set features that he was terribly angry.

John was talking, '… heard a sound, came out of the kitchen to investigate. Think she put up a fight. I shouted out "Hoy!" Guy beat it, out through the end door.'

'Which leads to?'

'The back yard.'

'You didn't follow?'

'Figured Alice was more important. She's unconscious but alive. Mrs Fry called an ambulance.'

Annabel looked into the storeroom somewhat fearful as to what she might see but in fact the scene was quite peaceful.

'She's in the recovery position.' Annabel knew about this from a first aid course she'd taken at school.

'I did that,' said John.

'You shouldn't have moved her,' said Grange.

'I thought it was more important to keep her alive,' said John evenly.

Presumably Grange also acknowledged that because he asked how Alice was positioned when found.

'Crumpled up against the back wall.'

'Who put the blanket over her?' Alice was covered by a blue and cream checked blanket and her head was laid on a tea towel.

'Mrs Fry – then she went to get you.'

Perhaps she carried out these caring and helpful acts in a state of suspended shock, a shock which only hit home as she came into the morning room. Annabel had heard of delayed shock.

'Can you describe the figure?' Grange asked.

'A man, pretty sure. Moved like a man.'

'Right,' said Grange to DS Idle, his voice coldly measured with an anger that was the more deadly because there was no increase in tone. 'I want everyone gathered together again and … I want to know how, with four constables in the house as well as ourselves, someone was able to attack a member of the staff.'

Idle disappeared without a word. The fizz had gone from his step.

'Why is it so dark?' asked Ferdy.

John pointed to the overhead light in the corridor. They looked up. The bulb had been removed. He fetched a stepladder and a spare bulb and rectified the situation.

'Premeditated,' said Grange. He stooped down in the improved light and inspected Alice's hands closely. 'Trimmed nails, doesn't look like she was able to scratch. Nasty bump on the back of the head, probably pushed against the wall, knocked senseless. Bruising on the throat, she was attacked from the front. Looks like you intervened just in time.'

'She'll be able to identify her attacker,' said Ferdy.

'When she comes round, *if* she comes round,' said Grange.

Annabel was remembering Alice's 'act' in the library on Saturday morning. Alice dreamt of wealth and riches. And when she and Mrs Fry brought in the coffee, hadn't Alice said something about not knowing what to mention to the police? Had that been a message to the murderer? Telling them that she had seen something?

'Blackmail,' said Annabel. 'I'm wondering if she was blackmailing him.'

Grange turned to her. 'Almost certainly, but what makes *you* think that?'

Annabel explained her thoughts.

'You should have mentioned that.'

Yes, she probably should have done.

'Was Alice looking at anyone in particular when she made her remark?'

If she was, Annabel hadn't noticed.

'I sensed she was hiding something,' said Grange. 'Gave her plenty of opportunity to tell us. I should have pressed harder. Fortunately for us all,' he looked at the recumbent Alice, 'she's still alive.'

Grange was being generous. Annabel was grateful for the reprieve. She wondered if the guilt she was feeling was a natural companion to this line of work.

DS Idle reappeared. 'The ambulance has arrived.' He carried a large flash camera and proceeded to take photos of the storeroom and of Alice with and without the blanket. The blanket was tucked back around Alice when he'd finished.

Alice was certainly the star of this scene. But it was probably not what she'd had in mind when she dreamt of being a film star.

A heavy footfall announced the arrival of the ambulance men and they all stepped back to make space. Two burly men carrying a stretcher proceeded with the minimum of fuss and a reassuring professionalism to inspect Alice then lift her carefully onto the stretcher.

Idle reappeared.

'I want a man with her at all times,' said Grange. 'And I want to be informed as soon as she comes round.' He moved along the passage to the back door and opened it, stepping outside and looking around then up at the building. From the outside, he closed and then opened the door before coming back inside. The murderer could have come in that way.

'Everyone is back in the sitting room,' said Idle. 'Lady Sarah and Mrs Fry are not going to say anything to the others about what has happened.'

'Good work,' said Grange. 'We'll speak to them all together this time.'

CHAPTER NINETEEN

Ferdy and Annabel entered the sitting room first, keeping up the illusion that they were not connected in any way with the police, although Annabel wondered quite how convincing that was now. The spy must surely suspect that they were hand in glove with them. John followed them in and lounged against the wall, his keen eyes surveying the assembled people beneath hooded lids. Mrs Fry was half lying on the sofa and looking very uncomfortable. She tried to rise up but was pressed firmly back into place by Sarah's hand on her shoulder. Violet was in Sir Terrence's chair and Sir Terrence, displaced, was standing in front of the fireplace which was Gerald's favourite spot. He had settled on a position beside the display case containing the snuff boxes. Alexi and Lucy were over by the French windows but didn't look as though they had been talking to one another.

Dorothy sat in an armchair nearer to the window. She had changed into a pair of black slacks and a short sleeved cream jersey. Matt joined her there, perching on the arm. 'Darling! You're wearing your ring again!' He took her hand gingerly in his and studied the finger closely. 'How odd, I can't see a wound.'

Dorothy retrieved her hand. 'Oh, yes, it's healed

really quickly.' She saw his brow crease and added hastily, 'Also, it's hidden under the ring.'

Matt looked puzzled but didn't attempt to take her hand again.

Humphrey was sitting in the armchair opposite Violet by the fireplace, an unopened book on his lap of the sort that Annabel would have classified as hard work. Perhaps books were, for him, a comfort; a reminder of normality. Certainly, there was nothing normal about the current situation. His hands clasped the book tightly. She could see the knuckles of his right hand shining palely white through his skin.

DCI Grange and DS Idle entered the room and instantly commanded attention.

'What is going on?' Violet burst out. 'We've been through all this!'

'Herded around like sheep ...' said Gerald.

'Have you discovered who killed Thomas?' asked Lucy.

'Alice, the maid, has been attacked,' said Grange. He let the sentence hang.

'What? Killed?' said Lucy, turning pale.

'Doesn't look good for you, does it?' said Alexi to Grange. 'Under your noses.'

'Oh for God's sake! What next?' said Violet.

'We could all be murdered!' cried Gerald.

'*Is* she dead?' asked Humphrey.

'She is not dead.' Again, Grange let the sentence hang.

'So …' Lucy spoke almost in a whisper, 'so, you know who did it?'

Annabel looked around at everyone's faces. They all appeared invested in knowing the answer to this question. By now, the murderer must surely be terrified of discovery.

After a significant pause Grange said, 'She is unconscious, and has been taken to hospital.'

'But she is all right?' asked Sarah. 'She's going to recover?'

'It is hoped that she will make a full recovery.'

Grange couldn't know that – another move in the game of cat and mouse.

'Thank God,' said Mrs Fry.

'So,' continued Grange, 'we'd like to know where everyone was during the last half an hour, starting with you, please, Sir Terrence.'

Sir Terrence knew that it was his job to set a good example and answer readily and without fuss. 'Of course,' he said. 'I was in my bedroom, working on some documents.'

'Can anyone corroborate that?'

'I'm afraid not. I was alone the entire time.'

Working round the rest of the people present, the answers revealed that nobody could provide an alibi. Sarah had been in her office. Alexi had been in his room, purpose undisclosed and, his tone suggested, nobody's business. Lucy had been wandering moodily around the garden. She didn't actually use that word, her tone suggested her frame of mind. Matthew had borrowed a first aid book from Mrs Fry and had been in his room trying to find a remedy for a cut finger that refused to heal. Dorothy had been in her room changing her clothes – presumably selecting something she least minded getting snagged by the ring. Violet and Gerald Harcourt had been here in the sitting room, sewing and reading respectively. The professor had been sitting on the terrace in the sunshine smoking a cigar.

Ferdy said that they were with Grange helping him with his enquiries until Mrs Fry had arrived with the disturbing news. It had the added merit of being true.

Annabel found that she was studying the men's hands, hands that a short time ago had been fastened around Alice's neck. Gerald's were strong enough, the nails manicured neatly. Alexi's were much smaller with long sensitive fingers. Humphrey's were uncared for and showed ink stains and the clear indentation of a pen on the middle finger of his right hand. They were the hands of a scholar. Matt's were … but it couldn't be Matt! And, as for John, he had raised the alarm so it was unlikely to be him.

A shiver ran down her back. If the spy had chosen to strangle, rather than chloroform her, there would have been nobody to come to her aid. She would be dead.

'It's one of us,' said Lucy in a whisper.

There was an uncomfortable shifting of bodies as everyone pondered on the truth of that statement.

'But why Alice?' cried Mrs Fry.

Alexi sighed. 'She saw something, I expect.'

'Oh, God,' said Sarah.

'But why didn't she say?' said Violet.

'That would have been the sensible thing to do,' said Sir Terrence.

'I don't think they can keep us here,' said Gerald. 'Not now they've been through all our things.'

'Perhaps not,' said Sir Terrence, 'but do you really want them turning up at your office? It's best, surely, to be patient.' The implication – that it should all be over soon – he left unspoken.

'Let's review where we are,' said Ferdy as he and Annabel once more circled the lawn.

'I can't see that we are any further forward.' said Annabel. 'We still have no idea who the spy is, we haven't managed to eliminate anyone as a suspect and we haven't found the camera.'

'We do know that whoever it is must be getting very jittery. That attack on Alice was risky as hell and only someone who feels they are being pushed into a corner acts like that.'

Annabel agreed. 'Which makes them even more dangerous,' she said. They had reached the lake and there was a nearby seat but Annabel didn't feel like sitting down. 'There must be *something*,' she said, 'something we've missed. Dorothy said something which made me think of something … sorry I'm not being very clear.'

'What did she say?'

'If I knew *that* I'd know the rest of it!'

'Look on the bright side, at least it wasn't you that found Alice.'

In spite of herself Annabel gave a gulp of laughter. She could just imagine Grange saying: 'Miss Staple, *three* bodies, in the space of one summer, is three too many.' But Alice wasn't dead.

'As soon as Alice comes round, we will know,' she said.

'Yes, and our spy knows that. The clock is ticking. I'm sure he expected to leave at the end of the weekend, negatives in hand, nobody any the wiser. He must be wondering now if he should make a run for it.'

Annabel hesitated. She wasn't sure if she should ask this, but then why not? 'What exactly is your background with Alexi? You say he is your friend but you think him capable of espionage. And how did you learn to speak Russian?'

Ferdy gave a wry smile. He took out his cigarettes and lit one using the lighter that used to belong to Alec. He drew the smoke in deeply and expelled it slowly.

'Smoking is very bad for you,' said Annabel. 'I'm just saying … my mother died of pneumonia and she smoked, a lot.' As usual when she thought about her mother she found it difficult to speak.

Ferdy didn't disagree. He regarded his cigarette with regret, 'Why does everything good in life seem to be bad for one?'

I wouldn't be bad for you.

'I got to know him when I was stationed out in West Germany on National Service.'

'Yes, you said that, but I always imagined it was a lot of routine square-bashing.'

'To start with it was, and very boring it was too. Happily my aptitude for languages was noticed, someone showed initiative and I was pushed into things I wouldn't otherwise have done, like learning to speak Russian. In the course of which I met Alexi ... and your father.'

'Alec? You knew my father then?' Annabel remembered Ferdy saying that he and her father went 'a long way back'. She hadn't realised it was *that* far back. 'I thought you said you'd met him through John Trevor.'

'Yes, but I knew him before that.'

Annabel was silent. So he had lied to her before, or at least not told her the whole story. But perhaps he'd been silent because of the sensitivity of the subject. 'I suppose it's another Official Secrets Act thing,' she complained. Ferdy had taken her to an anonymous looking office building in the city where she was presented with the necessary paperwork to sign. The single sheet of paper looked innocuous but she had felt a weight of responsibility as she signed her name.

Ferdy grinned. 'Very convenient, that Act.'

Annabel smiled politely but she was a bit shocked. There was a lot about Ferdy that she didn't know. Alexi had implied that Ferdy had picked up his Russian whilst working with him.

'I think we should go back in,' she said.

Ferdy reached out and took her hand. She felt as though a bolt of electricity had shot through her body. He must have felt it too, surely? Yes, she saw it in his eyes, he had. They stood for a moment looking at each other.

'Annabel, I …'

Sarah came out of the house. She looked troubled.

Ferdy cursed softly.

'You go on in,' Annabel said.

He cast a searching look at her, nodded, and went on in.

'Would you like a breath of air … a walk?' Annabel asked. Sarah seemed very self-reliant and self-contained, but Annabel felt that they had developed some rapport, enough at least to make the offer of a listening ear not unwelcome.

Sarah made a negative gesture with her hand but then stopped, 'Yes, I'd like that, if you can spare the time?'

'Of course.'

For the third time that afternoon, Annabel set out around the lawn. She felt she had carved quite a route around and across it that weekend, in various states of mind.

They walked for a few moments in silence. Then Sarah burst out, 'I feel terrible!'

'Terrible? Why?'

'Because it was my idea, all this. First Terry was hit on the head and now Thomas is dead and Alice … if she dies …!' She stopped and stared up at the sky biting her lip. 'I'll never be able to forgive myself.'

Annabel wondered how much she could tell Sarah and decided that Sarah deserved to know much more than she did.

'First of all,' she said, 'it wasn't your idea to stage this weekend. You were just kind enough to host it, and you did that with the best motive in mind. There is nothing to reproach yourself for. Secondly, I don't know if you know but Thomas was Special Branch and knew what he was getting himself into. And finally, well, Alice wasn't exactly blameless in what happened to her. She saw something that night. She may have seen who killed Thomas and she should have told the police. Instead it seems probable that she tried to blackmail the killer and that was why they tried to kill her. It was only because John intervened that she is still alive.'

'Terry told me Thomas was from Special Branch. But *blackmail*! What was she thinking! So dangerous when she knew he had killed once already.

'I think, if she did do it, it was because she wanted money,' said Annabel dryly.

'We pay generously. I make sure of that,' Sarah said quickly.

'I don't think it had anything to do with the salary you pay her. I think she dreams of being a film star.'

'A film star! Why?'

Annabel couldn't help smiling at Sarah's expression of incomprehension.

'Well, anyway, I can't have her working here any more,' Sarah continued.

Annabel looked at her in surprise. 'Surely, it was just one mistake?'

'No. It's out of the question. If she can do it once, she can do it again. I can't risk it where Terry and Jonny are concerned.'

Annabel was silent. This seemed extreme but then, why not? Sarah had been absolutely single minded when she ran off with Sir Terrence not counting the cost to his wife and family. And it was already clear that the comfort and safety of her husband and child were primary considerations.

'Would you like to sit down?' Annabel asked. They had reached the seat by the lake.

'Perhaps, for a few minutes.'

They sat in silence, the sun warm on their faces.

'So peaceful,' said Sarah. 'It's hard to believe all *that* going on back there.' She shifted on the seat. 'Are you any closer to knowing who might be behind it all?'

'Well, if John is right, it's a man and that means Gerald Harcourt, Alexi Galkin or Humphrey Calder.'

'Not particularly nice to think that one of them is a traitor and a cold-hearted murderer.' Sarah shivered.

You had to wonder what would lead a man to such an act. Although, of course, Alexi would be a straightforward spy acting for his own country, probably to return home to tea and medals. Or would it be vodka and medals?

'I can't see it being Gerald,' said Sarah. 'He just doesn't seem capable of it. He's not,' she smiled apologetically, 'clever enough, although he might be a really good actor.'

Annabel smiled in agreement. She had her own reasons for not suspecting Gerald. She thought his concerns were elsewhere. 'What about Humphrey?'

Sarah considered this. 'You know, it's not nice even contemplating that one of your friends might be a spy. But if I had to be objective I'd say that he was definitely clever enough except that … well, he's terribly forgetful. I can't see him remembering enough to be an effective spy.'

'What do you mean, "forgetful"?'

'Oh he's always leaving things behind whenever he comes to stay, his book, even his glasses once! It must be a real worry for him, being such a renowned historian. They rely so much on their memory for facts and details.'

'Has he ever said anything to suggest he might not be happy with Britain?'

'No, never, but he hasn't exactly said anything wildly for it either. In fact, he never says *anything* much.' Sarah grinned, 'I think that's why Terry likes him. He says he's restful. But, of course, it's also because they go back such a long way. I think they met at college.'

'What about Alexi?' said Annabel.

'Well, he *is* Russian.'

'Tick the box. Case closed,' said Annabel with more than a touch of cynicism.

'Yes, it is a bit too obvious,' Sarah agreed. She gave a half laugh, 'Of course there's Matt …'

'Matt!'

They looked at one another.

'No,' said Sarah, answering her own question.

'I really can't see it,' said Annabel with a gulp of laughter.

'I wonder if seeing me here, married to Terry, added to Alice's feelings of dissatisfaction?' said Sarah. She was clearly still puzzled by Alice's slide into criminal activity.

Annabel had wondered that herself but had not liked to say it. 'Perhaps, but you fell in love.'

'Yes I did. I was very lucky to find someone as wonderful as Terry … but his wealth almost put me off and it has caused a rift between me and my parents, my mother in particular.'

Annabel supposed that Sarah's marriage must have taken Sarah out of her parents' world and into a world where perhaps they didn't feel comfortable.

'They adore Jonny, of course, but they aren't at ease with Terry and they don't like coming here. I think Mum would have liked me to marry a school teacher or a bank manager, someone like that. This,' she swept her hand around them, 'is beyond their comprehension. We tried to move them here, there's a lovely house on the estate, but they won't move – and I can't blame them.'

'What do they do?'

'Dad's a fisherman – I grew up in Lowestoft – and Mum cooks at the local primary school. They were proud of what they'd achieved and proud of me. I hoped that decorating my bedroom might help my mother accept our marriage. I think she created the bedroom she'd always wanted. For a while it was as if we were together as we used to be.'

'But you're not very comfortable with it?'

'Oh dear! Did it show? I just find the roses a bit … too much.'

'The roses don't extend to Sir Terrence's room,' said Annabel.

Sarah laughed. 'His instruction to the interior decorator was, "Anything but roses" – or words to that effect. I have to say that I think he got Terry's room right. The rest all seem a bit …'

'If you don't like the roses, can't you just change them?'

'Oh no! Mum would be upset. And also, it all cost so much!'

So, now you're stuck with them. Perhaps all wasn't necessarily a bed of roses in the world of the super rich. Or maybe, in this case, there were just *too many* roses. 'Had you thought of asking Dorothy for help? She is really interested in interior design and I'm sure she'd love to help.'

Sarah looked interested. 'Do you think she would?'

'You could ask.'

'There's something I need to say …' Sarah started, then stopped. Then she stood up. 'Shall we walk?'

Annabel wondered what it could be that Sarah wanted to say. She understood the need to walk. It was always easier talking about difficult things whilst you walked.

They set off along the edge of the lake.

'I want to explain about Ferdy. You must have wondered how I could have done what I did?'

Annabel had indeed wondered.

'The truth is that I did love him. I still do.'

Annabel felt a sudden chill.

'But I'm not *in* love with him. I'd realised that by the time we went to his parents' house. At least, I knew that something was missing. I didn't want to hurt him. I felt terrible for not realising sooner, for giving him such false hope.' She took a deep breath. 'And then I met Terry and, well, the difference – from loving someone to *being* in love with them.'

Annabel understood the difference.

'I told Ferdy I couldn't marry him. It was the worst two weeks of my life. And then Terry turned up on my doorstep and said he'd left his wife and wanted to be with me.'

'So you hadn't spoken to Sir Terrence about it before? You didn't know that he was in love with you?'

'I had no idea. It was the most wonderful thing! He described it as like being hit by a thunderbolt. I felt the same.'

She turned back towards the house.

'But think how terrible it would have been if I had married Ferdy, and then he met you, as he almost certainly would have done, given his connection to Alec. I think that you and he are meant to be together … just as Terry and I are meant to be together.'

Did Sarah really believe what she was saying or was this just a convenient way of dealing with 'the Ferdy problem'? It was almost enough to make one want to do the exact opposite.

Annabel had the distinct impression that the subject was now closed. The ball had been passed to her and it was up to her to pass on Sarah's explanation to Ferdy. Part of her wanted to tell Sarah to speak to Ferdy herself – too many people had offloaded their problems onto her shoulders this weekend – but then, did she really want Sarah to have that particular discussion with Ferdy? No, she did not.

This morning the house had looked sinister, now the curved frontage seemed to be closing in on the occupants. Annabel thought of the locked gate and entry system, the high walls and the armed guards protecting Johnny. She longed to be back at Haddens.

'Maybe you could arrange for Alice to have acting lessons,' She suggested.

Sarah wrinkled her brow, 'Reward her for her attempted blackmail?'

'Just a suggestion.'

'You know,' said Sarah, 'one of reasons Terry fell for this house was its name. He said it was perfect for us because I "completed" him.'

CHAPTER TWENTY

Back indoors, Annabel ran up to her bedroom. She wanted, needed, to be on her own.

As she emerged some short time later she almost ran into Lucy who was in tears and running blindly along the passageway towards her room.

'Oh! Sorry!' Lucy cried. 'Oh, it's you.' She sounded relieved.

She's glad it's me, not someone else. But who?

'Is everything all right?' Annabel asked, concerned.

'Oh … I … yes everything is fine. Don't mind me.' She made as if to brush past.

What could have upset her? Perhaps it was Thomas' death?

'It's terrible about poor Thomas, isn't it?' she said.

Lucy stopped and looked back at her as if trying to remember who Thomas was, then said, 'Oh, yes, absolutely awful, the poor man.' She hovered, still wanting to get away but conscious that perhaps manners required her to stay.

So, not Thomas. Annabel wondered if she was the only person to mourn Thomas. Then she remembered her conversation with Gerald. Perhaps he had just told

Lucy of her mother's mental illness. That would be enough to make anyone cry.

'Have you seen your father?' she made her voice kind.

Lucy stared at her in surprise as well she might if her father hadn't spoken to her. 'No. Is something wrong?'

Annabel hastened to reassure her. So she wasn't crying about her mother either. What was it then that had made her cry?

With one final curious look, Lucy made her escape.

Annabel made her way slowly back towards the gallery. If she could get her thoughts in order, she might be able to make sense of it all. Instead of going back down the stairs she turned into the gallery and started to walk round the paintings, looking at them all in turn but not actually taking them in. The Monet was particularly mesmeric. The more she looked at it, the more unfocussed her eyes became, the more she saw. She felt that she was being drawn into the picture, into the water, the colour washing over her.

The sound of a door closing downstairs broke the spell and Annabel moved on to the dark portrait. She really didn't like this picture. It was sinister and brooding and the man's eyes seemed to follow you around the room. She wondered why Sir Terrence had bought it. Suddenly she remembered that she thought it had looked like Alexi. In all the turmoil of being chloroformed and finding Thomas and then the arrival of the police, she had forgotten. She drew forward and and studied the picture closely. It did look like Alexi! Then she looked afresh with mounting astonishment. The thing that had caught her attention when she'd looked at the painting before – that glint in the subject's eye – was missing. She squeezed her eyes closed and opened them again. Perhaps her eyes were tired? Perhaps it was just that the light was different.

Annabel was attuned to the possibility of works of art being reproduced, the originals having been stolen – it had happened to her father – but had that made her over sensitive to such things? Was she seeing reproductions where none existed?

But no, this picture was definitely different.

Art theft *as well as* jewel theft, industrial espionage *and* murder? It wasn't possible, was it? And if so, it would have to have been swapped sometime since she'd seen it the previous morning. That meant it must have been premeditated. Someone – Alexi? – had come with the reproduction in their possession ready to make the swap. But, really, it could be anyone.

What should she do? Tell Ferdy, but also Sir Terrence. Not the police, yet. She hurried down as fast as she could on the treacherous stairs, and tried the sitting room first. Sir Terrence and Ferdy were there but they weren't alone. DS Idle was there too. He and Ferdy were poring over a piece of paper.

'I'm not getting anything that makes any sense,' said Ferdy.

'"C. E. R. Loge",' offered Idle doubtfully.

'As I say, nothing likely,' said Ferdy. 'I've got "Col. E. Reg".'

Idle gave a smirk. 'It could just be "a Greek"?'

'It could be any bloody thing,' said Ferdy. 'I think we're barking up the wrong tree.'

Annabel drew near. Her old neighbour and friend Enid loved crosswords, and particularly, anagrams. They were trying to find the meaning of El Greco. She recognised the circles of letters, the separation of the consonants and vowels.

'No luck?' she said.

'I'll keep trying,' said Idle to Ferdy, 'but I think you're right. I'll be with the boss if you find anything new.' He left the room.

Annabel waited until he had gone before speaking.

'We have another problem,' she said.

They both looked up, Ferdy with interest, Sir Terrence with a degree of impatience. 'Yes?' he said.

'I don't think it's got anything to do with the espionage business' she began, and noted that Sir Terrence looked even more irritated, 'but, someone has taken your portrait upstairs and substituted a fake.' She didn't want to mention her suspicions of Alexi yet. Not to Sir Terrence, at any rate.

Now she had their attention.

'Nonsense!' said Sir Terrence.

'Are you sure?' said Ferdy.

Sir Terrence looked at Ferdy as though he were mad too.

'She knows about such things,' said Ferdy to his father.

Sir Terrence looked at Annabel. 'What makes you think that?'

Not pleased that he needed Ferdy's approbation to take her seriously, Annabel said, 'You'd better come and see.'

Patently unconvinced, Sir Terrence followed Annabel and Ferdy upstairs. They both studied the picture. It was then that Annabel realised Sir Terrence knew very little about art.

'Looks the same to me,' he said.

Or maybe she was wrong about the picture?

'There was a glint in the eye. It lifted the picture.' She was annoyed to hear a trace of uncertainty creeping into her voice.

Sir Terrence turned to go.

'Let's get Matt to look at it,' said Ferdy. 'He'll know.'

'Oh, very well,' said Sir Terrence. 'Where is he?'

They found Matt in Dorothy's room.

Without voicing her thoughts, Annabel asked him to look at the picture. Looking at her suspiciously he gave the picture a cursory look then paused, stepped closer and studied the picture carefully. A flush rose up his neck.

'Well, when I looked at this picture yesterday morning it was a very nice Holbein. This … this is not a Holbein. It's a good reproduction but it's missing …'

'The glint in the eye?' said Annabel.

Matt turned to her and smiled, 'Precisely!' Then he frowned, 'This seems to happen a lot around you.' It was not a compliment.

'Well, well!' said Sir Terrence. He looked at Annabel with dawning respect. 'Someone's been busy … presumably last night?'

'Can't see anyone carrying out the substitution in broad daylight,' agreed Ferdy.

'Whoever did this,' said Matt, 'came prepared with the replacement. They knew the painting was here.'

'The only person who's been here before is Humphrey,' said Sir Terrence. 'But I can't see him being interested in a Holbein. It's not nearly old enough.'

Annabel remembered the professor's threadbare dressing gown. He might well be interested in money.

'What about when you bought it?' asked Matt. 'Would anyone have seen you buy it?'

'Unlikely,' said Sir Terrence evasively.

Annabel recalled his reluctance to say where he had acquired the painting. She wondered if he had bought it through some illicit route.

Matt's expression showed that his thoughts were running along similar lines but she wasn't surprised when he didn't pursue the matter. Accusing your host and future father-in-law of dealing on the black market wouldn't rank high on his list of favourite actions. She imagined that discretion would always be his preferred course of valour.

'Thank you, Matthew,' said Sir Terrence. It was a dismissal and Matt took it as such, ambling away down the corridor back to Dorothy's room.

Idle came up the stairs and found them. 'We've

finished in the library,' he said. 'You can go back in if you want.'

They did want.

Sir Terrence led the way back down the stairs and they entered the library. Not much had changed. Annabel noted fresh finger print dust on the handle of the door to the French window and more on the desk, chairs, picture frames and desk lamp.

Sir Terrence stood in the middle of the room and looked around him with a bleak face. This was his room. Annabel could understand his feeling of displacement. She wondered how long it would take before he felt at home once more in the room.

He raised his head, 'So, where does this leave us?'

Ferdy also raised his head. 'I doubt if it was the same person. That means that we had two people wandering around last night.'

'As well as ourselves,' put in Annabel.

'Indeed,' said Ferdy. 'I suspect that the picture was exchanged after I went to bed and before our spy visited Annabel – so between eleven o'clock and two o'clock. Any later than that and they probably would have been seen by us or the spy.

'They may have bumped into one another. Neither would be wanting to reveal that they were up and about in the night,' said Annabel.

'Possibly,' said Ferdy, 'but wouldn't the one who nicked the painting have said something. It is murder, after all. And they could just say that they were looking for a drink – something to explain why they were up and about. They don't know that we know the painting has been substituted with a fake.'

'We're assuming that they are public spirited enough to care,' said Sir Terrence.

That was true.

'There's Alice as well,' said Annabel. 'Where was she when she saw Thomas being tipped over the wall?'

'Her bedroom is on the other side of the house,' said Sir Terrence, 'but there is a fire escape that runs down the end of the house. She might, conceivably have been standing out there and seen the murderer tip Thomas over the wall.'

'You don't think she might have stolen the picture?' Annabel suggested. 'Maybe that's why she didn't mention to the police about seeing the murderer. And if she is prepared to steal a picture, she mightn't think twice about trying her hand at blackmail.'

'The police have searched her room,' said Ferdy. 'They would have found the picture.'

'Once she recovers, we'll know everything,' said Annabel.

'It might be too late by then,' said Ferdy.

'Are we going to tell Grange about the picture?' Annabel asked.

Ferdy looked at his father. Annabel wasn't surprised when, after only the briefest of pauses, Sir Terrence shook his head.

'Can't see it's relevant to their enquiries,' he said.

DCI Grange tapped on the half open door and entered the room.

'Alexi Galkin is demanding to leave,' he said.

They all stared at him.

'But, we can't allow that. We think he might have photographed the documents!' said Sir Terrence.

'Unfortunately, there's little we can do about it.'

Ferdy walked over to the window and back again. 'I think we should phone Rosemary,' he said. 'This is her game.'

Grange nodded. 'I'll try to hold him off for a while.' He left the room.

'Is this line secure?' Ferdy asked his father.

'No, but the one up in my room is.'

'We probably should have phoned her before this,' said Annabel.

'Well, we didn't,' said Ferdy.

The house seemed strangely quiet as they made their way back upstairs.

'Where is everybody?' Annabel asked.

'Holed up in their rooms,' said Ferdy. 'Wouldn't you be with a murderer about?'

Once in Sir Terrence's bedroom with the door shut Ferdy spoke to his father.

'Do you want to speak to Rosemary?'

Sir Terrence hesitated, 'You're the one dealing with her.'

Annabel hid a smile. It seemed that Sir Terrence, who probably ate prime ministers for breakfast, had his limitations.

Ferdy rang and spoke to Phoebe. There was a short wait until Rosemary came on the line. Annabel moved closer so that her ear was next to the receiver. Ferdy adjusted the handset so that she could hear better. His hair tickled her ear and his hand brushed her chin. It was a distraction.

'Well?' Rosemary's voice was crisp. 'Has anything happened?'

'Quite a lot,' said Ferdy. He proceeded to explain everything that had happened including the reproduction Holbein but leaving out mention of Dorothy's ring.

Rosemary heard him out in silence.

'So, Thomas was Special Branch,' she said.

'Yes, Did you know?'

'No I did not! That bungling fool!' She spoke with venom.

'Who? Thomas?'

'No! Sir Richard. I presume it was he who introduced him into the household?'

'Yes, so Dad says.'

'Well, he's just got a man killed,' said Rosemary bitterly.

'Who? My father?' Ferdy was indignant.

'No, Sir Richard! Now be quiet, I need to think.'

Ferdy raised his gaze to the ceiling but said nothing. They waited.

'You say that Alexi wants to leave?'

'Yes.'

'Well, you might as well let him go,' she said.

Ferdy took the phone away from his ear and looked at it.

'Did I hear you correctly?' he asked. 'We think he might have photographed the documents!'

'I don't think so.'

Ferdy took a deep breath and held it for some moments. 'And why would that be?'

'Can't you work it out? Because of the Holbein, of course.' Rosemary clicked her tongue impatiently. 'Someone else has photographed the documents. You have to keep looking. And don't let anything happen to Alice. It's vital that we find out what she knows.'

'A few less riddles and a few more facts might help,' said Ferdy with asperity. 'We're not getting the whole picture here.'

Rosemary laughed. 'My dear young man, when do any of us get "the whole picture".'

'Maybe you'd like to come and take over?' he suggested.

'Maybe I should?' she said. 'In fact, yes, I will.'

The call ended and Annabel looked at Ferdy in horror. 'You had to say it!'

'Yes, but I didn't think she would take me up on it!'

'What did she say?' asked Sir Terrence.

'She's not happy,' Ferdy said. 'She's on her way over.'

Sir Terrence ran his hand over his face. 'Oh God, is she? I have to say that I am even less happy than Rosemary. I do not expect to be kept in the dark.' His voice had a dangerous edge.

Annabel could believe it. Sir Terrence had been kept in the dark about many things. No doubt someone would get an earful in due course.

'We're to let Alexi go,' said Ferdy. 'She doesn't think he's the spy. We're to keep looking for the negatives and guard Alice as though she's the crown jewels.'

'But what if Alice dies?' Annabel said. 'At the moment she's our only lead.'

'All our eggs in one basket,' Ferdy agreed. 'We'd better get Grange to double the guard, especially if Alexi is to be allowed to leave.'

'So you still think it could be Alexi, then?' she asked.

'I don't *want* to, but what if Rosemary's wrong?'

'I can't help wondering, *why now?*' Annabel said.

'What do you mean?' asked Sir Terrence.

'I mean why does Alexi suddenly want to leave now? You'd have thought that if he was going to leave he would have done so as soon as the police finished their searches.'

'Would have looked a bit obvious,' said Ferdy.

'It looks a bit obvious now,' countered Annabel.

Ferdy frowned, then shrugged. 'I don't know. But we'd better go and tell Grange.'

CHAPTER TWENTY-ONE

They found Grange in the morning room. He was standing over at the window, hands clasped behind his back. As ever, he gave off an aura of calm but his face, when he turned, looked troubled.

Ferdy quickly brought him up to date with what Rosemary had said. He listened to them in silence. His first words proved that he had grasped the nub of the issue.

'I have already arranged for a double guard on Miss Brown but I'll make sure that is reinforced. It's unsatisfactory to have to allow Galkin to leave but we can always pick him up at a later stage if necessary. We'll do our best to make sure he doesn't leave the country until we know, one way or another, if he's our man.'

'Let's hope your "best" is good enough,' said Sir Terrence.

Annabel remembered what Ferdy had said about how it was difficult to stop people leaving the country if they were determined to do so and had a support network. Grange was being realistic.

So, Alice's surname was Brown. No doubt that would be changed to something more glitzy if she ever became a film star.

'I think we should go and see Alexi,' said Ferdy. 'Any idea where he is?'

'I believe he's up in his room, packing,' said Grange. 'If you're speaking to him, you can tell him he can leave.'

Annabel and Ferdy made their way back up the stairs.

'I just want to have another look at that picture,' she said.

'Why? It's not the real one,' said Ferdy. 'That was good work on your part. I don't think Dad would have noticed the swap.'

Annabel agreed.

They stood in front of the portrait. Why would Rosemary have said what she had about the Holbein? Was she thinking about the telegrams received by Alexi? There had been a Holbein in the list but it had been in Amsterdam.

'Does he remind you of somebody?' said Annabel.

'Remind me of someone? No ... who?'

'Well, the first time I saw it I had the feeling that he was Russian. Then last night, in the observation room, it occurred to me that he looked like Alexi.'

Ferdy peered at the picture. 'Good God! You're right. He does look like Alexi.'

'I think that's why I thought it was Russian,' said Annabel. 'But I hadn't put two and two together.'

'Same nose, same eyes.'

'And do you remember on that first night at dinner,

Alexi talked about art work being stolen in the war? I think this might have been stolen from his family home.'

'Not by my father!' said Ferdy.

'No! But your father might have bought it from whoever stole it, or from someone who bought it from whoever stole it. It may have changed hands several times. I think he knows that it has a shady background. Matt said that, after the war, the question of provenance was often impossible to prove.'

Ferdy was looking deeply troubled. 'This is going to be awkward,' he said.

That was an understatement.

'But we need to speak to Alexi about it,' Annabel said. It was not a question.

Ferdy met her eyes, grimaced and nodded his head.

They knocked on Alexi's door, then waited for some time. Eventually the door was opened. Annabel's eyes widened in shock. Alexi looked a changed man; his face was drawn, his eyes had lost their light, his shoulders were hunched, he looked as though he had just received some very bad news.

'Are you all right?' Annabel asked.

He shook his head and turned away.

'Can we come in?' asked Ferdy.

Alexi shrugged. He stepped back to allow them in. Ferdy and Annabel exchanged puzzled looks. This was not how they had expected him to act. Could he already have a suspicion that they were on to him? Or was something else bothering him?

Alexi's suitcase was on his bed and it looked as though he had almost completed his packing.

'We gather you're off,' said Ferdy.

Alexi shrugged again but his eyes were watchful.

'We came to tell you that Grange says he's finished with his questions as far as you're concerned.'

'So, I'm free to go?' Alexi lifted an ironic eyebrow.

'But why now?' Annabel asked the question that had been bothering her.

'As good a time as any,' he replied. 'No point in hanging around.' His voice was bitter. He got his velvet jacket out of the wardrobe, folded it carefully and placed it in the suitcase.

If the painting was anywhere it would be in the suitcase. Annabel could see that Ferdy was also looking at the suitcase. He was pacing up and down, psyching himself up to ask the question that could end his friendship with Alexi.

'Alexi,' she stepped in, 'there's something we have to ask you.'

Alexi straightened up and faced them. 'What?' He looked tired, not guilty.

Annabel started to doubt herself.

At that point Sir Terrence entered the room. It was the worst possible timing. 'I understand you're leaving us,' he said to Alexi.

'I am.' said Alexi. 'I thank you for an … interesting …

weekend but I have things to do.' He turned back to Annabel, 'What must you ask?'

Horribly conscious of Sir Terrence's presence, Annabel forced herself to continue.

'There was a portrait out in the gallery. It has now been replaced. The man in the picture looks very like you and, we think … you might have taken it.' There, it was out.

Sir Terrence took an audible breath. 'Alexi, I –' he started.

'Portrait? What portrait?' said Alexi. Gone was his miserable expression. Now he looked fully engaged.

'The Holbein, the one with the black background.'

Sir Terrence stepped forward. 'Alexi, I don't know why Annabel is talking to you about this but –' He stopped as Ferdy made a brief but definite negating movement with his hand.

Alexi saw it too. '"We" includes you does it, Ferdy?'

Ferdy stepped forward, his face pale, 'Just let us look in the suitcase, Alexi, please.'

Sir Terrence looked from one to the other but this time kept silent.

After a moment, Alexi shrugged. 'Why not?' He stepped back.

Surely he wouldn't give way this easily if he were guilty? What if they'd got it wrong?

'Try not to mess up my packing,' Alexi's voice was dry.

Ferdy started to lift out the clothes revealing the base of the suitcase with its pattern of gold crests on a grey background.

They all looked into the empty suitcase. There was no painting. Annabel's head drained of blood. She wished she were anywhere but there, at that moment, facing such a failure. How could she ever have imagined that she had it in her to be a detective?

'Alexi, I can only … apologise …' Sir Terrence's words grated. 'Miss Staple was –'

Miss Staple

Ferdy interrupted, 'Come on, Alexi! That one's as old as the hills!' He reached into the bottom of the suitcase and pressed one corner. The base lifted up and revealed … the portrait.

Annabel swayed on her feet with a corresponding wash of relief that threatened to overset her, as the initial shock had not. Ferdy took her hand and gripped it. The warmth and strength of that grasp flooded into her body and soul.

Alexi looked up, his puckish smile appeared and he shrugged his shoulders much as a school boy might do when caught out in a prank.

Then he grew serious, reflective, his eyes seeing long ago images.

'It hung in my grandmother's bedroom on the wall above her old oak chest of drawers with the brass handles. She kept her silver-backed brush and mirror there and the carved wooden box which contained her hair pins. It was always dark in that corner of the room, away from the window, the sun fell the other way, across her bed and the patchwork coverlet. He is my many times great-grandfather. She said it … he … could have been my grandfather. When she thought nobody was looking she used to touch his mouth with her fingers. She always said that I had inherited the family face.' He turned to Annabel, 'You saw it, the likeness.'

His voice hardened. 'It was stolen by the Nazis. My family … I … have been searching for it ever since. I have friends out looking. One told me of seeing this here, said it looked like I'd described.'

The silence that followed this speech was deep.

Finally, Sir Terrence spoke. 'I don't expect my guests to steal from me.'

Alexi nodded acknowledgment.

'Don't leave yet. I'll have a think about this. In the meantime, I'll have it back.' Sir Terrence held out his hand.

With infinite care, Alexi lifted the painting out of his suitcase and handed it to Sir Terrence.

Ferdy cleared his throat. 'I assume you did the swap last night. Did you happen to see anybody else up and about?'

Alexi looked at him and his eyes were cold – not those of a friend. Annabel also saw interest in Alexi's eyes.

'Last night, at one o'clock, I saw no one,' Alexi replied. 'Why?'

'Just wondered.'

Sir Terrence left the room taking the portrait with him.

'Were you thinking of hiding it in your car?' Annabel asked, 'When you were working on your car yesterday?'

The look on Alexi's face told her that she was right.

Ferdy was lost in his own thoughts. 'What did you expect?' he burst out. 'This is family!'

'We're even now,' said Alexi.

What did he mean by that?

'I have never considered us anything but,' said Ferdy bitterly.

Ferdy and Annabel clattered down the stairs.

'Air,' said Ferdy, 'I need air.'

Annabel expected him to head for the back lawn but he went straight for the front door and they were out onto the drive and heading for a nearby copse of silver birch trees. It wasn't until they were in the shade of their light canopy that he slowed.

'That was … horrible,' said Annabel.

Ferdy gave a short laugh. 'I've had better experiences. Thank you, by the way. You stepped in, took the lead.' He stopped and took her hand. 'Really, I can't thank you enough.'

Annabel looked down. For a moment she felt unable to speak. 'Well, you repaid me by finding that portrait. A hidden panel! How do you know all this stuff?'

'Alec was a good teacher.'

He must have been. But did Ferdy know more than he had learnt from Alec?

'What did he mean when he said, "We're even now"?'

'Oh, he had this ridiculous idea he owes me.' He shrugged. 'I'm quite glad he's let that one drop. It was all a bit embarrassing.'

Annabel wondered if she'd ever get to the bottom of their relationship. Perhaps there were some things it was best not to know.

'And well done, *really* well done, for spotting the likeness to Alexi. I told you before that working with you was like being back with Alec. Well, that was exactly the sort of brilliance he would have shown.'

Brilliance?

'Seriously, you showed real courage back then, especially when my father ploughed in.'

Annabel didn't think she'd forget '*Miss Staple*', in a hurry.

'Do you think your father will let Alexi have the portrait?'

'I don't know. But the good thing is that he got Alexi to stay for a bit longer.'

True. She took a few steps away to distance herself from him. 'Sarah told me she didn't know your father was in love with her until after she'd broken up with you. She just knew she was in love with him. She's very sorry for the hurt she caused you.' She turned to face him.

He smiled wryly. 'I've known it ever since I saw them together. Three years of anger, wasted!'

'Three necessary years, perhaps?' Annabel thought of the three years she had mourned her mother and stepfather.

'Annabel, I …' Ferdy said.

Annabel held her breath.

'There you are!' Dorothy's voice sang out. 'I've

been looking for you everywhere.' Her slim figure, in black and white, stood out like a punctuation mark amongst the white-stemmed birches. She came closer and her face fell, 'What is it? Aren't you pleased to see me?'

Ferdy sighed. 'Always pleased to see you, Dodo. It's just your timing could have been better.'

Dorothy looked from one to the other her puzzlement turning to joy. 'Oh my God! Are you …?'

'No,' said Ferdy, flatly.

'Oh … well … shall I go away again?'

'Not necessary,' he said. 'What did you want?'

'Are you sure because …'

'I said no!'

'Oh … well, I only came to tell you that I've had a thought,' Dorothy continued, 'a *brilliant* thought! And, it's all down to you,' she beamed at Annabel.

'Me? What did I do? And what thought?'

'It's about my allowance. I've been puzzling and puzzling what to do and then it came to me. It was something you said to me about Lucy not having any money.'

'Lucy?' said Ferdy. 'She's loaded.'

'*I* know that,' said Dorothy, 'but Annabel didn't and if she didn't perhaps Matt doesn't either.'

'And this is going where, exactly?' said Ferdy.

'Well, I don't think I'm going to tell you *that*, in case it doesn't work. But I know you must have been worrying, so I thought I'd let you know.'

'Dear Dodo,' said Ferdy. 'Our minds are now at rest.'

'I knew you'd be pleased,' said Dorothy. 'Oh, and tea's been laid out in the sitting room.'

Annabel suddenly realised that she was ravenously hungry. It seemed ages since lunchtime. 'Tea!'

'Come on,' Ferdy grinned and took her hand. It lodged within his as though it belonged there. 'Let's get you some food. I've never known anyone to eat as much as you do.'

'I know,' said Dorothy ruefully. 'And where does she put it all? It's not fair.'

DCI Grange met them in the hall.

'A word,' he said.

Ferdy and Annabel followed him into the morning room. Dorothy looked intrigued but went on into the sitting room.

DCI Grange shut the door behind them. 'I don't know what you said to Galkin but he's staying, for the time being,' he said.

'That's good,' said Ferdy.

Grange let the silence hang.

'I think my father might have said something to him,' Ferdy offered.

'Hmph,' said Grange. 'Alice Brown has not recovered consciousness, yet.'

'Oh.'

More silence.

'Have you had tea?' asked Annabel.

'Yes, Miss Staple I have, thank you.'

CHAPTER TWENTY-TWO

'That didn't go well,' said Ferdy as they left Grange and went back into the hall. 'It's all very well working together but we can't tell him every single little thing.'

Hardly little, but she agreed with Ferdy that Grange didn't need to know about the Holbein.

The atmosphere in the sitting room was uncomfortable. The members of the household stood around like actors in a play where the clapper board is about to be closed to start the next scene. Only Violet, Humphrey and Sarah were sitting. Annabel wasn't surprised to see that Violet had bagged Sir Terrence's chair again. No doubt he would be glad when the Harcourts left. The possibility of leaving had been the subject of discussion.

'If he can leave, I don't see why we can't!' Violets voice was high and strained.

'You know that we can leave now, if we want,' said Gerald, an edge to his patience, 'but it might be better to stay until … everything is sorted.'

Annabel knew Gerald was imagining the police turning up at his office to continue their investigations. She could understand why he might not want that.

'Are you sure you don't want to leave?' Sir Terrence

spoke blandly but the underlying hint of hope was evident enough to make Gerald stiffen.

Sarah bit her lip to hide a smile. 'Would you like some tea?' she asked Ferdy and Annabel. 'And do help yourself to cake.'

Annabel helped herself to a generous slice of chocolate cake. Her hand hovered over the cake forks. She left them where they were.

'When are you off, then?' Gerald asked Alexi.

'I'm not.'

'Not what?' Violet stared.

'Not going,' said Alexi. 'Why leave, when we're all having so much fun?'

There was a crash as Humphrey's stick, which had been leaning up against his chair, fell on the floor.

Lucy bent down to pick it up. 'Sorry, so clumsy of me.'

He took it from her with a stiff smile of thanks.

Matt looked troubled. 'Seriously though, I am going to have to get back to Christie's tomorrow. How much longer do you think this is going to go on?'

'And how many more of us are going to have to die?' cried Violet.

'I know as much as you do,' Sir Terrence said. 'We must just try to be patient.'

'I'm tired of being patient,' said Violet, 'and my knee hurts. Gerald, I want to go back to our room.'

Gerald cast an angry glance at Sir Terrence and then stooped and helped Violet out of her chair. In fact, he practically lifted her since she did little to help him, and it didn't look as though he found it difficult. Perhaps they had written him off too soon. Perhaps he could have dragged Thomas out of the library and tipped him over the wall.

Why did she feel that the answer was within reach … if only she could cut through all the fog.

'I thought I might go out for a breath of fresh air after tea,' Sarah spoke to Dorothy, 'if you'd like to come along.'

'Oh!' Dorothy hesitated. 'All right, yes.' She was still being loyal to her mother. It would take time, perhaps.

Ferdy came over to Annabel. 'Let's go and have another word with chef John,' he said. 'Maybe there's something more he can tell us.'

Glad for something to do, Annabel followed him across the hall and through to the kitchen. The record player was playing 'Crazy' sung by Patsy Cline. Annabel loved this song. Ferdy was right, John did have great taste in music. They found him leaning up against the back door, smoking. He reminded Annabel of the American actor James Stewart. That same lanky, lazy elegance with a hard edge.

'Anything new?' asked Ferdy.

John cast a sharp glance at them from under his brows. 'I think that's for you to say.'

'Alice hasn't regained consciousness,' said Annabel.

'That's not good.' He took a deep pull on his cigarette and expelled the smoke out into the fresh air. 'She's OK. A bit off with the fairies, but OK.'

'We wondered if you'd had any more thoughts about when you found her?' said Ferdy.

The record came to an end, the needle retracted, the next record clunked down, there was a burr and then the thrumming first notes of 'The Great Pretender'.

John looked at them meditatively. 'Like what?'

'Well, you saw the man. Was he big? Small? Long hair, short?'

'If you'd listened the first time, I only caught a glimpse. No more than a shape.'

'So, nothing stood out.'

'If it had I would have said.' He drew on his cigarette. 'If I had to state an opinion, I'd say you're looking for someone athletic.'

'Athletic?'

'Just the way he moved. But then, as I say, I only caught a glimpse.'

They stood in frustrated silence.

'That was a delicious chocolate cake.' Annabel wanted to say something nice. Ferdy had been a bit hard on John.

He looked at her, his eyes crinkling, 'Thank you. Now, if you don't mind, I need to get on. Looks like we might have a full house again tonight.'

'What are you making?' Annabel asked with interest.

'Well … I thought we'd have the beef planned for lunchtime, then I've got the raspberry mouse, probably enough but it's always good to have a spare. So I thought …'

But Annabel was no longer listening. Spare …

another one … 'The Great Pretender'. All of a sudden the fog cleared.

'I've lost her,' said John to Ferdy. 'Everyone likes to eat but nobody, except Lady Sarah, cares about –'

'No,' Annabel interrupted, 'it's not that. I've got it! At least, I think I have.'

'Got what?' asked John.

'You know who did it?' asked Ferdy in rising excitement.

'She does?'

But Annabel was already out into the kitchen corridor. Ferdy caught up with her halfway along and grabbed her arm.

'Now hold on!' he said. 'This is where you go charging off without thinking and get yourself into all sorts of trouble. Where are you off to and who do you think did it?'

In the gloom of the hallway she could hardly see his face but she could hear the concern in his voice.

'I'm not sure of it myself yet but I *promise* I won't get into any trouble. You've got to trust me. Just get your dad into the library and I'll meet you both there.'

'But, where are you going?'

'The cloakroom,' she called back.

When Annabel entered the library some short time later she was pleased to see Ferdy and his father standing beside the desk. The sun shone in through the open French windows. All traces of the fingerprint dust were gone and the room appeared quiet and peaceful.

They both looked her way as she entered. The look of relief in Ferdy's eyes was painful to see.

Sir Terrence looked at what she was carrying in her hand and cried out, 'That's Humphrey's stick! He needs that. I've never seen him without it.'

'Yes,' she replied, 'I think it is his stick. Or, at least, it's *one* of his sticks. I think he has two and I think that this one contains a camera.'

She handed the stick to Ferdy who raised his eyebrows at her but took it without comment and started to press and pull the moulded handle. Under his administrations it clicked open and revealed … a tiny camera.

'Well, what do you know?' said Ferdy. 'Well done, Annabel. Well done.'

'But …' Sir Terrence stared at the camera, his face draining of colour. 'Not Humphrey?' He sat down hard in the desk chair.

'Whatever made you think of this?' asked Ferdy.

'It was lots of things and none of them made any sense, at first. I knew that Grange had checked everyone's belongings, including Humphrey's stick so it had to be something else. And then Dorothy said Matt had a *second* bookmark and Sarah said that Humphrey was forgetful and used to leave things behind when he came to stay. I think he did that deliberately to establish his poor memory and then on one occasion he left his stick behind. Over time, it would have just blended in with the other sticks in the cloakroom.'

'He probably had no idea, at that time, that this specific documentation would be here. He probably did it on spec in case something came to his attention that might be worth stealing. You said that he visited often. He could have known about your safes, where they were. He may have already worked out how to open them. And I'm sure,' she continued bitterly, 'that he knew about your observation room. And then John said he thought the man was athletic –'

'But, exactly, it can't be Humphrey,' Sir Terrence interrupted. 'He could never run or carry anything heavy with his bad leg.'

'Well, that's just it. Is his leg still bad? I think it has been probably been quite all right for some time now. It was John playing 'The Great Pretender' that was the final clue. All along we have discounted Humphrey because of his leg but what if he was just pretending?'

'It must be him. The camera in the stick proves it,' said Ferdy.

Into the silence that followed came a slow handclap from the second of the French windows, the one furthest away from them.

They all froze and looked towards it.

Professor Calder entered the room. It was immediately apparent that he walked with only the slightest limp – none of the hitherto leaning on his stick. But that wasn't what fixed their attention. What fixed their attention was the gun that he held in his hand. Annabel had never been faced by a gun before. The round, black hole at the end of the barrel drew the gaze with a ghastly fascination. This was a man who had killed already and who had nothing to lose by killing again.

CHAPTER TWENTY-THREE

Sir Terrence stood up on shaky legs. 'Humphrey …'
Humphrey looked almost as pale as Sir Terrence.
He took a few paces towards them and stopped. The sun
shining in through the second French window sent his
shadow across the richly coloured carpet.

'So,' he said, 'you know it all.'

'You don't deny it then?' Sir Terrence said.

A rhetorical question; the pistol told its own story.

'Oh no, I don't deny it. There would be no point now,
would there? You have it all worked out. I underestimated
you,' he said to Annabel. 'You're far more clever than you
look.' He gave a short laugh.

Annabel was fed up with people's assumptions concerning her.

'But why?' Sir Terrence said. 'Why did you do it? Why
betray your country?'

Humphrey appeared to consider this, his hand holding the gun lowered slightly. Annabel sensed Ferdy moving away from her to the right.

Humphrey's hand jerked back up. 'Stay where you
are. I'm not a perfect shot but from this distance I can't
miss. Why betray my country?' he continued. 'The answer is surely, why not? What has this country ever done

for me? It's a corrupt, capitalist, cesspit full of people like you.' He turned his gaze to Sir Terrence, who swayed in response.

'Hasn't stopped you eating at my table, smoking my cigars,' Sir Terrence responded trenchantly.

'And again, why not? It served my purposes. No doubt you considered me your friend?'

'Yes, I did. Clearly, I was wrong.'

'People like you make me sick to my stomach. All you think about is money, money, money. You grab and you take and you never count the cost.' His finger tightened around the trigger.

'And Russia is better?' said Ferdy.

Humphrey turned to him. 'Yes, Russia is better. It's not perfect, but it is better by far than …' he swept his hand around the room, '… all *this.*'

Why didn't Grange appear?

'I think you'll find there are money grabbing bastards everywhere,' said Sir Terrence.

The gun swung back his way.

'You would know, of course,' said Humphrey.

'I suppose you were recruited at college,' said Ferdy, 'and your work involves you in travelling all round the world. No doubt you had handlers lined up at various places to take the information you stole.'

The gun swung back to Ferdy. Every time it swung between Ferdy and Sir Terrence it moved across Annabel who stood between the two of them.

'I suppose, you'd like me to tell you everything,

wouldn't you? All the names, all my contacts, everything I've stolen over the years – and it is a lot. People are so stupid. It really has been laughably easy.'

'And yet, here you are unmasked,' said Ferdy.

'Humphrey shrugged. 'Well, all things must come to an end.'

An insect buzzed in through the nearer French window and did a circuit of the room.

'So, it was you who hit my father on the head,' Ferdy said.

'I couldn't resist. It's something I've been wanting to do for years.'

Sir Terrence drew in his breath.

'And Thomas,' said Annabel. 'He caught you at it when you were photographing the documents and you killed him.'

'I regret Thomas. I don't think he was expecting to see me. By the time he realised what he was seeing, it was too late. I think I put all my rage into that blow; in under the sternum and straight up into the heart. If it's any consolation, he wouldn't have felt a thing.' His voice sounded weary.

Why 'rage'?

'How many people have you killed over the years?' asked Ferdy.

'Strangely enough, he was the first.'

'But you knew about the observation room, I suppose I should be grateful you just chloroformed me, didn't kill me,' said Annabel. She could feel Ferdy's annoyance at her interruption. She knew that he was trying to deflect the gun from his father. It was now levelled directly at herself – an unnerving experience.

'I liked you,' said Calder. 'You weren't like the rest of them. But that was a mistake. I've been making too many of those recently.'

I liked you too.

'It wasn't just ideological though, was it?' Annabel said. 'It was the boy who was beaten to death when you were at college. His name was Jasper, wasn't it?' This was a guess, but she thought she was right.

Humphrey rocked back on his heels.

Ferdy took a half step forward.

'Jasper! That was his name!' cried Sir Terrence, suddenly enlightened.

Annabel had never seen such a look of hatred as she saw then in Humphrey's eyes.

'Yes, Jasper, that was his name.' Humphrey took a deep breath, and went on bitterly, 'He was the … brightest … of us all. He was set upon by four fascist thugs and he was beaten and kicked to death. So how could I have any *love* for a country that allowed that to happen. They made only a cursory attempt to catch those who did it.'

'So, he was a …' Sir Terrence stopped.

There was a horrible silence and then Humphrey spoke.

'He was a human being, a young man.'

'Yes, of course he was,' Sir Terrence mumbled. 'I didn't know that you and he –'

'You didn't care. Nobody cared.'

'I don't suppose you'll find Russia any more enlightened,' said Ferdy.

'Maybe not, but it's all a little late for that now, isn't it?' said Humphrey.

It did seem so. *Where* was Grange?

'You must have known that it was a trap. Why did you go ahead?' she asked.

'I wanted the documents. Why else? And, honestly, I didn't take you seriously. All that "we need to talk" nonsense. It was laughable. Amateur.'

'And yet, here you are unmasked,' said Ferdy again.

'Here I am holding the gun,' retorted Humphrey.

Yes, the gun.

'Where did the gun come from?' asked Ferdy.

The gun swung back to cover him.

'Forethought. You never know when a gun might come in handy. I hid it where I was reasonably sure no one would look – behind the poetry section on the bookshelves. Wordsworth and Coleridge.'

So much for the police search. Grange would not be happy.

'But then there was Alice,' said Annabel. Did she see you? Was it blackmail?'

'Alice. Yes, she saw me, out on the terrace with Thomas. She tried to blackmail me. A pathetic amount – one hundred pounds. I knew I could snuff her out … like a candle.'

There was silence whilst they all thought of Alice, putting her life in danger for one hundred pounds.

'But you couldn't, could you?' Sir Terrence took over. 'Snuff her out? Alice is still alive.'

The gun swung back to Sir Terrence.

'Yes, it's all over and, really, it is time. There are only two more things I wish to do now.'

Two things?

Ferdy stepped urgently forward but the gun remained trained on Sir Terrence.

'I think,' Humphrey spoke to Sir Terrence, 'yes, I think I can wipe that smug look off your face. I can show you how it feels to lose someone you love more than anyone in the world.'

Annabel froze in horror. Where was Sarah?

But the gun hand swung back and centred on Ferdy. Into Humphrey's face came a look of determination.

'Noooo!' Annabel hurled herself across to Ferdy. She was barely aware of Sir Terrence's strangled cry or of the pink shape that tore into the library through the nearer of the two French windows emitting an Amazonian roar and catching Humphrey sideways on, taking him completely by surprise.

There was a deafening report as the gun went off. Annabel, caught in Ferdy's arms, waited for the impact and for a moment wondered if it was as she had read – that you didn't feel the bullet that killed you.

Ferdy clutched Annabel to him and buried his face in her hair. 'Don't *ever* do that again,' he whispered.

They both looked at the two shapes on the floor. Humphrey was spreadeagled face down on the carpet and sitting astride him, resplendent in pink, was Lucy. One of Humphrey's shoes had come off revealing a hole in the toe of his sock through which a pale toe emerged.

Into the stunned silence, Lucy said, 'I don't like men who wave guns around.'

Ferdy stepped forward and kicked the gun away from the professor's twitching fingers.

Sir Terrence sank to his knees.

'Where did the bullet go?' asked Annabel.

Ferdy nodded towards the convex mirror on the wall. It was shattered into little pieces revealing, like a dark and shameful secret, the observation room behind.

The door burst open and DCI Grange, closely followed by DS Idle and Sarah rushed in. Grange took in the scene before him and spoke sharply to Idle, 'Keep everyone else out of here.'

Idle left the room.

Sarah stood momentarily rooted to the spot and then ran over to Sir Terrence. 'Terry! Are you all right? What's happened?'

Sir Terrence just shook his head.

'There's your murderer,' said Ferdy, pointing at the professor.

'Perhaps someone could explain,' said Grange.

Ferdy glanced at his father but Sir Terrence was

still on his knees and didn't look capable of explaining anything.

'Who fired the gun?' Grange asked.

'He did,' said Ferdy. 'But nobody's hurt.'

'Humphrey fired it?' Sarah sounded stunned.

Grange looked around. 'Where is it now?'

They all looked around. 'Safe,' said Ferdy. 'I kicked it away.'

Annabel spotted it. 'It's under the chair over there.'

Lucy spoke. 'I was walking past outside and I saw the professor with a gun in his hand. I thought I'd better do something before someone got hurt.'

'It was very brave, Lucy, and we're *truly* grateful,' said Ferdy.

Lucy smiled, pleased. 'That's good. I was afraid I might have made a complete ass of myself – if you were just play acting.'

'No. We weren't play acting. The professor killed Thomas.'

'So I gather. Pity, I quite liked him, but you can't go around killing people.' The professor gave a heave that rocked Lucy but didn't dislodge her. She took his left arm in an armlock. He groaned and subsided.

DS Idle came back into the room and stepped forward. 'We'll take over now, Miss Harcourt,'

'He's quite strong,' she warned.

DS Idle observed the armlock and decided to snap on some handcuffs whilst Lucy was still *in situ*. Then he helped Lucy to her feet.

Without Lucy on his back, Humphrey tried to right himself but with his hands handcuffed behind his back he was finding it difficult. DS Idle hauled him to his feet and sat him on an upright chair. Humphrey's eyes appeared unfocussed, his body hunched in on itself.

'Well,' Lucy looked around at them all, 'if that's all, I was on my way to see my father.'

'We'll take a statement later, Miss Harcourt,' said Grange.

Lucy left the room and Grange shut the door behind her.

'Remarkable woman,' he said. 'Now, perhaps, we could have the whole story.'

Ferdy explained what had happened. He didn't say that Humphrey had intended to kill him, or that he had believed Ferdy, rather than Sarah to be the person Sir Terrence 'loved the most in all the world'.

Annabel, glancing at Sarah, was grateful for that reticence. It was bad enough that Humphrey had threatened them with a gun. Sarah's eyes were like granite as she looked at the professor. Her stance, as she stood in front of Sir Terrence, was of a lioness protecting her pride.

Grange turned to the professor. 'I should like to hear what you have to say.'

It looked for a moment as though Humphrey hadn't heard him and Grange had opened his mouth to repeat the question when Humphrey spoke. 'What else is there to say?'

Grange turned to Annabel. He didn't look pleased. 'You should have brought the stick to me.'

'I was going to,' said Annabel, 'just as soon as Ferdy confirmed my belief.'

Grange frowned.

It was the second time she had intervened in a case that he thought was in his control. She realised that he had marked her down in his black book and was sorry for that. She also agreed with him. She knew that, for the rest of her life, she would have to live with that awful moment, when Humphrey had turned his gun on Ferdy. If Ferdy had been killed ... it was the stuff of nightmares.

But Humphrey had mentioned *two* things. What was the second?

Sir Terrence raised himself on shaking legs and gripped the edge of the desk for support. He looked as though he had aged ten years. He didn't look at the professor.

'Surely,' he said, his voice tired beyond measure, 'all's well that ends well?'

'That is a matter of opinion,' said Grange coldly. 'It's only chance that we didn't have another casualty.'

Sir Terrence's chin lifted. It was clear that he didn't take kindly to being criticised. His back straightened and the years fell from his face. Annabel supposed that he must have a remarkable ability to bounce back from adversity – to say nothing of having a very thick skin – to have got where he was in business, but it was an extraordinary recovery, nevertheless.

'The ... traitor is there,' Sir Terrence still couldn't bring himself to look at Humphrey, 'He has admitted it.

All we want is for you to take him away. I never want to see him again.'

There was a strange noise from Humphrey. It took a moment for everyone to realise that he was laughing. It was an other-worldly sound, soft and sad. 'Jasper,' he said. His shoulders began to shake, then his whole body. Froth started from his mouth and, as everyone looked on in horror, he toppled sideways from his chair onto the floor where he twitched for a few moments before lying still.

Idle leapt forward and felt for a pulse at his neck. He looked up in shock and disbelief. 'He's dead.'

CHAPTER TWENTY-FOUR

It was some time later and everyone was gathered together in the sitting room drinking cocktails prepared by Sir Terrence.

DCI Grange and the rest of the policemen had left, taking the professor's body and the gun with them. Statements had been taken from Sir Terrence, Ferdy, Annabel and Lucy.

'Heaven preserve me from amateurs,' Grange said, as he took his leave.

'We'll take that as a thank you,' said Ferdy.

The hospital had phoned to say that Alice had come round and should make a full recovery. The police had removed their guard now that the professor was dead and had confessed to attacking her. Grange looked sad but unsurprised when he learnt the amount that she had demanded in blackmail.

The Harcourt's suitcases were in the hall and Annabel knew that it was only curiosity that held them at Omega House. It was Dorothy, curled up on the sofa next to Matt and sipping a martini, who asked the question on everyone's mind – everyone, that is, who hadn't been directly involved.

'I just don't understand it. Why did the professor kill Thomas?'

A very good question and, in view of the fact that the whole matter of espionage must remain a secret, a difficult one to answer.

Sir Terrence had bowed to the inevitable and offered Violet his chair. Now he moved away from the drinks cabinet and took up position before the fireplace. He, Ferdy and Annabel had discussed this and decided that they neither could, nor wanted to, whitewash Humphrey's reputation entirely.

'Unfortunately,' he began, 'and entirely unknown to me, Humphrey has been suffering financially for some time. I say, unknown to me – had he told me I would, of course, have helped him. As it was, Thomas discovered him in the process of opening the safe that I have in the library.'

One of the three safes.

'Humphrey reacted ... unwisely ... I'm sure he had no intention of causing harm.'

When he grabbed the stiletto and plunged it into Thomas' chest.

'Then he panicked and tried to hide Thomas' body under the shrubs. And the rest you know.' He looked around at the raised faces blandly.

'Surely, the professor's leg ...?' said Gerald.

'... was not as badly injured as we had thought,' said Sir Terrence.

Or, as he had given us to suppose.

'Was anybody hurt when the gun went off?' asked Violet.

'Er ... no.'

Violet's mouth turned down. 'I was expecting something a bit more exciting. It's all rather a let down.'

Actually, it was quite exciting enough, thank you.

'I'm sorry to disappoint,' said Sir Terrence.

'Why did the gun go off?' asked Alexi.

'Ah. When confronted he tried to escape. The gun went off accidentally and he confessed.'

'So, he just confessed?' said Alexi, his tone reflecting his scepticism.

'He had a crisis of conscience, understandable in the circumstances.'

'And then he died?' Gerald's scepticism matched Alexi's.

'Unfortunately, he suffered a heart attack. There was nothing anyone could do.'

Brought on by a cyanide pill.

There was silence.

'So, we can go now,' said Gerald.

'Indeed you can.' Sir Terrence didn't try to hide his relief. 'All of you.'

'Well, it's been a …' Gerald struggled for the right words and gave up. 'Perhaps, when you have another snuff box to show me, we can meet at my club?'

'That is an excellent idea.'

Gerald looked at his watch, tossed back the remains of his drink and held out his hand to his wife. She allowed him to help her up from her chair and everyone moved out into the hall. Matt helped with their suitcases. Gerald led the way to the door.

Violet paused, 'Lucy!' she said peremptorily.

Lucy went forward and gave her mother a hug that rocked her on her small feet. 'I'll follow after, Mum.'

'But …' Violet's face creased up in puzzlement.

'It'll be all right, Mum. You'll see.'

'Come along, my dear,' said Gerald to his wife. 'Let's go home.'

'Nonsense, Gerald! Lucy is coming too.'

'Lucy has other plans.' With great gentleness, he guided his protesting wife out of the front door and into their car. Matt placed the suitcases in the trunk and they were away.

Annabel could see that there were tears in Lucy's eyes as she watched her mother depart. But then she turned and Annabel was astonished to see her face transform into a glow of love. It blazed out of her eyes and the object was … Alexi.

He stepped forward, disbelieving but hopeful, 'Does this mean …?'

'Yes,' she said simply.

He took her in his arms. 'Lucy, my little love.'

Annabel was sure she wasn't the only one with her mouth open. She checked. She wasn't.

'And,' said Lucy, turning to Annabel, 'we owe it all to you.'

They did?

'You do?'

'When I found out that Alexi and my parents would both be here this weekend, it seemed the perfect opportunity to introduce them. I knew my mother was worried about my marrying but I was sure that once she got to know Alexi, she would come round. But then, you saw how she was. And then when Alexi acted so strangely on the Saturday I thought he'd changed his mind.'

So it was Alexi that Lucy had been waiting for in the library, but with his mind on the Holbein he had missed not only their rendezvous but also their game of tennis. No wonder Lucy had been upset.

'But then you spoke to my father. He had no idea I wanted to marry but was holding back because of my mother. And I,' she paused, took a deep breath, 'I had no idea my mother was so ill. But, we both know now. And he has told me that I mustn't hold my own life back for one more minute. So,' she turned back to Alexi, 'I'm coming with you!'

'You are?' Alexi raised his face to heaven.

'I'm lost,' said Sir Terrence, 'totally lost. Could someone please explain.'

'Oh, Lucy,' said Dorothy. 'I knew you were in love but I didn't know it was with Alexi. This is perfect!'

'We'll get married on board ship,' Alexi declared.

'How romantic,' Dorothy sighed.

'What ship?' Sir Terrence demanded.

'I think it's a ship bound for Argentina,' said Annabel.

'Bariloche!' Light dawned for Ferdy.

Over Lucy's shoulder, Alexi frowned them down.

So Lucy wasn't in on the whole artworks rehabilitation exercise.

'Yes,' said Lucy, 'Argentina! Isn't it wonderful! A dream come true.' She hugged Alexi so tightly his face turned red. 'And earlier, he was going to go alone.'

That explained Lucy's tears and Alexi's misery.

Whilst Lucy went over to speak to Dorothy, Alexi sidled over to Annabel and Ferdy.

'An El Greco, eh?' said Ferdy.

'It was the crown jewel of our family and,' he looked meaningfully at them, 'it is the last. I have managed to track down and … repossess … the rest with the exception of the Holbein. Lucy knows nothing. Once I have that it will be over, I promise you.'

'Well, be careful. My father is one thing, ex-Nazis in Argentina is quite another.'

'When am I ever not?' Alexi spread his arms, his puckish smile in place.

Ferdy was unimpressed. 'Just make sure you are. You'll be a married man.'

'Isn't she wonderful?' Alexi gazed across at Lucy. 'I am the happiest man on earth.'

Surely Matt was already that? But no doubt it was a matter of personal perspective.

Alexi turned back to them and lowered his voice. 'I thought you were after me, but I see now that you had bigger fish to cook.'

'Fry,' said Ferdy, 'bigger fish to fry.'

'Of course,' he said, 'it sounds better doesn't it? I suppose it was the documents? Bait? A trap? They made sure

I knew of them too.' His face darkened, 'Do they really suspect me of spying? After all that I have done?'

'I don't think they did, seriously,' said Ferdy. 'It was those telegrams. They couldn't explain them.'

'Ah, the tortured mind of the security services. But,' Alexi looked searchingly at him, 'you didn't believe it could be me …?'

'Not for a minute.'

But you did. You didn't want to, but you did.

'You went to Amsterdam,' Annabel said, 'intending to acquire, or steal the Holbein but Sir Terrence got in first and bought it. How long did it take you to track it down again?'

Alexi looked at her wordlessly for a moment. 'Over a year.' He turned to Ferdy. 'You'd better hang on to this one, she's useful.' His face clouded again. 'Anyway, this is one that got away.'

Sir Terrence had slipped away. Now he returned, holding a rolled up painting which he handed to Lucy.

'A wedding present,' he said.

Alexi gave a cry, stepped across swiftly, unfurled the picture and gave a sigh of pleasure and gratitude.

Lucy's expression was somewhat different. It was clear that she was trying hard to look grateful. Annabel sympathised. Then Lucy looked again more closely. 'It looks like Alexi!'

'My ancestor,' Alexi said.

'Oh! Well, in that case … I love it! Thank you,' she said to Sir Terrence.

'It's a Holbein,' Sir Terrence couldn't help adding.

'Oh,' said Lucy. It was clear that this was of less interest to her.

'And the provenance?' Alexi said to Sir Terrence.

For a moment Sir Terrence stiffened in outrage but then his face relaxed into an expression of amused respect. 'I'll sort out something.'

Sir Terrence, Ferdy and Annabel stood in the drive and waved Alexi and Lucy off. Lucy continued to wave energetically until they were out of sight.

'Well, that was a surprise,' said Ferdy.

'Yes,' said Annabel.

'Generous gift,' said Ferdy to his father.

Sir Terrence looked after the parting car. 'She saved the life of my son. There is nothing I would not have given her.' The car now out of sight, he added, 'Love and fear of loss go hand in hand. You can't have one without the other.'

Annabel considered that statement. It seemed to sum up the events of the weekend.

Sir Terrence turned and walked back indoors.

Annabel looked away from Ferdy out over the surrounding birch trees. They really were incredibly beautiful. Simple, clean lines, fresh and uncomplicated. After a few moments she said, 'Do you think they'll be happy?'

Ferdy cleared his throat. 'I imagine so, ecstatically so. That is … it's not unknown for Alexi to wave guns around but,' he put his arm through Annabel's and turned her back towards the house, 'I'm sure they'll muddle through.'

Dorothy and Matt appeared on the threshold.

'Oh, are they gone?' Dorothy asked.

'Yes, Dodo, they've gone.'

'You know,' Dorothy continued innocently, 'without my allowance from Dad I'll be able to dress exactly like Lucy.' She turned to Matt. 'Won't that be nice!'

Matt blenched. 'Really? Like Lucy, er, why?'

'Oh, well, not *exactly* like, but you know, if you buy all your clothes the same colour they do mix and match well. It's much more cost effective. I wondered … purple perhaps? Obviously I can't have pink since Lucy's chosen that.'

'But, you look lovely in pink,' Matt protested.

'I know, but really, it's no bother. I don't mind at all.'

Careful, don't over-egg it. You might get stuck wearing purple for the rest of your life.

'Or maybe not purple. It can be a bit ageing. Maybe grey? That wouldn't show the dirt at all.'

'But really, Dorothy, is that going to be necessary?' Matt looked concerned.

'Well … yes, to be honest. But really and truly, I don't mind … I know!' she cried out as if inspired, 'black! *That's* the answer.'

Matt was starting to look suspicious.

'Second hand,' Ferdy chipped in. 'Loads of bargains to be had.'

Matt peered at him.

'Second hand, yes!' Dorothy corroborated with glee. 'I'm sure Lucy knows lots of jumble sales.'

Working together, brother and sister were formidable.

'Maybe we need to rethink the allowance question,' said Matt.

'Oh, do you really think so, darling? We can if you want.'

Perhaps Dorothy wasn't so bad at subterfuge after all, but Annabel wished her friend had felt able to tell Matt that she simply didn't want to wear the ring.

An old, pale blue, Daimler eased its way up the drive towards them.

'Ah,' said Matt, 'here come the parents.'

Ferdy and Annabel looked at him in astonishment.

'Were you expecting them?' Annabel asked.

'Well, that was the plan.'

'Why on earth didn't you put them off?' Ferdy asked, not unreasonably.

'Tried but couldn't get hold of them. Must have left home early; probably called in somewhere on the way. It doesn't matter now, surely? The police have gone.' He ambled forward towards the car which had drawn up in front of the house.

'Do you think Sarah knows?' Annabel whispered to Ferdy.

'Well, if she didn't, she does now,' he replied, as Sarah emerged from the house behind them.

But if Sarah objected to the arrival of yet another set

of guests at the end of a trying and emotionally tiring day, no trace of it showed on her face as she stepped forward to greet Matt's parents.

Mr Lloyd clambered stiffly from the driver's seat and straightened himself up, rather as an old concertina player might draw open his instrument with arthritic hands. They saw an older version of Matt, tall and stick thin. His smile, when Sarah walked forward, proved to be as sweet as Matt's. Meanwhile, from the passenger seat his wife, with much puffing and effort, extracted her substantial body. Clad in tweed skirt and paisley patterned shirt stretched tight across a massive bosom, she was almost as tall as her husband but twice as wide. She arranged a particularly beautiful silk shawl around her shoulders, and then surged forward.

Sarah performed the introductions. Mr Lloyd nodded amiably, Mrs Lloyd beamed.

Nobody could object to such genial guests.

Dorothy in particular received a special greeting, being enfolded in Mrs Lloyd's arms.

'My daughter to be!'

Unused to such behaviour, Dorothy at first stood stiffly then she appeared to melt and … *nestled*. There was no other word for it. Annabel looked on with delighted approval. Perhaps, at last, Dorothy might have found a worthy parent.

The perfect moment was rudely interrupted by Matt who stepped forward saying, 'Mother! Dorothy cannot wear that ring!'

It was Mrs Lloyd's turn to stiffen. Her arms lowered.

'She's wearing it?' She squinted down at Dorothy's head in horror. 'You're not wearing it, surely?'

Dorothy nodded. She looked like a duckling that'd been welcomed into the nest only to be cast out into the cold once more. Tears started in her eyes.

'Dorothy, dear, please lower your arms, very carefully, and step away,' said Mrs Lloyd. 'This is my favourite shawl.'

Dorothy stepped away in bewilderment but hope glimmered in her eyes.

Safely distanced from the ring, Mrs Lloyd turned on her son. 'What were you doing allowing her to wear it?'

'But …' said Matt. 'You gave it to me for her. You said all brides wore it!'

'I said all brides *wore* it. I didn't say they *wear* it. Good God! That thing's a menace to mankind!'

Mr Lloyd sidled up to Matt. Annabel inched closer to hear.

'Almost lost the "family jewels",' he muttered out of the corner of his mouth. 'Nasty moment.'

Matt looked at him in horror, although whether this was because of the direct reference to his parents having sex – which, let's face it, no child wishes to hear – or because of his own close call, Annabel wasn't quite sure.

'You might have warned me!' hissed Matt.

His father winked. 'Call it the Lloyd "rite of passage". I did.'

CHAPTER TWENTY-FIVE

Mrs Fry appeared at the sitting room door where drinks were being handed out to the new guests. 'Miss Hutton has arrived at the gate. Shall I let her in?'

'And so it continues,' said Sir Terrence, as he stood at the front door with Sarah, Ferdy and Annabel. They watched as an old and battered black Ford made its way up the drive towards them. 'Are all your weekends like this?' he asked Ferdy.

Ferdy grinned. 'No, thank God.'

'We must all be thankful for that,' said his father.

The car drew up in front of them and Phoebe, looking slightly harried, got out.

'Hello,' she said. 'Lovely to see you. She's a bit …'

There was a hammering on the windscreen which proved to be caused by the handle of Rosemary's stick. Phoebe hurried round to the passenger side and helped Rosemary out. This was quite a performance but eventually Rosemary stood upright, or as upright as her arthritis allowed, on the gravel. She scowled across at them.

'Of all the complete cock ups! This one beggars all belief.'

Sir Terrence intervened hastily, 'Perhaps we can continue this inside?'

'I'm sure you'd love something to drink?' Sarah offered.

'Tea would be lovely,' said Phoebe.

Sir Terrence led the way through to the morning room, so recently vacated by the police. Progress was slow as they crossed the hall but they met no one except Mrs Fry who hurried off to the kitchen to prepare some tea and, no doubt, to inform John that whilst five visitors and all the police had left, a further four had arrived. Once in the morning room they sat at the table. Annabel was not surprised that Rosemary took the chair with its back to the window. Phoebe sat to her right, the rest of them arranged themselves around in the other seats.

'Complete and utter cock up,' repeated Rosemary once she was settled and tea had been produced by Mrs Fry.

'Perhaps you would allow us to explain before you leap to judgement,' said Sir Terrence with tight lips.

'Well, Thomas is dead. I don't suppose you can bring him back to life?'

She had a point.

'That was hardly our fault,' said Sir Terrence. 'I should like to make it clear right from the start that I take extreme umbrage over Special Branch operatives being foisted onto my staff without my knowledge … or consent.'

Rosemary's eyes narrowed. Dishing out fire was *her* modus operandi and she didn't like being on the receiving end. 'I didn't know that he was being employed on this job,' she said. 'If Sir Richard had told me I'd have put a stop to it. The man's a fool.'

Sir Terrence's silence made his own feelings on the subject clear.

'It should have been a straightforward sting exercise,' she said. 'And now we have nothing.'

Ferdy cleared his throat. 'Actually, that's not at all the case. We've uncovered the spy and the police have just taken him away. He's dead, by the way.'

'You have? What do you mean, dead?' Rosemary stared.

'Cyanide pill, and it wasn't either of the two that you put us onto, it was –'

'Humphrey Calder,' said Rosemary.

They all stared at her.

'You knew it was him?' said Annabel.

'Of course, I knew it was him,' Rosemary was scornful. 'I just needed the proof.'

'In other words,' said Ferdy, 'you had a hunch.'

Rosemary glared at him. 'I never indulge in hunches.'

'Well, you now have the proof. He confessed.'

Rosemary sat for a few moments in silence. An expression of deep satisfaction settled over her features.

'Good. Good. Although, it's all taken far too long. Far too many secrets lost. If people had only listened.'

'But, if you suspected him, why didn't you say so when you briefed us?' asked Annabel.

'Because I didn't trust you not to give the game away.'

'Well, that's a ringing endorsement!' said Ferdy exasperated.

'But why didn't Sir Richard tell Thomas that Humphrey was a suspect?' said Annabel. 'If Thomas had known, he might have been more cautious.' He might still be alive.

Rosemary shifted in her seat. 'Sir Richard didn't know.'

'You mean you didn't tell him,' Ferdy's voice was heavy with accusation. 'It seems to me that you've both been playing games and keeping secrets from one another, and Thomas has been the unfortunate fall guy.'

'If you knew the background to this you wouldn't be so quick to judge,' said Rosemary crisply. 'I have been saying for years now that I believe Calder to be a spy and nobody, including Sir Richard, has listened. When he approached me for help, I saw an opportunity to prove my point and prove it I have. If Sir Richard had known what I intended he would probably have pulled the plug on the whole operation.'

'So you never suspected Alexi or Gerald Harcourt?' said Ferdy.

Rosemary huffed. 'There was the outside possibility, I suppose, but I never credited it. There seemed to me to be other much more likely explanations for their conduct.'

'Well, you were right,' said Ferdy. 'Care to hazard a guess? What did your *hunch* tell you?'

'I don't enjoy *games*, Ferdy' said Rosemary frostily.

'No? Gerald's wife is a kleptomaniac and Alexi is busy retrieving his family's artwork stolen during the war.'

Rosemary raised her eyebrows. 'Interesting.'

'But how did the professor know about the documents?' asked Annabel.

'Oh, I made sure of that,' said Rosemary.

'Talking of which,' said Ferdy. He pulled the documents out of his jacket pocket, 'What do I do with them?'

'Chuck them in the bin. They've served their purpose.' The sun lit up her hair like a halo. 'You don't think I'd have risked real documents do you?'

CHAPTER TWENTY-SIX

Annabel sipped at her martini as she looked around the sitting room. The evening sun was sending warm light across the oak polished floor, over the dove-grey sofa and up onto the white walls. A huge bunch of orange, yellow and red dahlias on the side table provided a counterpoint of colour to balance the modern painting above the fireplace in the otherwise neutral colour scheme. The overall effect was comfortable, cosy even. Annabel had not thought to use such a word when describing Omega House. She wondered if the effect was as much to do with the lightening of tension as the low evening sunshine.

From the group around the fireplace, Ferdy's laughter rose up. It was a carefree sound. Annabel had never heard him laugh like that before. For a moment she felt excluded, then he looked up, their eyes met and he smiled. It was a smile that reached out and drew her in.

She found that Sir Terrence had joined her. Together they looked at Sarah, Ferdy and Dorothy, all talking and laughing together. Annabel thought that, once again, Sir Terrence had got what he wanted. He was reunited with his son and Sarah was happy. She wondered if that had been his motivation behind the weekend all along and the trap to catch a spy had been incidental.

'I was never happy with Ferdy's old business partner –' he said.

Annabel knew this.

'– and I wasn't happy with his new choice –'

Annabel knew this too.

'– but I've changed my mind and I don't often do that.' Sir Terrence took a sip of his drink. 'I think that you and he will do well together.' He took a step away then paused. 'If you can get him to accept his allowance, I'll be in your debt.'

What was wrong with this family? Why didn't they talk to one another? Surely it was up to Ferdy to accept his allowance, or not, as he chose?

Ferdy joined her. 'All right?' he smiled.

She smiled back. 'Yes. And you?'

'Very much so. We did well.'

Had they done well? They had fulfilled their brief and identified the spy but then things had got out of hand. And she had made mistakes, silly mistakes that could have cost Ferdy his life.

'Stanhope and Baxter are back in business!' he said.

Perhaps, for all his words of encouragement, he had shared her own doubts of her abilities as a private detective.

'We work well together, don't we?' she said.

'We do.' He lifted his glass, 'Here's to us!'

She chinked it with her glass. 'To us.'

'I wonder what our next case will bring?' he said.

Whatever it was, Annabel was sure it would not be dull.

EPILOGUE

Ferdy dropped Annabel off at Haddons on Monday afternoon and headed into London to the office. Mrs Summers would have left at midday and Annabel had the house to herself. She stood in the hall and let the quiet of the house settle about her, savouring the clean smell of the wax polish, the soft light falling across the oak floor from the open library door, the steady tick tock of the grandfather clock. Nothing had changed. Then she went through to the kitchen.

Something had changed.

On the kitchen table stood a small glass jar with a red and white checked gingham cover secured with a bow of red ribbon. The label on the jar read 'Rhubarb and Ginger Chutney 1964'. There was a note beside it in Mrs Summers' scribbled handwriting. 'Goes best with Proctor's honey roast ham but you'll probably like it with your cheddar.'

Annabel threw her bag and coat on the chair, untied the ribbon, removed the cover and with difficulty unscrewed the lid of the jar. It came loose with a muted pop, releasing a nutty aroma. Annabel took a teaspoon from the drawer, scraped back the greaseproof circle and dipped into the mixture.

It tasted tangy and sweet. It tasted of belonging.

ACKNOWLEDGEMENTS

To Michael Laskey and the Leiston writing group and to all at the Stradbroke writing group, thanks for sharing skills, laughter and the joy of writing. Thanks to my kind friends Lynn Gulliver, Julie de Jong, Lynn Eldrett and Amanda Marks for giving so generously of their time, reading and providing invaluable feedback during the development of The Omega Trap. My thanks also to Michael Lansbery for advising me on Ferdy's backstory. Michael, you have lived an extraordinary life! Grateful thanks to Dr Susan Bodgener for advising me on some of the medical aspects of this story and then absolving me for taking a wide author's interpretation of that advice. To Ellie Stevenson and Barbara Archer, my thanks for their professionalism and excellent editing skills and to Vidya at ebookpbook thank you for prompt and skilful formatting. To Franky Peck, my especial thanks for the perfect 1960's style cover designs which have made the Annabel Staple series so distinctive. Your graphic skills are amazing! Most of all, I wish to thank my husband Geoff for his constant input, encouragement and support at all stages in this, the second Annabel Staple mystery.

Printed in Great Britain
by Amazon

58021334R00189